SUNDAYS IN FREDERICKSBURG

FOUR-IN-ONE COLLECTION

Eileen Key
Lynette Sowell
Connie Stevens
Marjorie Vawter

BARBOUR
PUBLISHING

Hope's Dwelling Place by Connie Stevens
Amelia Bachman wants no part of a loveless marriage like she observed growing up in her parents' home. Instead she chooses to become a schoolteacher since teachers aren't permitted to marry. Hank Zimmermann hopes to build a successful carpentry business but discovers what he wants even more is a home of his own and a family to fill it. If Amelia is to be a part of that family, God will have to change her mind and turn the Sunday house into a home.

A Shelter from the Storm by Marjorie Vawter
A nurse in World War I Europe, Mildred Zimmermann returns to Fredericksburg, which is dealing with an outbreak of Spanish influenza. Drawn into the hometown battle, Mildred opens her family's Sunday house as an overflow to the small, overcrowded clinic. Death seems to plague those she loves, and she is determined not to allow herself to fall in love...until war hero Nelson Winters is placed in her care.

Letters from Home by Lynette Sowell
Trudy Meier has her hands full during the summer of 1943. While Mama volunteers at a hospital and Papa is away at war, Trudy watches over the home front, even though she yearns for adventure. Reporter Bradley Payne rents the Meiers' Sunday house to write his weekly column and finds the Texas Hill Country slowing him down and making him imagine what life would be like with Trudy. But when he hears the call of the open road again, can he take Trudy's heart with him?

A Hint of Lavender by Eileen Key
Gwendolyn Zimmermann tends the family's peach stand since her college plans were interrupted by her dad's illness. Her aunt's consignment shop needs a manager and a steady salary would help her family, so Gwen leaves the stand, moves to town, and lives in the loft over her family's Sunday house. But she's surprised when her aunt asks her to carry meals to injured geologist Clay Tanner. As Gwen cares for Clay, Clay's faith deepens. Will love also bloom in the fertile soil of their hearts?

SUNDAYS IN
FREDERICKSBURG

HOPE'S DWELLING PLACE

by Connie Stevens

Dedication

To my nieces and nephews: Kris, Brad, Matt, and Esther.
You are all so precious to me.

Chapter 1

Amelia Bachman braced herself against the jarring ride of the stagecoach and peered out the window. The stage was scheduled to arrive in Fredericksburg before dark, but the deepening purple, gold, and magenta streaks in the western sky hinted the sun might be in deep slumber by the time she reached her destination. She'd had no way to notify Mr. Lamar Richter, chairman of the Fredericksburg school board, that her arrival was delayed by a broken wheel. She hoped he didn't interpret her tardiness as a change of mind.

Amelia pulled two letters from her reticule and held them up to the waning sunlight. The well-worn edges and bent corners testified to the number of times she'd unfolded and refolded each one. She'd nearly memorized the first, from her father. His disapproving frown the day she left home to attend Normal School in Austin lingered in her mind. He couldn't understand how she could ignore the opportunity to marry a prosperous rancher in favor of becoming a schoolteacher—a menial occupation at best, and one where she would be required to remain single. Her throat tightened as she read his berating words once again. If she'd followed the same path as her parents, she might live a comfortable life in a fine house with servants to do her bidding. But she couldn't erase the images from her childhood of the misery etched on her mother's face, trapped in a loveless marriage. She'd long ago promised herself she'd never marry for the sake of social status.

She folded the letter and stuffed it resolutely back into her reticule and opened the second letter. The words scrawled in this letter brought a smile to her face.

Dear Miss Bachman,
    We school board of Fredericksburg, Texas, offer to you teach der school to end of der school year.

Amelia shifted her position on the hard, dusty seat, thinking of the teacher she was replacing. Mr. Richter had stated in a previous letter that their teacher had turned in her resignation just after Christmas. Seemed the woman was getting married and didn't want to wait until the end of the term. Well, Mr. Richter wouldn't have to worry about Amelia doing such a thing. She squinted at the rumpled paper once again.

    You must stay at der Richter family Sunday haus. *There is a place for* schlafen *up der stairs side. Stagecoach bring you and der town familys is glad.*

A tiny smile tweaked Amelia's lips when she remembered struggling to recall the little bit of German she knew, relieved to translate *schlafen* to mean there were private *sleeping* quarters for her. She cast another glance out the window at the quickly disappearing sun and imagined Mr. Richter growing weary of waiting for her stage to arrive.

As she feared, darkness shrouded the town when the stage finally drew to a halt amid swirling dust. Amelia brushed the gritty film from her skirt and smoothed her hair the best she could. The driver grunted as he climbed down and opened the door, kicking a wooden crate over for her to step on. He didn't wait to help her down, but rather climbed back up to retrieve the luggage. She unfolded her stiff muscles, closing her lips to stifle an unladylike groan, and disembarked the conveyance. Lanterns flickered on either side of the depot, casting ghostly shadows across the boardwalk. Amelia glanced around but only the stage driver was within sight.

Where was Mr. Richter?

"Oh dear."

The driver lowered her trunk to the ground. "Beg your pardon, miss?"

She turned. "Do you know Mr. Lamar Richter?"

"Nope."

She bit her lip. "I wonder where I might inquire after him."

Her carpetbag plunked at her feet as the driver jumped down. "Iffen you can rattle the depot door loud enough, the old German fella that runs the place might can help ya. Name's Humble, Hurmole, Hummerol. . ." The man knocked his hat askew scratching his head. "It's somethin' like that."

He climbed over the wheel and collected the reins. His

sharp whistle made the horses snort in protest, but they lurched forward, leaving Amelia standing alone in the chilled February night air.

She scanned up and down the street. The whole town seemed to have retired for the night. She longed to do so as well, but first she had to find this Sunday house of which Mr. Richter wrote.

She drew her thin shawl tighter and tapped at the depot door. No lights glimmered from within. She knocked harder, rattling the glass in the door window. "Hello? Is anyone here?"

A faint glow spilled from a back room and moved slowly toward the door. Candlelight never looked friendlier. A wizened old man clad only in a nightshirt shuffled to the door, holding the candlestick aloft.

"*Wer gibt es?*"

Wer? Amelia prodded her brain. . . . *Who.* No doubt he was asking who was knocking on his door in the middle of the night.

"My name is. . .um, *ich bin* Amelia Bachman." What was the German word for *teacher*? "Mr. Richter was supposed to meet me."

"Richter, *ja.*" The man set the candlestick down, gripped Amelia's hand and pumped it. "*Fraulein* Bachman. You am. . . uh, teacher, ja?

Relief rippled through her. "Yes! I mean, ja."

He drew his shoulders back and clapped his hand to his chest. "I is Humbert Schmidt." A beaming smile accompanied Mr. Schmidt's broken English.

"Very nice to meet you, Mr. Schmidt." She pulled the

school board chairman's letter from her pocket. "Mr. Richter says I'm supposed to stay in the Sunday house, er, *Sonntag haus*. Can you tell me—" She furrowed her brow trying to think around the headache that had weaseled its way behind her eyes. "*Wo ist das haus?*"

"*Ja, ja*—" He pointed and gave her directions, half in English and half in German, but she caught the words *gelb haus*, so at least she knew the house she was looking for was yellow.

"*Sie brauchen*—" Candlelight danced against the elderly man's thick gray eyebrows as he shook his head. "Bah! Englisch, Schmidt!" An apologetic smile wobbled across his countenance. "You need lantern. *Hier ist.*" He scurried to a cabinet and returned with a lantern, lighting the wick with his candle.

"Thank you, uh, *dank*, Mr. Schmidt. I'll bring your lantern back in the morning." She picked up her satchel and pointed to the larger trunk. "I will send someone for the trunk tomorrow—*morgen*, all right?"

He nodded. "*Morgen ist fein. Gute nacht.*"

"Good night." Clutching her bag in one hand, she looped her small cloth purse over her arm and picked up the lantern. Its flaming wick cast a swath of light before her.

Unfamiliar with her surroundings and weary from the hours of travel, she couldn't be sure if the shiver that ran through her was from the cold or the eerie shadows. Either way, all she wanted was a warm bed behind a sturdy door.

Mr. Schmidt had told her to take the second street—that much she understood. She held the lantern higher to get a better look at the tiny houses that lined up for her perusal. She trudged on, her carpetbag growing heavier by the minute. Finally, the lantern light fell on a small yellow house. Amelia ventured closer and shone the light on the door. Above the lintel was an ornate sign that read: RICHTER HAUS.

Fatigue wilted her shoulders. "Thank goodness."

She climbed the steps to the narrow porch, but hesitated at the door. It didn't seem fitting to enter the house without knocking. Was the Richter family sleeping inside? She held the lantern up to one window. The light glared off the wavy glass.

She rapped on the door but there was no response. For good measure, she knocked again and listened for stirring from within. Satisfied the house was empty, she gripped the door latch and pushed.

"It's locked!"

Her arrival was expected. Why would Mr. Richter tell her she would stay here, and then lock the door without providing her a key? She worked the doorknob again to no avail.

The frustration of the day crawled up from her gut and she clenched her jaw. Leaving her satchel and reticule by the door, she tried the two front windows. Neither of them budged. She huffed out a breath of annoyance and took the lantern around the side of the house. She held the lantern high and continued to make her way along the side of the house.

Near the back corner, she stumbled into a pile of firewood stacked against the house. "Oh!" Pieces of split stove wood tumbled down with a noisy clatter. A yowling screech split the air as a cat scrambled off the unstable woodpile.

An involuntary scream strangled in Amelia's throat and a stabbing pain shot through her foot. She managed to hang on to the lantern as she hopped on one foot and leaned against the corner of the house.

Her breath heaved in and out as she waited for the pain to subside. Between the stagecoach's delayed journey and the turbulent ride, Mr. Richter's absence, struggling to communicate with Mr. Schmidt, and finding she couldn't gain access to her promised living quarters, seething tears burned behind her eyelids. She squeezed her eyes shut and forced the tears to retreat.

Drawing in a deep, steadying breath, she hobbled around the scattered firewood and found another window on the back wall of the house. She set the lantern on the ground and pushed at the window. It gave a piercing squeak as wood scraped against wood, but at least it opened.

"*Wer sind sie und was machen sie?*" The deep, masculine voice boomed through the still night air.

Amelia squawked and spun around. She understood the first part of the challenge: Who are you? "I'm Miss Amelia Bachman, the new schoolteacher. Mr. Richter?"

Two large, booted feet carried the man out of the shadows and into the lantern light. "You're a woman!"

Under the circumstances, his observation was so ludicrous she didn't know whether to laugh or throw the lantern at him.

He reached for the lantern and drew it up where it illumined both their faces. His disheveled sandy hair flopped in his eye. If this was Mr. Richter, he was a lot younger than she expected.

15

"What are you doing?" His tone lost a bit of its gruff edge, but his dark brown eyes still held an air of suspicion.

She was getting ready to climb through the window. What did it look like she was doing? "Are you Mr. Richter?"

Skepticism flitted across his face. "No. I'm Hank Zimmermann." He jerked his thumb over his shoulder. "My family's Sunday house is next door." He narrowed his eyes. "You didn't answer my question. What are you doing outside the Richter's' Sunday house in the middle of the night?"

Indignation pulled her chin up. She resented Mr. Zimmermann's accusing tone.

"Mr. Richter's letter said I would be staying in the Sunday house belonging to his family. The stage arrived late and nobody was at the depot to greet me. I had to find this house by myself in the dark, and the door is locked." The tears that threatened earlier returned to taunt her but she refused to give in to them.

"Locked?" His frown pulled his eyebrows into a *V*. "Folks around here don't lock their doors."

Her voice cracked with emotion but she latched on to the frayed edges of her composure and hung on. "Well, it wouldn't open and I have no way of getting in. I can show you Mr. Richter's letter if you don't believe me."

Chapter 2

No, no, I believe you."

Hank had never called a lady a liar before, especially not one this beautiful.

"I know Mr. Richter and the school board have been looking for a new teacher since Miss Klein left. But I didn't know. . .that is, I didn't expect—" He couldn't very well say he didn't expect someone as pretty as her to be a schoolteacher. The teacher he'd had as boy was as homely as a mud fence.

"Let me check the front door for you." He stepped back and allowed her to precede him. Before she took three steps, he blurted, "Hey, you're limping. Did you—" He clamped his hand over his mouth while heat filled his face. She might have some physical impairment that caused her to limp.

She lifted her shoulders. "I stubbed my toe on the wood-pile when that silly cat startled me."

"Oh, good. I mean, it's not good that you stubbed your toe, but. . .I thought, that is, I was afraid I'd insulted you."

A befuddled look marred her features. Perhaps he could smooth over his clumsy remark by offering her his arm. To his surprise, she laid her gloved hand on the crook of his elbow while he held the lantern. They picked their way around the house and when he sneaked a peek at her from the corner of his eye, he caught her looking up at him.

"So you speak both English and German?"

He grunted. "Everyone around here speaks German. Most speak English, too. You'll encounter both in the classroom." He handed her the lantern and stepped up on the front porch, certain the door was not locked. He twisted the doorknob and pushed, but the door didn't budge.

"Hmm. The wood is probably swollen." He angled his shoulder and pushed hard against the stubborn door. It popped open. "It was just stuck. I can fix it if you like." He bent to pick up her satchel. "Would you like me to carry this upstairs?" He tilted his head to the side of the house opposite of the way they'd come.

Confusion flickered over her face as she moved the lantern inside the door and perused the small space. "There are no stairs."

He pointed to the end of the porch. "The stairs leading to the sleeping loft are on the side of the house."

She blinked and raised her eyebrows. "Oh."

Even in the dim lantern light, he saw a rosy blush steal into her cheeks and the impact of his statement struck him. "I'll—I'll just put the bag at the top of the stairs for you. If you have any trouble with the door to the sleeping quarters—"

Embarrassment cut off his words and they stuck in his throat. He plowed up the steps two at a time and plunked the satchel on the landing. When he descended the stairs, she finished the sentence for him.

"I'll push it open with my shoulder. Thank you, Mr. Zimmermann."

"Hank."

"Uh, yes, well, good night." She picked up her skirt and scurried up the steps as quickly as one could with a painful toe.

He stood in the shadows and watched until she was safely inside and had closed the door. Wisps of light drifted past the small upper window.

"What are you doing, Zimmermann?" Hank muttered, shaking himself back to consciousness. Sweat prickled out on his upper lip like it was a sultry July night instead of a frigid February eve. He prayed Miss Bachman didn't get the wrong impression of his offer to help with the door.

The front door of the house still stood open. He tried to pull it closed as quietly as possible but the place where it stuck previously hit with a thud. He cringed and strode off the porch before the pretty schoolmarm hollered down, wanting to know what he was doing.

Dawn's first rays had barely broken through the slate sky when Hank's feet hit the floor. He couldn't remember the last time he'd tossed and turned all night, but when he'd climbed into his cot after the encounter with Miss Bachman, he couldn't quiet his thoughts.

Her wide, hazel eyes lingered in his mind. How could a woman with whom he'd spent less than ten minutes drive away sleep and confound his thinking? She wasn't the first pretty woman he'd ever met, but there was something distinctly distracting about her.

He pulled on thick woolen socks and padded to the tiny kitchen. Coals still glowed in the small stove. A few sticks of kindling coaxed them to life. While he waited for the coffeepot to boil he ran his hand over the cabinet he'd spent the past few days working on, the satiny smooth grain of the wood submitting to the will of his fingers. The result of his labor pleased him. He only hoped the customers of Horst Braun's general store agreed. If the samples of Hank's work generated enough interest, perhaps his father wouldn't look on him with disappointment.

Needles of guilt jabbed him. Tradition dictated that the eldest son worked side by side with his father and eventually took over the family business—in this case, their farm. But Hank's heart didn't find contentment in working the soil or growing crops. Instead, his hands itched to create fine pieces of furniture. His brother, George, on the other hand, loved planting and harvesting, and longed for their father's approval. George should be the one to partner with *Vater* on the farm.

He ran one finger along the curved edge of the intricate carving he'd done last night. The pattern mimicked the one on the cabinet in his parents' home, crafted by his mother's grandfather. His father had always admired the piece. Hank prayed for God to help him prove his skill so Vater would be more accepting of his chosen occupation. Would his father ever subscribe to the belief that a son could pursue a different vocation and still adhere to the fifth commandment?

"Must I be a farmer in order to honor my father? Lord God, please guide my hands and help me to show Vater that I can still honor him without following in his footsteps."

The coffee boiled over and hissed as the liquid hit the hot metal plate of the stove. Hank grabbed a towel and moved the pot to the dry sink. What a mess.

After a breakfast of dark bread, cold sausage, and strong coffee, Hank set to work on the cabinet. Thoughts of the pretty, new schoolteacher next door continually distracted his focus and had him peering out the window at the Richter's Sunday house.

He poured another cup of coffee and blew on the steaming liquid before taking a noisy sip. As he set the cup down on the windowsill, he saw her.

Miss Amelia Bachman stepped onto the porch and pulled her shawl around her. When she hesitated a moment, it gave Hank the opportunity to stare at her without her knowledge. Fascination arrested his attention. Even her name sang in his subconscious—*Miss Amelia Bachman*.

She set off resolutely down the street and Hank followed her with his eyes. As he watched, he realized she was headed toward the depot. Consternation filled him. What if she'd decided not to stay? What if she was going to buy a one-way ticket back to where she came from? He hoped she wasn't judging Fredericksburg by the awkward late-night meeting with her neighbor. Admittedly, he hadn't made a very a good impression last night, but Fredericksburg needed a teacher. He couldn't let her leave.

He grabbed his leather jacket and hat and ran out the door after her. By the time he caught up to her, she was knocking on the depot door.

"Mr. Schmidt?"

"*Ja, gut morgen, Fraulein Bachman.*"

"Good morning. I've come to—"

"Miss Bachman."

She turned and the moment she made eye contact with him, her cheeks turned bright pink. "Mr. Zimmermann."

"Miss Bachman, please don't leave. The town needs you. I apologize for surprising you last night and I hope you don't think—"

"Mr. Zimmermann, what are you talking about? I'm not leaving." She cast a dubious look at him. "I'm returning Mr. Schmidt's lantern."

Hank's tongue tangled around his teeth. "Oh." He took a step backward. "I, uh, suppose I should just mind my own business."

The tiniest of smiles twitched across her lips. "That's quite all right. It's nice to know I'm needed." She glanced past him and scanned up and down the street. "I was hoping to meet Mr. Richter this morning."

"*Nien*," Humbert Schmidt spoke up. "Richter don't come. . ." He cast a glance at Hank. "*Stadt?*"

"Town." Hank supplied the English word. "What Mr. Schmidt is trying to tell you is the Richters don't ever come into town except on the weekends."

"But I don't understand." Lines of puzzlement deepened across Miss Bachman's brow. "I sent him my itinerary. He knew I was arriving yesterday." She turned to the depot agent. "You mean Mr. Richter wasn't here waiting for my stage to arrive yesterday?"

The elderly man scratched his head and looked at Hank.

"*Wartete Richter hier gestern?*" Hank translated her question, but he already knew the answer. Richter wouldn't rearrange his weekly routine for anyone.

"Nien." Mr. Schmidt shook his head. "He work at farm. He come. . ." He scowled as if trying hard to think of the word he needed, then brightened. "Tomorrow. Richter come tomorrow. *Samstag.*"

"Saturday?" The schoolmarm aimed her inquiry at Hank. "He wasn't planning on coming to town until Saturday?"

Hank shrugged. "Probably." Clearly, she didn't understand the life of a farmer in this area of Texas. "Most of the farmers live a ways out of town. For some, it's a two- or three-hour journey. So they only come to town on Saturday to do their trading, stay overnight at their Sunday house, attend worship and socialize, and then go back to their farm Sunday afternoon."

Mr. Schmidt nodded even though Hank knew the man only understood about half of what he'd said.

Miss Bachman appeared as if trying to hide her embarrassment. "I see. If I'd known, I wouldn't have made such a fool of myself."

Hank opened his mouth to assure her she had no need to be embarrassed, but Schmidt beat him to it. The older man shook his head so vehemently, his unkempt gray hair flopped over one eye.

"Nien, nien, I know das word, fool. You ain't fool." He patted her hand. "You is. . .*klug.*"

"Smart," Hank supplied.

Schmidt nodded. "Ja, you smart. You teach"—he bounced his hand, palm down, indicating several young ones—"*kinder.*" He poked his thumb into his chest. "Schmidt *dummkoff.*"

He rapped his forehead with his knuckles. "Fraulein Bachman, you *sehr hubscher*...teacher."

"Mm." Hank murmured in agreement despite the expression on Miss Bachman's face that indicated she didn't understand the full meaning of Schmidt's statement. He ducked his head to hide the smile he couldn't suppress.

"Mr. Zimmermann, since you're here—"

Hank jerked his head up and met her enchanting hazel eyes.

"Could you give me a hand with my trunk?" She pointed to the battered piece of luggage that sat just inside the depot door.

"Sure." He grabbed one leather handgrip and hoisted the load, clamping his lips on the grunt that tried to escape. The thing must be filled with rocks.

She thanked Mr. Schmidt and led the way back to the Sunday house. Hank followed with the rock-laden trunk.

"I hope it's not too heavy." She glanced over her shoulder. "I packed quite a few books."

That explained why it was pulling his shoulder out of joint.

She tipped her head and looked sideways at him. "May I ask you a question?"

He nodded and hiked the trunk up a tad higher.

"What does *sehr hubscher* mean, and why did you find it amusing?"

Heat raced up Hank's neck. Sehr hubscher meant *very pretty*.

Chapter 3

Saturday morning, Amelia sat at the small table with her books. The *clip-clop* of hooves and jingling harness announced the arrival of a wagon, and moments later the door crashed open. A husky woman with ruddy cheeks nearly fell into the room. Amelia leaped to her feet.

"*Was ist dies?*" The woman's eyes widened. "The door is not stuck?"

"Hank Zimmermann fixed it."

The woman eyed her with suspicion. "You are the new schoolteacher?"

"Y–yes." Amelia didn't know whether to extend her hand or stand there like a statue. "I'm Amelia Bachman. May I help you carry anything?"

"I am Olga Richter." The woman eyes snapped and she pointed to the small table. "You may carry those books upstairs. There is no room for them."

Before Amelia could collect her things, another woman, as wide as she was tall, waddled into the room, fussing over the cluttered table and scolding Amelia in German.

A burly man stepped in behind her. "*Mutter, stoppen sie sich zu beschweren*—stop complaining. Pardon my mama, she speaks no English. I am Lamar Richter. This is *meine mutter*, my mother, Winnie. You are Miss Bachman, ja? So—you are here." The man didn't appear bothered in the least that Amelia had arrived with no one to meet her or escort her to the Sunday house, for he said little else.

Amelia spent the remainder of the day dodging out of the way as Olga and Winnie bustled around, her attempts at conversation rejected. Evening brought the uncomfortable realization that she was expected to share the tiny sleeping loft with the two women, while Mr. Richter slept downstairs on a pallet.

Sunday afternoon as Amelia helped Olga carry things to the wagon, agitated voices carried on the air. Next door, Hank Zimmermann stood beside his family's wagon while his father berated him.

"The Zimmermanns are famers. When will you stop with your playing and come back to the farm where you belong?"

Hank ran his hand through his hair. "Vater, building furniture is not playing. It's my hope that one day you'll respect my choice to be a carpenter."

"Respect! It is you who should respect your father and work the land as you were born to do."

Mr. Zimmermann's harsh tone made Amelia flinch with the memory of her own father's disapproval of her chosen vocation. Empathy trickled through her. Sometime after the Richters left, the Zimmermann wagon pulled out, but Hank wasn't on it.

The first two days of classes required some adjustments. Most of the children were sweet, but some of the older boys attempted to play a prank or two, taking advantage of Amelia's unfamiliarity with the German language and culture. The class snickered when Bernard Braun tried to convince her that Mr. Richter went by the name *alte ziege*. Between the laughter and the devilish smirk in Bernard's eyes, it wasn't hard to figure out the reference wasn't flattering. She knew *alte* meant "old" and she was fairly certain *ziege* was some kind of animal. Bernard and his best friend, Paeter Lange, appeared panic-stricken when she replied that she'd make sure Mr. Richter knew the boys were kind enough to tell her his nickname. She ducked her head to hide her smile.

As she prepared to leave the little house on Wednesday morning, she heard the ring of Hank's hammer. Sending a furtive glance toward the Zimmermann's Sunday house, she caught a glimpse of Hank perched on a ladder, hammering a board into place at the back of the house. She paused and watched for a moment, fascinated by the way Hank's tools seemed an extension of himself. Pieces of wood conformed to the mastery with which he used his skill.

What a wonderful lesson to teach her students—that their hopes and dreams could grow and develop when surrendered to the hands of the Master. She tucked the thought away, but before she stepped off the porch, Hank straightened and looked her way. He tugged the brim of his hat then raised his fingers in a slight wave.

Her heart hiccupped. There was no point in pretending she hadn't been staring at him. She returned a polite nod and scurried down the street.

She'd barely gotten the fire started in the potbellied stove in the middle of the classroom when a wagon rolled into the yard. She cracked open the door to see who was arriving early. To her surprise, Hank's father sat on the wagon seat and three blond heads peeked just above the sides of the wagon bed. The gruff farmer pulled the team to a halt in front of the schoolhouse and barked at the youngsters to get out while he climbed down.

Amelia met him at the door, glancing past his shoulder to watch a little girl with golden pigtails help the two younger ones slide off the end of the tailgate. The oldest child couldn't have been more than seven or eight years of age, yet Mr. Zimmermann left them to fend for themselves. They were undoubtedly siblings, their resemblance being too uncanny to miss.

Amelia disciplined her features to not show disapproval of the man's inconsideration. "Good morning, Mr. Zimmermann."

Instead of returning the pleasant greeting, he merely grunted and gestured to the children. "These are startin' school today. That one"—he pointed to the eldest—"is Elsie. Next is Joy, and the boy is Micah. Last name's Delaney." He almost sneered when the name fell from his lips. "You kinder mind what the teacher tells you, or I'll take a strap to you."

Three pairs of eyes glistened with tears and the little boy's lower lip trembled. Mr. Zimmermann climbed back onto the wagon seat. "You go find your Uncle Hank when school's out." With that Mr. Zimmermann released the brake and whistled to the team.

The trio stood huddled together, eyeing Amelia with fear-filled eyes. Only then did she realize she was scowling, but the children had no way of knowing her displeasure was not aimed at them. She fixed a smile in place and stepped toward them. The little boy started to cry.

"Now there's nothing to be afraid of." She reached to pat Micah's head and the child shrank from her.

She pulled her hand back and tried a different approach. "Elsie? You must be the oldest. It looks like you're doing a fine job of taking care of your sister and brother." She sent the little girl a beaming smile. "Come inside where it's warmer and you can tell me all about yourselves. I brought some sugar cookies to school today."

At the mention of cookies, Micah wiped his nose on his sleeve and followed his sisters into the schoolhouse.

Amelia glanced at the little watch pinned to her bodice. The other students wouldn't begin arriving for at least another fifteen minutes. She directed the three siblings to one of the front benches and retrieved a cloth-covered pail from her desk.

She offered each child a golden-edged cookie. Elsie and Joy whispered a thank-you, but Micah observed her with wide, solemn green eyes, as though weighing her trustworthiness. Her heart twisted within her breast. She wanted to take the little fellow and hug him. Instead, she held out a cookie.

"My name is Miss Bachman, and I'm very happy to meet you." They munched their cookies while Amelia continued. "Elsie, can you tell me how much schooling you've had?"

Elsie wiped crumbs from her mouth. "We ain't never went to school before, but Mama taught us letters and numbers, and I can read."

"I can read, too." Joy lifted her chin and straightened her shoulders.

Elsie clucked like a hen. "No, you can't. You just know all the letters."

Amelia smiled, but in the back of her mind, Elsie's reference to *Mama* intrigued her. Where was their mother and why was Mr. Zimmermann carrying them to school? "Well, that's a very good start. Do you have a paper tablet and pencil?"

Elsie and Joy shook their heads in unison, their yellow braids flopping against their chins.

"That's all right. You can borrow mine today." Amelia's heart lifted just a little when a hesitant smile poked a dimple into Joy's cheek.

"Can I learn to read today?"

Amelia couldn't stay her hand from reaching out to cradle the side of Joy's face. "It will take more than one day, but we'll get started today." The glow in the little girl's eyes reflected her name.

Amelia instructed the three Delaney children to wait until she had cleaned the chalkboard and swept the floor so she could walk them to the Zimmermanns' Sunday house. Mr. Zimmermann's harsh tone and uncaring attitude still irked her, but she wasn't going to allow the children to wander the town searching for their uncle Hank alone.

Elsie wanted to carry Amelia's lunch pail, and Joy begged to carry her paper tablet, while Micah shyly tucked his hand into Amelia's. The four of them walked uptown and turned on Lincoln Street. As they approached the Zimmermann house, Amelia's eyes widened. The few boards and posts that Hank had nailed in place that morning had expanded into an extension off the back of the house. It still lacked a roof and one wall, but the structure was definitely taking shape.

"Mr. Zimmermann." Amelia raised her voice to be heard above Hank's hammering. Instantly, all three children halted and hung back.

When Hank poked his head around the corner to respond, Micah cried out, "Uncle Hank." The child dropped Amelia's hand and raced toward his uncle. The girls also relaxed and ran to claim a hug from the man whose blue-plaid shirt was speckled with sawdust.

Amelia's heart smiled.

Hank squatted to corral all three children in his arms. He tugged on the girls' pigtails and ruffled Micah's hair. "What are you rascals doing here?"

Amelia stepped forward. "Your father dropped them off at the school this morning and told them to *find you* when class was dismissed." She raised her eyebrows in a silent question.

Hank stood and pointed toward the door. "Elsie, there is some bread in the cabinet and a jar of jam on the table." The siblings trotted inside, leaving Amelia waiting for an answer to her unspoken inquiry.

Hank glanced over his shoulder and blew out a stiff breath. "First of all, let me explain. I'm not their *uncle* Hank. They are actually my cousins, but my father thinks it's disrespectful for them to call me Hank without some kind of title in front of it." He brushed sawdust from his sleeve. "My father's baby sister, Laurene, was fifteen years younger than him. My parents disapproved when she married an Irishman about nine years ago. Last week my father got a telegram saying Aunt Laurene and her husband had been killed in a wagon accident and the three children were being sent here."

Amelia's stomach clenched in sympathy for the three orphans, but misgiving filled her as well to think of them growing up under Mr. Zimmermann's harsh hand. "They were very frightened this morning."

"I'm not surprised." Hank muttered the remark that sounded more like he was talking to himself than to her. He shoved his hands in his pockets. "My father doesn't want them. He said he's already raised his children and doesn't intend to raise these. On Sunday, he said he was going to send them to the orphanage, so I'm a little surprised to see they are still here."

The disturbing revelation made no sense to Amelia. "He told me they were starting school today. Maybe he changed his mind."

Hank snorted. "Nothing changes Thornton Zimmermann's mind." Instantly, regret softened his features. "I didn't mean that the way it sounded."

Amelia's insides churned at the uncertainty the children faced. At least they appeared to love their "uncle" Hank, and if the way he greeted them was any indication, the feeling was mutual.

Chapter 4

Vater, how could you say such a mean thing to those kids?"

Thornton Zimmermann thumped his coffee cup down on the table and turned to face his son with rage in his eyes. "I am the head of this house. I make the decisions. Der kinder are not my responsibility. My sister and her Irish husband whelped them and now I am expected to raise them? Nein! I already raise my kinder." He cast a withering look at Hank. "Ja, I raise my son to be a farmer and he wants to be a *woodcutter*."

Hank sucked in a breath. He would not shout at his father no matter how angry he was or how much he disagreed with him. Instead, he pointed across the room at his brother, who waited in silence for their father to head out to the fields. "Vater, can't you see how much George loves planting and harvesting? He's the one who should take over the farm one day. I came here this morning hoping I could make you understand the gift God has given me to craft things out of wood, but this isn't about me being a craftsman."

"Bah! Craftsman!" The elder Zimmermann turned away. "I have fields to plow."

Hank took three strides and blocked him. He pointed out the door where Elsie, Joy, and Micah huddled together, crying.

"Look at those children out there. They've already lost their parents. We are the only family they have. How could you tell them you're sending them to an orphanage?"

His father's face mottled beet red. "You do not question what I decide. I have fed them for over two weeks. The letter finally comes and says there is no room at the orphanage in San Antonio. The director says he writes to Austin and Abilene. Or maybe kinder will go to Dallas, but they will go! As soon as I have word from the place"—Vater pointed his finger in Hank's face—"they *will* go."

Hank stared at his father. When had the man become so hateful? Was this his fault? Was Vater so angry at him for not following in his footsteps that he'd take it out on innocent children? Hank clenched his fists at his sides as anger boiled within him.

Hank glanced across the room at his mother, but Lydia Zimmermann shook her head at him, a warning in her eyes. There was no point in trying to talk to his father like this. He turned and stalked out the door.

Three tear-stained faces tipped up to look at him when he approached. His heart splintered at the sight of their blotchy cheeks and red-rimmed, swollen eyes. A cool March wind stirred the dust, creating muddy streaks tracing their sorrow.

Hank pulled out his bandanna and dipped it in the horse trough. Lowering himself to one knee, he blotted each child's face, talking in low, soothing tones.

"We can't have you going to school with dirty faces. What will Miss Bachman think? Besides, if you climb up on old Fritz with stripes on your cheeks, he's liable to think you're a tiger and buck you right off." He wiped the last of the dirty tears away from Micah's cheeks and the little boy looked up at Hank.

"Fritz won't buck me off. You said he's too old to buck."

Hank feigned surprise. "Did I say that?" When all three children nodded, he forced a smile he didn't feel and stood. "Well, maybe I did. Now, if we don't hurry, you're going to be late for school."

"I don't want to go to school today." Tears again filled Joy's eyes.

"Here now." Hank bent to cup her chin. "Miss Bachman would miss you something fierce if you didn't go to school. She told me you're learning to read."

Joy nodded.

"How about if you come to the Sunday house after school and read to me what you learn today?"

Joy shrugged. "I guess so."

"All right, then. Do you have the lunch pail Aunt Lydia packed for you?"

Elsie held it up.

"Then we're ready to go." Hank scooped Elsie up and lifted her onto Fritz's swayed back while the gray horse dozed at the hitching rail. He positioned Joy behind her sister, and Micah sat in the front where Elsie could hold on to him.

"Everybody all set?" He swung up onto his own horse. "C'mon, Fritz. It's time to get these kids to school."

Amelia led the first and second graders as they recited their addition tables in unison, but her gaze continually wandered to the three empty seats the Delaney children usually occupied. Although she tried to convince herself not to worry, her heart refused to listen.

"All right, first and second grade. Take out your tablets and copy the addition problems I've written on the chalkboard. Third and fourth graders, come to the front bench for reading. I want the older grades to go to the back corner where you will find some maps of the United States to study. When you've—"

The clopping of hooves cut her instructions short and she glanced out the window. A sigh of relief rippled through her.

"Freda Braun, you will be in charge of the reading group. Page thirty-seven. I must step out for a minute. Everyone has their assignments."

She exited the classroom in time to see Hank help the Delaney children off the swaybacked plow horse. The instant she caught sight of their puffy, red eyes, fear gripped her heart.

Hank bent to tuck Micah's shirt into his pants and smooth the boy's unruly straw-colored hair. "Come to the Sunday house when class is dismissed. I'll see you then."

Amelia touched the top of each child's head and gave them a reassuring smile. "Go on in and find your seats. I'll be there in a minute. I want to talk to your uncle Hank."

Elsie took Micah's hand and led him toward the door, but Joy wrapped her arms around Hank's waist and clung.

"Are you gonna make us go away, Uncle Hank?" A fat tear trickled down her cheek.

Amelia met Hank's gaze, holding her breath and waiting for his answer. His smoky eyes were a study in anger. The fear she felt when she first saw the children doubled. What had transpired to make the children so late and upset them so? She was afraid to ask.

Hank stooped to speak to Joy at her eye level. He brushed loose tendrils of hair from her face. "If it was up to me, you wouldn't have to go anywhere, sweetheart. But it's not my decision to make." He cupped her chin. "Do you remember the Bible story we read last night?"

Joy sniffed and nodded.

Hank thumbed her tears away. "Jesus is the Good Shepherd and He knows His sheep. No matter where His sheep are, He looks after them." He folded her fingers within his. "That means wherever we are, Jesus promises to take care of us, even if we are far away from each other."

The child buried her face in Hank's shirt and mumbled, "But I don't want to be far away. I want to be here."

Amelia gently peeled her away from Hank. "Joy, sometimes hard things happen in our lives and we don't have a choice. But the hard things don't mean that our love for each other goes away."

A twinge of guilt stabbed her. Growing up watching her parents' cold hearts and resentful demeanor was hard, and when she left home she didn't have the love of her parents to take with her. But Joy didn't need to know that.

She pulled the child into a hug. "Suppose you go behind the schoolhouse to the pump and wash your face. Then we will have our reading lesson."

Joy dragged her sleeve across her soggy cheeks and sniffed again. "Yes'm." She trudged away to do her teacher's bidding.

As soon as she was out of earshot, Amelia spun to face Hank. "What happened?"

He turned away as though looking her in the eye was painful. "Micah heard my father say something this morning about an orphanage, and he asked what an orphanage was." The dejection in his tone made Amelia shiver. He removed his hat and fidgeted with the brim. "So my father told him and the girls that they weren't his children and he wasn't going to be saddled with them, and as soon as he could make the arrangements, they were going to live in an orphanage."

Amelia covered her mouth and a gasp slipped between her fingers. "Oh no. How could he be so heartless?" She bit her lip, fearing her outburst may have offended Hank.

He snorted. "I asked him the same thing. He just blustered that it was his decision. We argued—" He shook his head. "I don't know what else to do."

Amelia plunked her hands on her hips. "Couldn't you take the children?"

Hank jerked around to face her. "What?" His eyes widened. "You can't be serious. I don't know anything about raising children."

"What do you have to know?" She cocked her head. "You need to love them and provide for their needs."

Hank's fist crumpled the brim of his hat. "How am I going to do that? In case you haven't noticed, I'm working out of my family's Sunday house and I don't have customers beating down the door."

"But those children need to know they are wanted and loved. Who is going to do that?"

He opened his mouth but apparently changed his mind. He plopped his hat back in place. "Look, I can't do what you're suggesting. How am I supposed to take care of three little kids? Do you really think my father would let me move them into the Sunday house like I owned it? He doesn't even like me using the place for my woodworking." He heaved an exasperated sigh.

Discouragement wilted her posture. She shrugged and turned back toward the schoolhouse. "I just wish. . ."

"I know. I wish the same thing."

She turned to face him. "Wishing won't change a thing, but praying might."

He looped Fritz's reins over a low-hanging branch. "Sometimes I'm not sure God hears my prayers."

Amelia glanced over her shoulder. She needed to return to the classroom, but Hank's remark disturbed her. "Of course, He hears you. Why would you think otherwise?"

He turned to his own horse, gripped the saddle horn, and swung astride. "Sometimes I wonder if God is as angry at me as my father is." He spoke absently, as though more to himself than Amelia. "My father refuses to listen to me because I'm not doing what he wants me to do. Does that mean I'm out of God's will? Wouldn't He refuse to listen as well?"

As if suddenly remembering she was there, he straightened and reined the horse around, tugging on the brim of his hat before nudging the horse into a gentle lope.

Amelia watched him ride away and felt a check in her spirit. Unconsciously, wasn't she doing something similar? She felt like a hypocrite. She'd encouraged her students to trust

God with the new skills and knowledge they were learning, and let Him be the Master of their hopes and dreams. But her own hopes and dreams remained tucked away in a secret place in her heart—like unplanted seeds.

"Lord God, I couldn't do what my father wanted to me to do. I just couldn't." She paused by the schoolhouse door and fingered the pull rope on the bell. Becoming a schoolteacher was a noble occupation, one in which she could influence young lives and mold their character.

And remain single.

She, too, had gone against her father's wishes. Did that mean she was out of God's will, and therefore beyond the reach of His ear?

Chapter 5

Amelia swept her tiny pile of dirt out the back door of the Sunday house, noticing as she did so that Hank was nowhere to be seen. She'd grown so accustomed to hearing the song of his chisel gliding along a length of wood, or his mallet beating out staccato taps, the absence of the sounds felt lonely. The lean-to addition he'd constructed off the back of his family's Sunday house testified to his skill. Amelia paused for a moment and studied the lines of the new space he'd created, and wondered if the inside was as efficient and functional as it appeared from the outside.

Her face warmed with the thought. Why in heaven's name was she so fascinated by this man? She ordered her attention back to her tasks. Now that the sun was up, she wanted to polish the windows before the Richter family arrived for the weekend. The Saturday morning air held a bit of a chill for late March. She propped open the windows so the house would smell as fresh and clean as the spring breeze.

As the sun climbed higher in the eastern sky, Amelia took rags soaked in a vinegar solution to the windows, angling her head to peer sideways, checking for streaks. She wanted to give Olga and Winnie nothing to criticize.

The sounds of wagons arriving to the melody of birdsong, children's laughter, and folks calling out greetings to each other began filling the air. Amelia hurried to finish her preparations. Her final chore was filling the woodbox. She picked up as much stove wood as she could hold, but as she turned to carry it into the house, the breeze blew the door shut.

She stamped her foot. "Drat!"

"Here, allow me."

Amelia jerked her head around. Hank stepped onto the small stoop and reached for the load in her arms.

"When I saw what you were doing, I came to help."

"Oh, th–thank you, Mr. Zimmermann."

"Hank."

"Mr.—Hank. I didn't realize you were. . .your house looked empty."

He cocked one eyebrow and his silent query caused flustered embarrassment to twine up her throat—she'd just told him that she'd been looking for him. She put her composure back in place.

"You don't have to do this."

He shrugged and grinned. "I'm setting a good example for my young cousins."

She allowed Hank to relieve her of the load of wood and she propped the door open.

He tipped his head toward the wood piled in his arms. "Toss me a few more pieces."

She obliged, and he carried the firewood inside and emptied his arms into the box beside the stove, filling it to the brim.

"Thank you, Mr.—Hank."

"My pleasure." He dusted off his hands as he exited, then paused on the stoop. "It's a beautiful day."

She murmured her agreement with his observation.

"Perfect morning for a stroll. If you aren't too busy—"

"Oh but I am." A sliver of guilt over the fib poked her. She ignored it and continued. "The Richters will be here any time, and I still have things to do before they arrive. Thank you for your help. It was very kind of you. Good day." She pasted a polite smile on her face and closed the door on his disappointed expression.

Filling the woodbox was her last chore of the morning, but Hank's warm brown eyes sent strange ripples through her. The inclination to explore the feeling teased, but she purposefully shoved it into submission.

Reverend Hoffman stood at the door of the church and shook hands with the parishioners as they filed out. Amelia fell into line behind the Richters and expressed her appreciation to the pastor for a fine, inspiring sermon.

"I hope my students were listening as you spoke about compassion. It's a virtue I hope to instill in all the children." She didn't add that she hoped Thornton Zimmermann was listening as well. She'd seen the man, three rows ahead of her, thump Micah's head when the five-year-old squirmed.

"Thank you, young lady." Pastor Hoffman grinned broadly. "My daughter loves going to school since you began teaching. Whatever you're doing, don't stop."

The preacher's praise sent warmth scurrying into her

cheeks. "Your Gretchen is a fine student. It's a pleasure having her in my class."

They bid each other good afternoon and Amelia stepped out into the early spring sunshine.

"Miss Bachman!" A joyful chorus of childish voices greeted her. The Delaney children ran to her with smiles. How good it was to see them happy, even if it was for only a few moments.

Elsie, usually the serious one, tugged at Amelia's sleeve. "I learned a Bible verse today."

"Why, that's wonderful, Elsie. I'd love to hear it."

The little girl twisted one braid around her finger and dipped her fair brows in concentration. "For He shall give His angels charge over thee, to keep thee in all thy ways. Psalm ninety-one, verse eleven." A grin filled her face as she finished.

"Excellent, Elsie. I'm very proud of you."

"You are?" The child's eyes widened with wonder.

"I am." Amelia bent and slipped her arm around Elsie's shoulder. "Do you know what the verse means?"

"I think so." The little girl cocked her head. "It means God tells His angels to take care of us wherever we go." She leaned close to Amelia and whispered, "Even if we have to go to the orphanage."

Amelia's throat tightened at the child's courageous spirit. "We're still going to pray that doesn't happen, but if it does, yes, God will take care of you wherever you are."

Elsie fingered the lace edging on the sleeve of Amelia's green, flowered dress. "I ain't never seen such a pretty dress."

She tipped her face up. "Green was my mama's favorite color. She woulda looked beautiful in a dress like this."

Amelia pressed her lips together and forced the corners upward, blinking hard. She didn't dare try to speak.

"Good morning."

Amelia looked up to find Hank Zimmermann's deep brown eyes fixed on her. Had he heard Elsie's heart-wrenching appraisal? She gulped.

"Elsie was just reciting her scripture verse for me." She took Elsie's golden braid between her thumb and forefinger.

"Oh?" Hank bent down, his hands on his knees. "Will you recite it for me, too?"

Elsie leaned to one side and peeked around Hank to where Mr. Zimmermann stood talking with another man. "All right, but just you."

A smile stretched across Hank's face, but an ache invaded Amelia's heart. Elsie and her siblings had only been living with the Zimmermann's for less than a month and already the child knew whom she could and could not trust.

Hank slid the last of the newly finished pieces of furniture through the yawning double doors of the general store and turned to face the proprietor, Horst Braun. The man grinned and slapped Hank's shoulder. "This is good work, ja. You will have many customers when they see this beautiful craftsmanship." Horst ran his hand along the intricate design at the top of the cabinet Hank had labored over for two weeks.

Hank swiped his sleeve over his forehead. "I hope you're

right, Horst." He didn't add that if he didn't get orders for more pieces, he'd find himself back on the farm doing what his father wanted. Doubt swirled in his stomach and he besought God again for direction. A silent prayer ascended from his heart.

Lord God, I want to be certain this is Your will. Why else would You have put the skill in my hands and the desire in my heart if You did not intend for me to use it? Please make peace between Vater and me, Lord. Can I not honor him and still be a carpenter?

Horst positioned the smaller piece, a pie safe with punched tin door inserts and gingerbread trim, near the entrance of the store. "There." Horst turned to Hank and beamed. "The customers can't miss it when they come in."

"Are you sure you have room for the cabinet?"

"Ja, we just move a few things over." Horst's gap-toothed grin stretched the man's beard into a crescent. "You push *der* pickle barrel there, and I move *dies* display of boots."

The two men shoved and maneuvered items here and there, opening up a space into which they slid the cabinet. Hank stepped back to survey the position of the piece at the same moment the front door opened and hit him in the backside.

"Oh, pardon me. I'm so sorry."

Hank turned to see Amelia's contrite expression turn to one of mortification. Her eyes widened and color stole into her cheeks and for the briefest of moments, Hank thought she was prettier than the sunrise he'd admired that morning.

Amelia clasped her hand over her bodice. "Oh dear, I

should watch where I'm going. Do forgive me."

A grin tweaked his face. "No harm done." His pulse quickened. "I didn't realize it was time for school to be out. Are the youngsters at the Sunday house?"

She shook her head and looked out the window. "They were headed out of town on their old farm horse. I believe they call him Fritz." When she turned back around, she'd regained her composure. A polite smile curved her lips.

"Ja, Fritz is too old to pull the plow, but he doesn't mind the kids riding him." Hank shuffled his boot against the rough-hewn floor, trying to find the words to ask Amelia to join him for a stroll. "Vater must have told them to come straight home." Perhaps she'd agree to walk down by the creek with him before going back to. . .

"The children are—"

"Would you have time to accompany—"

Nervous laughter bubbled from Amelia, and Hank gestured with his hand. "You first."

The rosy glow crept into her cheeks again. "I was just going to say the children are doing well with their studies. Joy loves learning to read, and Elsie excels in spelling and vocabulary. Micah needs a bit more help with his letters and numbers, but he's a bright little boy. He'll learn quickly."

Hank shrugged. "They sure seem to like school and I thank you for that, but I don't know how much longer they'll be here. My father is waiting for letters from the orphanages at Abilene and Dallas." He scowled and studied the toes of his boots. "I'm afraid he won't even try to keep the kids together.'

"But the children *must* stay together." Her voice broke.

"They've already been through so much. If they are sent away—all they have is each other."

Her plea carried with it a thread of challenge and Hank gritted his teeth. He would take all three children in a minute if he could, but he'd already told her he didn't have the means to support them.

Distress over the children's future pressed her lips together and tiny lines appeared across her forehead, but she straightened her shoulders and lifted her chin slightly. "You were about to ask me something."

Hank swallowed the sudden dryness in his throat. "Would you consent to walk with me to Baron's Creek? It's not far from the Sunday house and we'd be in plain view for propriety's sake."

Amelia's eyes widened and she blinked twice. Her lips parted but she hesitated to speak, and the same flustered expression he saw when she hit him with the door returned to her face.

"It's very kind of you to ask, Mr. Zimm—I mean, Hank. But I've come to Fredericksburg to teach, and I don't wish to give any other impression. Good afternoon."

She hastened down the steps, apparently forgetting whatever it was she came to purchase.

Chapter 6

Almost a week after Amelia's conversation with Hank in the general store, the words she'd spoken to him still haunted her. She hadn't lied to him—not exactly. Teaching school had brought her to Fredericksburg, but there was no denying the underlying motive. Becoming a schoolteacher afforded her a perfectly reasonable excuse for refusing invitations from would-be suitors, including the prosperous rancher with whom her father had attempted to marry her off.

As evening fell she crossed the small kitchen area to prepare her simple supper. A light winked from the window of the Sunday house next door, testifying to Hank's presence. She fixed her gaze at her neighbor's window and felt a whisper of defiance ripple through her.

"I came to Fredericksburg to teach."

A twinge of foolishness poked her since there was nobody to hear her repeat the declaration she'd already delivered to Hank. If she were honest, she'd admit her decision had as much to do with her desire to control her own destiny as it did with molding the minds and character of children. In the five weeks she'd been in Fredericksburg, she'd thrilled to see her students learn and grow, but Fredericksburg was also a refuge. She was safe here.

She released a soft snort. "Safe from what? Marriage? Or just life in general?"

She lit the oil lamp on the table and cut a thick slice of the dark bread she'd purchased at the German bakery and slathered it with peach preserves. A chunk of cheese and small piece of cold sausage rounded out her supper. She set the kettle on the stove for her tea.

An image tiptoed into her mind. What would it be like to put supper on the table for a husband and children? The silent suppers she'd endured all her life, with her father at one end of the table and her mother at the other, faded from her memory as a fascinating scene unfolded and drew her. Blond-headed children with smiles of anticipation welcomed the culinary offerings she placed before them, and the man at the head of the table beamed at his family and bowed his head to pray. When he said amen and lifted his head—it was Hank Zimmermann's face.

Amelia startled and covered her warming cheeks with both hands. "Mercy!" *Such nonsense.* But the more she tried to push the thought away, the more strongly it insisted on manifesting.

Amelia heaved a sigh. A distraction. That's what she needed. Her canvas satchel sat gaping open on one of the chairs. She dug deep past the books and folders, and felt around the bottom of the bag. Her fingers found the small cloth pouch and she pulled it out. While she waited for the kettle to boil, she untied the strings that held the pouch tightly closed and shook an assortment of seeds into her open palm. A dozen different kinds of wildflower seeds given to her by one of her professors when she graduated—to commemorate her new beginning and opportunity to blossom.

As she rolled the seeds around in her hand, a plan began to form. Why not use the seeds as a science lesson, coupled with an outing for her students before the end of the school year? She glanced at the calendar on the wall. First week of April. Plenty of time to plan. She smiled and slid the seeds back into the pouch, pulling the strings snug. Her thoughts were back where they belonged.

Steam rose from the kettle's spout in lazy wisps that fogged the window. Amelia wiped the condensation away and the lamplight from Hank's window became visible again.

Amelia stepped out the door of the post office clutching two envelopes. The first one bore her mother's distinctive flowing script. The arrival of the letter—the first she'd received from either parent for more than six months—sent hope surging through her. But anticipation over the contents of the letter sparred with dread in her heart. The last conversation she'd had with her mother was not a happy one. She tucked the letter into her satchel along with her books, lesson plans, and papers to be corrected. The privacy of the Sunday house was the place to read the letter, in case her parents' opinion of her career choice had not changed.

She didn't recognize the handwriting on the second letter, and the return address was smudged. Pausing on the boardwalk, she broke the seal on the envelope and extracted the single sheet of paper, scanning downward to the signature.

"Uncle Will?" The corners of her mouth lifted. Her father's brother, widowed a year ago, was her favorite relative. He and his wife had worked together in his medical practice in McAlester, Oklahoma. She read his scrawled words.

> *I hope this letter finds my favorite niece happy and well.*
>
> *It's been difficult for me to continue living and working here in McAlester since your aunt's passing. I can't walk down the street without her presence accompanying me. Everything I see reminds me of her, and while I desire to cling to her memory, I seem to be bogged down in grief.*
>
> *I need a fresh start. After corresponding with a few colleagues, I've made the decision to close my practice here and move to Fredericksburg.*

"Uncle Will's coming here?" Happy anticipation lifted her heart. She read the last line of his missive.

> *It may take some time to finalize everything, but I hope to be there perhaps by late May. Fondly, Uncle Will.*

While she'd been sad for Uncle Will at the passing of her aunt, joy tickled her stomach at the prospect of him coming to Fredericksburg. She slid Uncle Will's letter into her satchel with the one from her mother and hurried toward the general store.

A brisk spring breeze flapped the brim of Amelia's bonnet

as she stepped through the bright blue door. Two ladies stood admiring the pie safe near the entrance of the store while Horst Braun walked over to them, wiping his hands on his apron.

"*Das ist verkauft*—that one is sold, ladies, but I'm sure if you speak with the craftsman, he will be happy to build another for you."

One of the ladies examined the gingerbread trim. "*Wer ist es?* Who does this fine work?"

Horst grinned. "Hank Zimmermann. He is very skilled, ja?"

A swell of pride for Hank danced through Amelia as the ladies exclaimed over the piece of furniture. The instant she recognized the emotion for what it was, heat filled her face. She ducked her head and pretended to examine a bolt of dress goods.

Foolishness.

Certainly Hank would be pleased to know people praised his work, especially in light of the argument she'd overheard between him and his father. She'd caught glimpses of him working hard at his craft, but to experience prideful flutters in her belly over the compliments from Horst and the women was just plain silly. So why did an absurd smile insist on stretching across her face? She shook her head.

"What can I get for you today, Miss Bachman?" Horst's voice boomed directly behind her. Amelia jumped as if he'd read her thoughts and knew why she was smiling.

"Oh, uh…" Why *did* she come into the store? She gawked at Horst for a moment. "Thread."

His indulgent smile was punctuated by a slight arch of

his thick eyebrows, and he remained in place. The ends of his mustache wiggled and he pointed to the shelf a foot away from her right elbow. She jerked her head around.

"Oh." Her face burned and she could have sworn it was the middle of summer. "Oh my. I admonish my students about daydreaming and here I am, guilty of the same pastime. Forgive me, Mr. Braun."

The burly man tilted his head back and belly-laughed. "*Es ist gut*—it is good, ja, to daydream sometimes. My little Freda, she likes to watch the clouds. Her mutter grows impatient with her when she imagines stories drifting across the sky instead of doing her chores." A wide grin elongated his mustache.

Amelia imagined her student cloud-gazing with her father. A tiny ache began in the pit of her stomach. She'd never known such frivolity as a child, and especially not with either parent. Amelia hastily chose spools of thread, one of green and one of white. She opened her reticule to pay, but paused and pointed to a glass jar on the counter.

"Please give me two scoops of those gumdrops. I think I'll let my students do some daydreaming and reward their creativity."

Horst shoveled two large scoops into a paper bag. "I won't tell Freda's mutter you let her daydream in school." A twinkle in his eye accompanied his conspiratorial whisper.

Amelia paid for her purchase and dropped the thread and confection into her satchel. She hesitated for a brief moment at the door to take a better look at the pie safe. Horst was right. Hank was a fine craftsman. The silly flutters began again.

Hank couldn't keep the grin from his face three days ago when Horst Braun told him the pie safe was sold and two other women were interested in having one made. But when Mayor Ehrlichmann knocked on the door of the Sunday house and inquired about having a rocking chair crafted for his wife's birthday, Hank's heart soared. This was God's answer. After countless prayers asking for heaven's affirmation of his dream, Hank had cash in his pocket from his first sale, an order in his hand, and the possibility of two more, lending true credibility to the choice he'd made. Gratefulness filled his heart.

A soft spring rain fell outside the lean-to workshop. Hank ran his hands over slabs of burr oak, choosing the best pieces for the rocking chair. Interesting waves and curves flowed along the wood grain, interrupted by an occasional knot. He carefully selected each cut for its beauty and strength. Once the chair was finished, rubbing linseed oil deeply into the grain would enhance its radiance. The classic lines and intricate detail came alive in his mind—a chair to hand down to the mayor's grandchildren and great-grandchildren.

The smile in his heart faded. If his young cousins were split up and sent to different orphanages, they would likely never possess a family heirloom like the one he planned to create for Mayor Ehrlichmann. A scowl tugged on his brow with the disturbing thought. Raising his heart heavenward, he sought God's ear.

"Lord, I know I got angry at Amelia for suggesting I take the children, but how can I do that without a way to support them? I'd have to sell a whole lot more pieces of furniture. Amelia doesn't understand how a man feels about taking care of a family, how he wants to give them everything they need and put a decent roof over their heads, to be able to feed them and clothe them, keep them safe and warm and protected."

He halted his list of things God already knew. Since God was already aware of every desire of his heart, it seemed futile to hide the one thing he'd neglected to mention.

"God, if it's not asking too much, could you send me a helpmate?" The entreaty had barely escaped his lips when he caught sight of Amelia fetching firewood from her back stoop.

Chapter 7

Olga and Winnie Richter each grunted a greeting to Amelia and brushed through the door of the Sunday house. Winnie muttered something in German Amelia didn't catch. Olga turned and sent a sour frown in Amelia's direction.

"She wants to know if you've been cooking on her stove."

Before Amelia could admit to using the stove to heat water for tea or to warm leftover stew, Winnie waved her chubby hand.

"*Sprechen sie auf Deutsch!*" She followed up the challenge with a torrent of German, none of it sounding the least bit complimentary in tandem with her derisive tone.

Amelia understood the first demand. Winnie wanted German spoken and became angry whenever Olga had to translate into English.

Lamar Richter entered, lugging a loaded crate. "*Mutter, beruhigen sie sich.* Calm down." He plunked the crate on the table and faced Amelia. "Der is a matter I must talk to you."

"Yes, sir?"

The school board chairman pointed to the back door. "Outside."

It wasn't a request.

Amelia sucked in a breath. Had she done something

wrong? She hated the way her heart hammered, much the way it used to do when her father berated her for speaking her mind or disagreeing with him.

She exited the back door with Mr. Richter on her heels. He stepped in front of her the moment he closed the door. His bushy eyebrows resembled a fat, gray caterpillar wiggling over his hooded eyes, but she didn't dare smile.

Mr. Richter cleared his throat and thumbed his suspenders. "Some parents complain to me. You do not teach der class in German. This is true?

Was that all? "Yes, it's true." Amelia clasped her hands at her waist. Frankly, she didn't see the problem.

"You know our community is German. All der schools in every district always teach in our mother tongue." Mr. Richter lifted his chin and raised his voice a decibel, injecting a demanding tone into his words as if daring her to state otherwise. "Der parents"—he struggled to find the word— "expect der kinner learn in German. Der young ones must grasp their heritage."

Amelia lifted her shoulders and opened her hands, palms up. "You knew when you hired me that my German was very limited. I didn't make a secret of that fact. Neither do I recall reading anything in my teaching contract about German being mandatory."

"It is who we are." Mr. Richter's voice boomed through the cool spring air, disturbing a few birds in the overhead branches.

Lamar Richter's inflection and the pitch of his voice intensified, but Amelia refused to be bullied. "I agree. But you and your families are living in a country, and in a state, that speaks primarily English. These children will have to learn to function in an English-speaking society. If they don't, some unscrupulous person may try to take advantage of them or cheat them."

The man's face reddened and his jaw worked back and forth. "You refuse to speak German in der classroom?"

Amelia was certain most everyone up and down the street could hear him bellow. "I'm not refusing, and if speaking German is that important to the parents, I will do my best to improve my understanding of the language and conduct classes in both English and German."

"Nien! This is not acceptable."

"And what *is* acceptable, Mr. Richter? That I do exactly what you say, no more and no less?"

If the man's face grew any redder, he'd explode. Judging by his clenched fists and sputtering lips, he obviously wasn't accustomed to his word being questioned.

"Mr. Richter, you must remember, I have some students who do not speak German. All of my German-speaking students understand English. But the ones who speak no German would come to a standstill in their learning. I won't allow that to happen."

"You won't allow—? Who are you to decide what is allowed?"

Amelia lifted her chin and folded her arms across her chest. "I am their teacher. It is my job to see to it that they learn, and I will use whatever means necessary to impart knowledge to them. If that involves teaching in two languages, I'll do it, even though it will require a great deal more lesson preparation time."

Mr. Richter blustered. "You can take some of dat time you use now teaching foolish things and learn better German."

"Foolish things?" Amelia's ire tightened her jaw. "What have I been teaching that you deem foolish?"

"Some parents tell me der kinner must draw maps of der whole United States. And others complain about der kinner reciting poetry." He leaned slightly forward. "Paeter Lange's father say his son must know a long list of many dates. Foolishness!" Richter waved his hands as if erasing a lesson plan from the air. "None of those things teach a child to plant and harvest a better crop."

Amelia plunked her hands on her hips. "Are you suggesting that I don't teach geography or history or literature?"

"Ja! Dat is just what I suggest. The young ones, dey only need to know how to read and write and cipher." Mr. Richter's fingers clutched his waistband and he hiked up his britches and threw out his chest.

"I disagree."

Predictably, the red blotches mottling Mr. Richter's face turned purple. He huffed and stammered, his anger tying his tongue in a knot. Amelia took advantage of his rattled state and continued.

"The children will become much better citizens, and much better people, if they know how our country came to be. Understanding the boundaries and rights of each individual state teaches the children to respect the diversity among us. Literature and science help expand young minds. They are learning to be productive people."

She uncrossed her arms and held her hands out in front

of her, beseeching the man to understand her point of view. "Don't you see? Some of these children will follow in their parents' footsteps and become farmers, and that's wonderful, if it's what they want to do. But some will become merchants or skilled craftsmen. Others will want to go to the university and become doctors or scientists. Some might grow up and learn the law or become part of our system of government. Some may even become teachers."

Mr. Richter started to open his mouth, but Amelia put her hand up. "Yes, teachers, Mr. Richter, because every *parent* should be a teacher."

Checkmate.

Exasperation etched hard lines in the school board chairman's face, and for now, he had no retort. He stared, unblinking, at her for several long moments. Finally, he waved a stubby, sausage-like finger under her nose.

"You think about what I said."

With that, he turned on his heel and returned to the house, slamming the door in his wake.

Amelia shook her head. "I wonder if he will think about what *I* said." She started to follow the man into the Sunday house but caught sight of Hank Zimmermann standing, arms akimbo, by his back door, staring in her direction. Dismay filled her when she realized he must have heard every word.

Hank lingered outside the front door of the church as the parishioners filed out. His three young cousins romped in a circle around him like colts in a spring meadow.

"Catch me, Uncle Hank!" Micah jumped up and down, shrieking with giggles when Hank grabbed the child around the middle and tickled him.

Elsie and Joy dodged out of his reach in a silly game of tag, their laughter spilling out to rival the singing of the birds.

Hank emitted a mock growl. "When I catch you two, I'm going to tie your pigtails together."

The little girls squealed and dashed between the parked wagons. Hank had just crouched behind one of the wagons, lying in wait to jump out and surprise the girls, when Lamar Richter rounded the corner.

"Zimmermann." The school board chairman leveled a glare at Hank crabby enough to wilt the spring flowers. Richter shifted his gaze to the children who stopped short, colliding into one another.

"Good Sabbath to you, Mr. Richter." He glanced down at his cousins. "Laughter is music in God's ears, is it not?"

Richter snorted. "Sacrilegious. Children should be seen and not heard."

"You know, Mr. Richter, I'm glad you brought that up, because there is something I'd like to discuss with you." He turned to the children. "Elsie, you and Joy take Micah and go to the wagon. Uncle Thornton will want to leave soon."

At the mention of his father, the smiles on all three children's faces drooped.

"Are you coming, too, Uncle Hank?" Joy tugged at his hand.

"I'll be along shortly. You three scoot now, and go get into the wagon."

As soon as the children were out of earshot, Hank returned his gaze to Richter. "I heard you yesterday—in fact, I think half the town heard you—bellowing at Miss Bachman for not conducting her classes in German."

Richter scowled. "It is no business of yours."

Hank leveled a steely gaze at the man. "You made it everyone's business hollering at the top of your lungs. And I beg to differ with you." He gestured in the direction the children had gone. "Three of the children Miss Bachman was talking about were my little cousins. Granted, they've picked up a few German words since they've been here, but if classes were taught purely in German, they would cease to learn. I don't think that's what you want, is it?"

"All der school districts teach in German. Der old ways are best." The volume of Richter's voice rose with each word until nearly everyone in the surrounding churchyard stopped what they were doing and stared at the school board chairman.

Hank cocked an eyebrow at the man. "Seems to me your first consideration should be to the children and their education. You have a teacher who is doing an excellent job. The children—*all* the children, are learning."

"*Was es ist*—What is it to you?" The veins in Richter's neck bulged. "You have no children in der school. You have no say in the matter. Mind your own business."

Pastor Hoffman hurried across the yard to where the two men stood toe-to-toe. "Gentlemen, please. It is the Lord's Day and we have just come from worship. Can this not be settled in a Christian manner?"

Hank turned to the preacher. "You're right, pastor. Forgive me. I only meant to clear up a misunderstanding. You see, it is my business to ensure that the children I love get the best education possible."

Richter smoothed one hand through his hair and drew in a deep breath. "Hank Zimmermann is not a parent—"

Pastor Hoffman held up both hands and spoke in a quiet but firm, even tone. "I'll not allow our day of worship to be disturbed by uncontrolled tempers. Both of you go home and examine your own hearts, and let God rule in this issue."

Hank chewed on his bottom lip and gave a curt nod. He turned on his heel and strode across the churchyard past the gawking parishioners. At the edge of the street, Amelia stood with her fingertips covering her mouth, and wide, unblinking eyes fixed on him. His step slowed as their gazes locked and his heart squeezed. He prayed he hadn't made things worse for her by confronting the pigheaded school board chairman, but a small voice within pressed him to take a stand for his cousins. In doing so, he supposed he also stood up for Amelia. The thought caused no small stirring in his heart.

Chapter 8

Hank waited outside the schoolhouse until the children came spilling out the door at the end of the school day. The Braun children, Pater Lange, the Hoffman girls, and the Werner twins chased each other around the yard in a dizzying game of tag, but Hank's cousins were apparently still inside.

"Hope they didn't get into trouble," Hank muttered to himself as he approached the door. Sometimes his father made the children do extra chores in the morning before they left for school, which made them late. The door stood open and Hank peeked in. His three cousins encircled their arms around their teacher in a collective hug.

"G'bye, Miss Bachman."

"See you tomorrow, Miss Bachman."

"I love you, Miss Bachman."

Hank's heart tumbled end over end. A twinge of jealousy nipped at him. The children held no inhibitions when it came to expressing their affection for their teacher. How Hank wished he could do the same.

"Uncle Hank!" Joy and Micah squealed their delight when they spied Hank standing in the doorway. Elsie, more sedate, held Miss Bachman's hand and walked like a little lady. Was it his imagination, or did Amelia's eyes light up when she saw him? Probably just wishful thinking.

He tweaked Micah's nose and tugged on the girls' pigtails as they clamored for his attention. "Did you three rascals behave yourselves today?"

"I learned to read some new words." Joy tugged on his arm.

Micah grabbed his other hand. "I can write the whole alphabet."

Hank raised his eyes and found Amelia's soft smile and tender eyes on him. The moment their eyes met, she dropped her gaze and her cheeks pinked.

He gathered the children and pointed them toward the door. "There is some apple *kuchen* on the table in the Sunday house. You may each have a small piece, but then you must go straight home. Uncle Thornton will expect you to do your chores."

The siblings grabbed their slates and McGuffey's, Elsie snatched the lunch pail, and they skipped out the door, calling out their good-byes to their teacher.

Hank watched them scramble aboard Fritz. "They're very fond of you, Miss Bachman. You've helped ease their grief with your kindness." He turned to face her. "Thank you for that."

She looked past him through the open door. "I have affection for all my students. But those three. . .I suppose as a teacher, I'm not permitted to have favorites, and I try to be impartial, but your cousins are very dear to me." Her voice quavered and she straightened her shoulders and marched back to her desk. "So, what brings you to school today?"

Hank gulped. Her sweet voice and enchanting eyes so

mesmerized him, the answer to her question was momentarily lost in his fascination of her charm.

Why did I come to. . . "Oh yes. Mr. Richter asked me to see if I could repair a broken hinge."

Amelia's eyes widened. "I wasn't sure Mr. Richter heard me when I mentioned the cabinet hinge needed fixing." She walked to the cabinet in the corner and cautiously opened the door with both hands to prevent it from falling. "See? I hope you can mend it. The door almost fell off and hit Gretchen Hoffman in the head last week."

Hank gave the hinge a cursory inspection, but Amelia's nearness proved quite distracting. Some kind of sweet fragrance clung to her, like a field of wildflowers—those purple ones that bloomed in late May. He drew in a surreptitious breath, hoping she didn't realize he was drinking in her scent.

"Can you fix it?"

Hank startled and the door slipped from his grip onto his toe. He gritted his teeth and bit back the *ouch* that sprang into his throat.

Amelia uttered a soft gasp. "Oh my, are you all right?" She impulsively laid her hand on his arm.

No, I'm not all right, but it has nothing to do with the door falling on my foot. "Sure thing. I'll have to bring some tools back with me to fix this properly, but it shouldn't take more than a few minutes. In the meantime, I suggest you leave the door off."

"Of course. Thank you—Hank." A rosy blush accompanied his name on her lips.

His heart rat-a-tatted like a busy woodpecker. "I'll be back first thing in the morning." He couldn't stop the silly grin that pulled the corners of his mouth at the thought of seeing her again.

He walked the few blocks to his Sunday house with the memory of his cousins hugging their teacher and declaring they loved her. He glanced at the windows of the houses and shops he passed, certain the occupants could hear his heart proclaiming that he loved her, too.

The rocking chair for Mayor Ehrlichmann came to life in Hank's hands. He savored the gratification of watching the grain of the wood take on a character for generations of the Ehrlichmann family. Inhaling the aroma of the freshly sanded burr oak, he stroked his fingers along the satin surface of the armrests. Tomorrow he'd begin coaxing linseed oil into the grain.

"Uncle Hank! Uncle Hank!"

Without pulling out his pocket watch, he knew it was 3:30. Who needed a watch with his cousins around? He wiped his hands on a rag and met the children at the door of the lean-to. Elsie and Joy wore look-alike dresses of green calico he didn't remember seeing before. His mother sewed, but certainly Hank's father wouldn't allow his wife to spend money on yard goods for children that weren't his.

"Look, Uncle Hank." Elsie's eyes sparkled. "Look what Miss Bachman made for us." She held out the edges of her skirt and pirouetted, her straw-colored braids flying and her face beaming as if she'd just been given a precious treasure.

Hank's heart arrested as he gazed from one sibling to the other. There was something familiar about the dresses. "Miss Bachman made them?"

The sisters nodded and Elsie fingered her sleeve. "Green was Mama's favorite color."

Recognition rang in Hank's mind. Two Sundays ago, he remembered Elsie admiring Amelia's green calico dress, telling her teacher that her mama "would have looked beautiful in a dress like that." A tender ache tangled through Hank's chest when he realized what Amelia had done.

Micah sported a new white shirt. The boy tipped his beaming face up to Hank with a gap-toothed grin. "My shirt used to be Miss Bachman's apron."

Hank ruffled the boy's hair. "You look like a fine gentleman in that shirt. Don't get it dirty, all right?"

"I won't, Uncle Hank."

Amelia Bachman was an extraordinary woman. Was there no limit to her giving heart? How could anyone—his father or Lamar Richter or any of the parents who'd complained—doubt her love and compassion for these children? How many of them gave pieces of themselves to enrich a child's life the way Amelia did? Hank's heart groaned within his chest. How he wished he could declare to her the love God had already revealed to him.

Elsie hugged Hank's waist. "We have to get home so Uncle Thornton won't be mad, but we wanted to show you our new dresses." Even the thought of their tardiness stirring their uncle's wrath couldn't erase the smile from her face.

Hank boosted them up onto Fritz's back and made sure Elsie had a firm grip on Micah. "I'll see you tomorrow. Be careful going home."

Three small hands waved as Fritz plodded down the street. Their childish voices created a woven tapestry as they called out to him "Bye, Uncle Hank. I love you, Uncle Hank."

Hank's heart turned over. Those ornery, adorable youngsters had wrapped their fingers around him and there was no escaping their clutches—nor did he want to.

"Oh Lord, I hate the thought of those kids being sent to an orphanage—maybe separate orphanages. Please provide some way for them to stay together with a family who will love them."

Amelia wished she could stamp her foot to express her frustration, but she'd not give Lamar Richter the satisfaction of knowing he'd irritated her. All she wanted was to borrow the man's wagon for the outing she'd planned. Shouldn't the school board chairman be the greatest supporter of the teacher and her efforts to educate the community's children? The man's narrow-mindedness caused her no end of vexation.

"Reading, writing, and ciphering. Dat is all der pupils need to learn." He flipped one hand out in a derisive motion. "Planting flower seeds. Bah! Such foolishness."

"Mr. Richter, planting seeds and nurturing plants is a science. Every time a farmer sows seeds for his crop, the conditions have to be right to ensure a successful harvest. This exercise will show the children how seeds germinate, put down roots, develop into plants, and propagate new seeds." She paused, trying to read his facial expression. Surely he could see how beneficial the planned outing was for the students.

He muttered something in German she didn't understand. She bit her lip. She'd spent more time studying the language like Mr. Richter demanded, but her vocabulary was still lacking.

His thick eyebrows knit together into a deep scowl. "Der kinder learn about planting at home."

Amelia sucked in a breath. "I had planned to combine the science lesson with a picnic to celebrate the end of the school year. It's only for one day, Mr. Richter. Certainly you could spare your wagon for one day."

"Nein." He waved his hand as if shooing away the very idea. "I have no time for picnics. If you must do this, have your picnic in der school yard." A sharp bob of his head punctuated his declaration before he stomped off.

Amelia plopped her hands on her hips. She couldn't remember ever meeting a more stubborn man.

Amelia set the McGuffey Readers on the front bench and then began writing arithmetic problems on the chalkboard, when a soft knock drew her attention. Hank filled the door frame, his toolbox in one hand.

"I've come to fix that hinge before the students arrive." He stepped into the schoolroom and left the door standing open for propriety's sake.

Butterflies danced in her stomach at the sight of his

boyish face. She sent a silent reprimand to her heart and ordered the flutters to cease. They didn't. "Th–thank you, Hank. I appreciate this."

A lopsided smile pulled a dimple into his cheek. "My pleasure." He set the toolbox down and rummaged through it, extracting a chisel and hammer. "I'd like to thank you for what you did for the kids—the new dresses for the girls and the shirt for Micah. That was mighty kind of you."

Warmth skittered up her neck and tickled her ears. "I couldn't help noticing all three of them were outgrowing their clothes. It was nothing."

Hank's hands paused in their task. "I disagree. What you did meant a great deal to them." His eyes smiled at her and a shiver darted up her spine.

Stop that! You're a teacher. You aren't looking for a beau.

He tapped the hammer against the chisel and removed the broken hinge. "I wish there was something I could do to repay you."

"Actually there is." She pressed her lips together. Dare she ask?

He looked over his shoulder at her. "Name it."

She clasped her fingers together to stop their jittery fidgeting. "I'm planning an outing for the children in a couple of weeks to plant some wildflower seeds. It will be a combination science lesson and end of the year picnic."

Hank tipped his head in a most appealing way. "I'm not very good at frying chicken."

A nervous giggle escaped her lips. "No, the children will bring their lunches as always, but I need a wagon to carry all the children out to our picnic spot."

He took on a thoughtful pose. "When is this?"

"Sometime in mid-May."

He fit the new hinge into place. "I don't own a wagon, just a buckboard, but I'll see if I can borrow my father's wagon."

His smile tied her stomach into a knot.

Chapter 9

Hank rubbed linseed oil into the sideboard he'd been working on for Karl and Gerta Schroeder. Since finishing the rocking chair for Mayor Ehrlichmann, four new orders now hung on the workshop wall. Hank sent another prayer of gratitude heavenward for the way God was blessing his business. But in the midst of his joy, a dark cloud of gloom hung about his shoulders like a heavy cloak he couldn't shed.

He glanced at the afternoon sun. Amelia would be arriving home soon. The anticipation with which he normally watched for her was markedly absent today. He dreaded having to tell her about the letters Vater had received.

The linseed oil's pungent odor stung his nose. He watched the intricate detail of the wood grain emerge as he rubbed the oil deeply into the oak, as if the very tree that provided the wood left its fingerprint. He wished God would write His answer to this matter with which Hank struggled as clearly as the oil revealed the wood grain.

"Lord, I need an answer. I don't know what to do."

As if hearing the whisper of God's voice, Hank raised his head and looked out across the narrow expanse of yard that separated the Richter Sunday house from his. Amelia walked up the limestone path to her front door. A groan that started in the pit of his stomach rumbled past his lips.

"God, I'm not ready to face her. I've been turning this over in my mind for two days and I still don't know how I'm going to tell her."

The unmistakable impression of God's Spirit blew across Hank's conscious thought. *"Go tell her. You won't be alone."*

The assurance of God's presence fortified Hank's courage and he set the oil-soaked rag aside. Before Amelia could step inside her door, he jogged across the yard.

"Amelia."

She lifted her eyes in his direction when he called to her. The smile that glowed across her face felt like a punch in Hank's gut. His news would erase that sweet smile.

"Hello, Hank." Her cheeks flushed with pleasure. "My students are excited about the picnic. I'm looking forward to it as much as they are. In fact, we've been studying about—" The delight faded from her expression. "Is something wrong?"

He shoved his hands in his pockets. "I have something to tell you."

A flicker of panic crossed her face and she set down her book satchel. Breathlessness tinged her voice. "What is it?"

This is going to hurt her, Lord. Please comfort her.

Hank drew in a tight breath. "My father has received replies to his letters. The first is from the orphanage in Dallas. They have room for the girls, but their boys' dormitory is already overfull."

As he expected, distress carved furrows in Amelia's brow and she covered her mouth with her fingertips.

Hank went on to deliver the rest of the bad news. There

was no gentle way to say it. "The orphanage in Abilene said they could take Micah."

Moisture glistened in her eyes and she shook her head mutely. She turned away from him. A slight shake in her shoulders defined her sorrow. He longed to wrap her in his arms to deflect the cruelty of his message. A soft sob reached his ears. He could stand it no longer. He reached out and ran his hand up and down her arm, despising his own helplessness.

"I wish I didn't have to tell you this. I know you love those kids as much as I do."

She didn't shrug off his hand so he slid his fingers up to her shoulder and squeezed. "The director of the facility in Dallas said to wait until the school year had ended. My father grumbled about it, but at least the children will be here another month."

She sniffed and wiped her eyes before turning around to face him again. But instead of the despair he expected to see in her expression, her eyes grew dark and stormy.

"Hank Zimmermann, I simply cannot understand why you don't take those children yourself. Even if your father doesn't want them, there's no reason for you to stand by and watch them separated and sent away."

Hank yanked his hand back. His earlier excuse of not having the means to support his cousins wouldn't wash anymore. The furniture orders he'd received the past few weeks kept him plenty busy. He'd even spoken to his father about the possibility of purchasing the Sunday house. Vater hadn't agreed yet, but he hadn't said no. Still, none of that meant he was in the position to take on three children.

"I can't take care of those kids by myself." He blurted out the retort before he could temper his words. "What about you?"

"Me?" Her brow dove downward in disbelief. "What are you talking about?"

Hank thrust his upturned palm in her direction. "How can you do something so loving for those children—making clothes for them out of your own clothing—and then do nothing to try and keep them together?"

She lifted her arms away from her sides. "What can I do? I'm only their teacher."

"You could marry me and then we could take them."

If every muscle in his body hadn't frozen at that moment, he would have turned around to see who had spoken those words. The realization that they'd come from his own lips startled him, but judging by the expression on Amelia's face, she was even more dumbfounded than he.

Her mouth fell open and wavered closed like a fish gasping its last on the end of a hook. Her wide, unblinking eyes nailed him.

"Wh–wha–what?"

Hank grappled with his composure. He couldn't say the idea hadn't crossed his mind before. Imagining Amelia as his bride had caressed his dreams more than once. But his dream hadn't included shocking her by blurting out a clumsy proposal of marriage.

"You've said yourself that you love the kids. We could adopt them, they could stay together, and they wouldn't have to go to the orphanage." The word *we* pushed past the growing lump in his throat and came out unnaturally high-pitched.

He swallowed hard but the lump remained.

Deep red flushed her face and she gasped like she'd just finished a footrace. "Do you have any idea what you're saying? Lifelong relationships must be founded on something greater than good intentions." She leaned down to grab her satchel. "Yes, I love those children, but to make them the basis for a marriage is—it's. . ."

Something painful flashed through her eyes and she took a step backward. When she finally completed her sentence, Hank barely caught her strained whisper. "It's not right."

She turned and marched in the front door.

Anticipation and dread swirled in Amelia's stomach. Her students had enthusiastically prepared for today's outing, but after the heated exchange with Hank over two weeks ago, she now regretted asking him to transport her and the students in his wagon. Since Hank had uttered his "proposal" to her, Amelia avoided making eye contact with him across the yard and at church. She'd tried in vain to dismiss Hank's words from her mind, but her heart refused to comply. She muttered as she slipped her lunch and the wildflower seeds into her satchel.

"Lord, You know I grew up watching my parents endure a loveless marriage. Joining with Hank in such a union for the sake of the children might be unselfish, but they would grow up seeing the same resentment in both of us that I observed in my parents."

A deep sigh whooshed from her lungs. She couldn't

deny her attraction to Hank, beginning with the night she arrived in Fredericksburg. Despite trying to push the unintended feelings away and refuse them acknowledgment, they persisted. Hank occupied her thoughts more than she wanted to admit. She repeatedly asked God to remove this unreasonable captivation, for surely it was nothing more than admiration, or perhaps infatuation. But God allowed the feelings to persist and grow. Certainly her secret feelings for the man didn't mean he reciprocated.

She couldn't shake the nagging prick of melancholy over Hank having asked her to marry him with no expression of tenderness. Not that the children staying together and having two parents who loved them wasn't important, but she refused to become the woman her mother was—trapped in a marriage with a man who would never love her.

"God, I became a teacher so I could remain single." She suspected her adamant statement only caused God to smile. She huffed and snatched her shawl from the peg. "This is foolish. Why am I arguing with God? He knows why I became a teacher." She stepped toward the door, but stopped short. Talking to herself was as foolish as arguing with God.

Hank halted the wagon near the door of the schoolhouse. Amelia had the children lined up by grades. Hank had to admit that, despite their excitement, Amelia maintained order and discipline as she directed one group at a time to the wagon. Hank boosted the younger ones up to the tailgate.

Amelia had avoided him ever since the afternoon of his

awkward proposal and she didn't appear anxious to converse with him now. Once again he berated himself for the bumbling manner in which the words had fallen from his lips. After spending considerable time communing with God, he determined that he didn't regret his suggestion at all, only the way he'd spoken it. In fact, the longer he thought about it, the deeper and more steadfast his conviction that he was in love with Amelia Bachman. He'd spent the last week praying God would grant his petition to make Amelia his bride. The opportunity to speak privately with her today didn't seem likely with twenty-two children listening. If only she'd look in his direction, he could at least offer her a smile.

The last student scrambled into the wagon bed and Hank held out his hand to the teacher to help her up to the front seat. She hesitated momentarily, deep pink flooding her cheeks. She gathered her skirts and accepted his hand to aid her up over the wheel.

He settled himself beside her and picked up the reins. "I'd like to speak with you later, Amelia."

She folded her trembling hands primly on her lap. "As you wish."

He drove out past the edge of town and turned the team northwest toward his parents' farm.

Amelia jerked her head in his direction. "Where are you going?" She pointed northeast. "The spot I found is that way."

He smiled sideways at her. "If you'll allow me—there's a hillside lined with oaks and mesquites about halfway to my folks' place that has a beautiful view of a small lake. I think you'll agree it's a perfect spot to plant your wildflower seeds."

She arched her eyebrows and he half expected her to argue, but she nodded. "All right. I'll concede that you know the area better than I."

Forty-five minutes later the wagon rounded the curve of a hill, bringing into view a little pristine lake reflecting several burr oaks along the water's edge.

"What a beautiful spot." It was the first time he'd seen her smile since he'd told her about Vater's letters. Hank's heart pinched. How he wished she'd smiled in response to his proposal.

He set the brake and aided her down from the wagon seat. The children clambered off the tailgate and began an impromptu game of tag.

Hank cast an eye to the west. A few white puffy clouds gathered on the horizon. He hoped rain wouldn't ruin their outing. "I'll be back to pick you up around three."

"Thank you, Hank." Her hazel eyes fixed him in place. "It was kind of you."

Why did he get the distinct feeling she wasn't talking about driving them to their picnic?

Chapter 10

Hank pushed the plane along the edge of a cedar plank, producing thin curls that reminded him of the tendrils of hair that fell around Amelia's ears. He closed his eyes and invited her image to grace his musings. Her soft voice echoed in his memory.

Perhaps this afternoon—what would he say to her? How should he broach the subject? Certainly he owed her an apology for the tactless way he'd spluttered out his proposal.

He couldn't fault Amelia's statement. A real marriage needed a foundation much stronger than good intentions. Giving the children a home was a fine thing, but he should have told her first how much he loved her. He reckoned most women wanted to be courted and romanced. There just wasn't time. He prayed God would prepare Amelia's heart to hear what he wanted to tell her.

"God, if You'll give me another chance to say it right, and if Amelia says yes, I'll romance her for the rest of my life. Order my words, Lord, so she'll know she's loved."

A rumble of thunder interrupted his prayer. Muted, murky light replaced the earlier sunlight. He poked his head out the door. What happened to the bluebonnet sky and cottony clouds? Angry greenish-gray mounds churned across the sky where the sun should have been. Ominous swirls billowed in from the northwest.

Alarm clenched his stomach and a chill sliced through him. He grabbed his jacket and jogged to the backyard where the horses stamped and snorted in nervous agitation. His fingers flew through the task of hitching the animals to the wagon. The team tossed their heads and whinnied as Hank leapt into the wagon seat. He released the brake and blew a piercing whistle through his teeth, slapping the reins down hard. The horses lurched forward.

"Lord, please protect Amelia and the children until I can get there."

He turned onto the street and met Emil Lange, the father of one of Amelia's students, coming the opposite direction.

"Emil, follow me! I'm going out to get the children. This storm is coming up mighty fast."

The man nodded his head. "Lead the way."

Before Hank reached the edge of town, he heard a sickening shout.

"*Twister!*"

Hank rose up from the seat and hollered at the horses. "Giddyap. Go!" He slung the ends of the reins down across the animals. He didn't know if Emil still followed behind him. He focused solely on Amelia and the children.

The sky unleashed driving rain and crashing thunder. "Oh God, please hedge them about with Your mighty hands." He urged the team on and shouted above the tempest. "Lord Jesus, You spoke peace and the storm stilled. You walked on the water. Overpower this storm with Your might. Protect them, Lord."

He struggled against the buffeting wind to remain in the wagon and the horses slowed to a nervous, high-stepping trot, shying in their traces. Hank forced them forward. "Go! Go!"

Lightning slashed across the sky accompanied by immediate explosions of thunder, shaking the very ground over which he traveled. Air pressure nearly burst his eardrums. Bits of hail now pelted his face, and the wind and rain so hampered his visibility, all he could do was pray he was headed in the right direction.

"Guide me, Lord. Cover Amelia and the children with Your hand and lead me to them." His voice broke as he cried out his gut-wrenching plea. "Oh God, please protect them."

The wind slowed and the rain diminished enough for him to see and he pushed the team to pick up their pace. Thunder rolled through the hills in the wake of the storm.

Broken limbs and uprooted trees littered the landscape. Hank's heart hammered and his lungs heaved in their effort to draw breath. Water dripped from his hair and saturated clothing.

A child's bonnet swung from the ripped branches of a scrub pine. A lunch pail sat upside down in the dirt. One of the quilts Amelia had stacked in the back of the wagon wrapped around the twisted trunk of a mesquite.

His heart in his throat, Hank hauled on the reins and pulled the team to a stop. He jammed the brake lever forward and leapt from the wagon, running through the now-soft rain, shouting Amelia's name.

"Amelia! Where are you?"

Small heads poked upright from a gulley along the base of the hillside.

Elsie and Joy screamed in unison. "Uncle Hank!"

Hank charged in the direction of the children. Others now raised their heads, some crying, some simply staring wide-eyed. A few of the older students comforted the younger ones. Micah scrambled to his feet and launched himself into Hank's arms, sobbing.

"Uncle Hank, I was scared. The wind roared real loud and it almost blew us away." He looked down at himself and his cries intensified. "The shirt Miss Bachman gave me is all wet and dirty."

"It's all right, buddy. That was a bad storm, but it's gone now." Hank squeezed Micah, but his glance bounced wildly about. "Where is Miss Bachman?"

Elsie's panicked voice reached him. "Uncle Hank, Miss Bachman won't wake up."

He lowered Micah to the ground and ran down the slope where Elsie and Joy sat on either side of Amelia. A violent shudder rattled through him when he caught sight of her motionless form. Bits of leaves and grass clung to her and the stains on her dress testified that she'd crawled through the mud, presumably trying to protect the children.

Hank knelt and brushed tangled hair and debris from her face. "Amelia. Amelia, open your eyes. It's Hank. The storm is over."

The children crowded around their teacher, begging Hank to make her wake up. Behind him, Hank heard the other wagon pull up, and some of the children ran to meet

Paeter Lange's father, but Hank remained in place patting Amelia's face. He slid his fingers around the back of her neck, searching for injury. Inch by inch, his hand traveled upward until he located a large lump on the back of her head. Ever so gently, he parted her hair and found matted blood.

"Der kinder seem to be all right." Emil jogged down the slope, his belly heaving with exertion. "Miss Bachman, she is—"

"She's unconscious." Hank's throat was so tight he could barely push the words out. He indicated the back of her head, and Emil bent to look.

"Ja, she got pretty bad goose egg."

Hank rose. "Let's put her in the back of my wagon. Elsie, see if you can find one of the quilts from the picnic." The little girl ran to do as Hank bid her and Hank turned to Emil.

"Can you take the children back to town?"

Emil bobbed his head. "Ja, I make sure they all get home safe." He paused a moment. "My Paeter, he say Miss Bachman told all der kinner to lay flat, and she keep them down." His voice turned husky. "She save their lives, ja?"

Indeed, when Hank came up on the scene, all the children were in the safest possible place in the gulley at the base of the hill. "I believe so."

"Uncle Hank." Elsie called to him. "I found a quilt, but it's wet and dirty."

"That's all right." He instructed her to spread it in the back of the wagon.

While Emil gathered the rest of the children and directed

them to his wagon, Hank slid his arms beneath Amelia's shoulders and knees, lifting her as if she were made of fragile porcelain. She didn't stir. He carried her to the wagon and laid her gently on the soggy quilt.

He let his fingertips stroke her cheekbone momentarily before securing the tailgate.

God, please let her be all right.

"Uncle Hank, is Miss Bachman gonna die like my mama?"

Hank jerked his startled gaze around to see Elsie, Joy, and Micah standing behind him. He knelt and gathered the children close.

"She just has a bump on her head. We're going to pray and ask God to make her better."

Tears filled Elsie's eyes. "But I prayed for Mama and Papa to get better and they didn't."

Elsie's statement slammed into Hank with a force so intense, he lost his breath for a moment, and his heart ripped in two. How could he make promises to these children he wasn't sure he could keep? They'd already endured much more pain than children ought.

"You three go with Mr. Lange. I'm going to take Miss Bachman to Dr. Keidel."

He hugged each one and nudged them toward Emil's wagon. "Go on, now."

With his heart bleeding for the youngsters and fearful for Amelia, Hank climbed up and whistled to the team, steering them back around toward town.

He held the horses to a less reckless pace, not wanting to jar Amelia any more than necessary. He glanced at her over his shoulder every few minutes, longing to see her eyes flutter open, but they didn't.

Hank lifted his voice to heaven's throne. "Please, God, let her be all right." He repeated the prayer until he pulled up at the doctor's office in town. A small crowd gathered as he gently lifted Amelia into his arms and carried her inside.

Quiet voices pierced through the dull ache in Amelia's head. Fragments of memory slowly came together: the children, the swirling storm clouds, the wind. . . She forced her eyes open despite the pain and she struggled to sit up. Her vision swam and blurred.

"Whoa there, where do you think you're going, young lady?"

"The children—"

"Are safe, thanks to you."

The voice was familiar but the cobwebs in her head prevented recognition. She lay back down and rubbed her eyes. Gradually the face in front of her came into focus.

"Uncle Will?"

Her favorite uncle grinned at her. "It's me. Thought I'd surprise you by coming a couple of weeks early, and you surprised me by being my first patient."

Confusion still spun in her brain. "But when—"

"I arrived on the stage this morning just ahead of the storm. The man at the depot told me the schoolmarm and students were on a picnic today." He leaned closer. "Amelia honey, don't you know you're supposed to pick a sunny day for a picnic?"

The regular town doctor leaned over Uncle Will's shoulder. "Miss Bachman, I'm Dr. Keidel. You gave us a bit of a scare. You have a concussion, but you're going to be all right."

She looked from one to the other. "You're sure the children are all right?"

"They're just fine," Dr. Keidel said. "But you have a very impatient visitor waiting to see you."

Uncle Will winked at her. "I'll bring him in." He shook his finger at her. "But you have to promise to lie still." He followed Dr. Keidel out of the room.

A moment later Hank slipped in. The sight of him set her pulse to dancing. He closed the distance between them in four long strides. The lines across his brow softened as he reached her side. He picked up her hand and held it between both of his own.

"Amelia." His breathless whisper was bathed in relief. "Praise God you're all right."

Hank's nearness coupled with the warmth of his hands enveloping hers drew a perception of safety over her. A tiny smile tugged at the corner of her mouth. "I am now."

Air whooshed from Hank's lips in a deep-throated chuckle. He lifted her hand to his lips.

Her breath caught when he placed his gentle kiss on her fingers. An apologetic prayer formed in her heart, recanting the times she'd asked God to take away her growing feelings for this man. She understood now why God hadn't granted what she thought she wanted.

His eyes glistened. "I begged God for another chance to do this right because I bungled it the first time."

Still holding her hand, he lowered himself to one knee. "Amelia Bachman, I want to spend the rest of my life with you, not just because of the way you love the children, but because of the way I love you. Will you marry me?"

Epilogue

Amelia straightened Joy's hair ribbons and smoothed Elsie's dress, while Hank tucked in Micah's shirt. Pastor Hoffman waited patiently in the white gazebo Hank had built in the middle of the field of wildflowers.

The preacher grinned. "It's not every day I get to marry an entire family."

Amelia's bouquet of bluebonnets, daisies, and white dogtooth lilies trembled slightly in anticipation. Her foolish declaration of becoming a teacher so she could remain single echoed in her ears. How silly she'd been to try to limit God. She never dreamed being a teacher would lead her to three precious children and a fine, godly husband who loved her.

Pastor Hoffman smiled as the five of them stepped into the gazebo. Elsie and Joy, the bridesmaids, stood to Amelia's left, and Micah, the best man, stood to Hank's right.

"This gazebo is Hank's wedding gift to Amelia," the pastor announced to all the assembled townsfolk. "The stone foundation is indicative of the faith we have in Jesus Christ." He gestured to the gleaming white gingerbread trim adorning the uprights. "This structure reminds us of how beautiful love is—God's love to us and our love for each other."

Hank smiled down at Amelia and her heart turned over.

Pastor Hoffman continued. "Finally the roof represents

the canopy of God's faithfulness, always sheltering us from the storms of life."

Hank took both Amelia's hands in his and they repeated the ageless vows, pledging themselves to one another and to God. At the pastor's prompting, Hank bent his head toward Amelia's. He paused, an inch away from her lips.

"I love you, Amelia Zimmermann."

Connie Stevens lives in north Georgia with her husband of over thirty-five years, John. She and John are active in a variety of capacities in their home church. One cantankerous kitty—misnamed Sweet Pea—allows them to live in *her* home. Some of Connie's favorite pastimes include reading, sewing, browsing antique shops, collecting teddy bears, and gardening. She also enjoys making quilts to send to the Cancer Treatment Center of America. Visit Connie's website and blog at www.conniestevenswrites.com.

A SHELTER FROM THE STORM

by Marjorie Vawter

Dedication

To my paternal grandparents, the real Nelson and Mildred,
from whom I borrowed their first names, portions of their
characters, and one small part of their love story. I miss you,
and I look forward to the day when we will be reunited
in our precious Lord's presence.

Special thanks to Rebecca Germany and Joyce Hart and
my own hero, Roger, for believing in me and
encouraging me in my writing journey.

*For thou hast been. . .a refuge from the storm,
a shadow from the heat.*
ISAIAH 25:4

Chapter 1

Hill Country, Texas
December 15, 1918

Mildred Zimmermann looked out the railcar window, vainly searching for a speck of light to indicate home was within reach. Nothing. They had to be getting close. She glanced at her military-issue wristwatch and sighed. Ten thirty. Too late for any of her family to meet her.

But Harold might be there. Surely he was home from the war now.

"Fredericksburg, next stop," the conductor called out as he entered the railroad car.

He shut the door behind him, closing off the cool draft before walking up the aisle toward her. He stopped to speak to a man Mildred had noticed as soon as she entered the car in San Antonio—absolutely the most handsome man Mildred had ever laid eyes on. Not that she was looking. But after serving nearly two years in field hospitals in Belgium and France, she could safely say she'd seen her share of men, good-looking and otherwise.

The train slowed, and steam from the locomotive billowed past her window. Finally home. Excitement tickled her stomach as she reached down to grab her pack—all her worldly goods in one small bag. She hadn't needed much outside of her navy nurse's uniform, but it would be nice to wear something different for a change.

"Excuse me, miss."

A man's rich baritone startled her out of her musings. She looked up into steely blue eyes that contrasted sharply with his dark brown hair. Her handsome fellow traveler. Heat rose from the pit of her stomach, and she prayed it would stop before it reached the top of her high-necked blouse.

Swallowing hard to dispel the rock stuck in her throat, she mentally shook herself for her reaction to this stranger. "Yes?"

"The conductor said you might know if there is somewhere to stay the night, a hotel or boardinghouse? I didn't expect to get in so late."

"You must be new to Fredericksburg not to know that this train never keeps its published schedule." Mildred smiled. "But surely someone is expecting you."

"Dr. Bachman, yes. I am his new assistant."

"Dr. Bachman needs an assistant?" Neither her parents nor her doctor uncle had mentioned it.

The train lurched and slowed as the whistle blew its warning, and the stranger grabbed at the back of the seat to steady himself. Only then did she see his cane. "Oh my." She scooted closer to the window. "How rude of me to make you stand. Please, sit down."

Relief shone in his smile as he sank into the seat next to her. "Thank you. I'm still getting used to this." He raised the cane in the air.

"What happened?" She winced. "I'm sorry. I have no right

to ask. Just my nurse's training."

With more heat radiating from her cheeks, she looked out the window as the train bumped to a stop. A handful of people stood on the platform, but not her parents.

"Oh look." She nudged her companion. "There's Dr. Bachman. You won't need the hotel after all."

"Yes." The man's voice was hesitant. "Are you here to give Dr. Bachman a hand with nursing?"

Mildred lifted her eyebrows. "Why on earth would you think that? As soon as I can get out of this uniform, my nursing career is over."

"Oh, well. . .I thought that in light of. . ."

His hesitation made her stomach clench in unease, and she looked more closely at the elderly doctor on the platform. Now she saw his tired—no, exhausted—stance. Exhaustion etched his wrinkles deeper than she remembered in the beloved face. After seeing so many fatigued military doctors, she hadn't expected to see her uncle in the same state.

Turning back to her companion, she struggled to keep the alarm out of her voice. "Who are you?"

"Dr. Nelson Winters." He stood and held a hand out to help her rise.

But she ignored it. Tightening her grip on her bag, she stood without his assistance. And immediately noticed he was a head taller than she. She'd long ago gotten used to the fact that she was taller than many men. Even Harold, at five foot eleven, looked her straight in the eye.

A blush rose up her neck at Dr. Winter's close scrutiny, and she lowered her gaze and made her way past him, taking care not to knock into his cane.

"Spanish influenza," he said as she started down the aisle to the car door.

She looked at him over her shoulder. "Excuse me?"

"Have you heard of it?"

"Yes, of course. We had several cases at the last field hospital where I worked. But surely that's just in Europe." She stopped and turned toward him, catching his solemn demeanor. "Oh no. . ."

He nodded. "It's here in the States. And here in Fredericksburg." Shrugging, he added, "That's why I'm here and why I thought you. . ."

Mildred forced her feet to move her toward the door and down the steps, wondering at the tingle in her elbow as Dr. Winters steadied her from behind.

"Mildred, *liebchen*. Welcome home." Uncle's gravelly voice greeted her when she stepped onto the station platform, and he wrapped her in a warm hug. "I see you've already met Dr. Winters. I hope he's brought you up-to-date with our current problem."

Clutching her uncle's sleeve, Mildred nodded and looked over his shoulder at the others milling around. "But Uncle Will, Mama and Papa—are they all right?"

"Uncle? Dr. Bachman is your uncle?"

Mildred barely spared a glance for Dr. Winters. "And Harold?"

Her uncle wrapped his arm around her shoulder and pulled her close. "Harold. . .I don't know. We've not seen him. Everyone is fine at the farm, liebchen." A chuckle rumbled in his throat. "Did you not tell Dr. Winters our relationship?"

Mildred shook her head. "There wasn't time. We just. . ."

Uncle hugged her closer and spoke to Dr. Winters, who looked a bit confused. "This is the great-niece I spoke to you about. Mildred Zimmermann."

"Ah."

The syllable held a wealth of meaning that Mildred couldn't fathom. What had her uncle said to the man?

"Pleased to meet you at last, Miss Zimmermann."

Heat rose in her cheeks, making them tingle in the cool night air. "I seem to be always apologizing to you, Dr. Winters. Forgive me for not telling you of our relationship when you first mentioned my uncle."

"No need to apologize. I could hardly expect you to enlighten me at first acquaintance." He turned to her uncle. "I will get my other bags from the baggage car. Where should I have them taken?"

"There's one bed left at my place. It is yours until we can make further arrangements."

As Dr. Winters walked away, Uncle Will said, "Your parents want you to stay at the Sunday house until they can get into town. Do you have more bags? We should have told Dr. Winters to get them with his."

"No." She looked at the bag she'd dropped at her feet. "This is all I have. I'll be fine." She looked around the thinning crowd. "You haven't heard anything from Harold?"

"When did you last hear from him?"

Uncle Will's eyes reflected his weariness, and Mildred

hated to add to his burden. Harold should have been here to meet her.

"He telegraphed a week or so after Armistice Day. Said he was headed home already; he would meet me here." Uncle Will didn't need to know the rest of the message. *Plans have changed. Letter to follow.* Only it hadn't. Mildred swallowed hard.

"*Ach ja.*" Her uncle reached into his coat pocket and drew out a telegram. "This arrived for you today. Maybe it has the answer you seek."

Taking the distinctive Western Union yellow envelope, she ripped it open with shaking fingers.

MISS ZIMMERMANN. YOU ARE LISTED AS CAPTAIN HAROLD BADER'S NEXT OF KIN WITH THE UNITED STATES WAR OFFICE. WE REGRET TO INFORM YOU THAT CAPTAIN BADER DIED NOVEMBER 20. CAUSE OF DEATH—SPANISH INFLUENZA. HIS BELONGINGS WILL FOLLOW.

Her nerveless fingers released the telegram. As it floated to the platform, the words echoed in her head: *Harold. Dead. Spanish influenza.*

Welcome home, Mildred.

Chapter 2

Nelson sat on the edge of the bed and reached for his cane. The pale light edging around the window shade told him morning had finally arrived.

And none too soon. When Dr. Bachman showed him to the small room last night, Nelson had gratefully eased his aching leg under the quilts on the comfortable bed. But instead of the sleep his body so desperately craved, his mind remained alert, his thoughts so jumbled even he couldn't keep them straight.

Nelson sighed and rose, balancing on the cane until his bad leg would agree to carry him across the room to the washstand. The cold water on his face startled his muddled thoughts and focused them sharply on one picture. Mildred's face.

She had to be the Millie Harold talked about so much, though she was much prettier in person than in Harold's blurred print.

His heart winced at the thought of Harold. Dr. Bachman had told him of his friend's death last night, after they had seen a very distracted Mildred to her family's Sunday house.

Sunday house. That was one oddity Harold had never mentioned in all his talk about Fredericksburg. He'd have to ask why these people called the small houses by that name. Maybe it would ease his guilty conscience whenever he thought of Harold.

Grimacing at his reflection, Nelson ran a comb through his thick hair. Then, as he finished tying the knot in his tie, a sharp knock on the door startled him. His leg gave way as he turned toward the sound, and he grabbed at the side of the wardrobe to keep himself from collapsing on the floor.

"Dr. Winters?" The elderly doctor's voice sounded strained. "Are you awake?"

"Yes." Nelson gripped his cane. "Come in, sir. And call me Nelson, please."

Dr. Bachman eased the door open but didn't come in. "Didn't you sleep at all, son?"

Nelson shifted his weight and indicated the unmade bed. "Not much." His mouth tightened. "But not because of the bed, sir. Just the leg talking to me."

Dr. Bachman nodded. "I hate to disturb you so early, but we have a problem."

Nelson followed his superior to the kitchen where Dr. Bachman motioned him to a seat at the table.

"Coffee?"

"Please." Nelson sniffed the air. The coffee smelled rich and strong, just the way he liked it.

"Cream? Sugar?"

"No, sir. Thank you. Just black."

Dr. Bachman nodded his approval as he poured coffee into two large mugs and brought them to the table. Then he lowered himself into a chair across from Nelson.

After a cautious sip, Dr. Bachman asked, "Are you ready to get to work?"

Nelson nodded his assent. Anything to keep his mind

occupied and away from the distraction Mildred posed.

"I had planned to ease you into the workload, but this blasted influenza isn't slowing its attack on the people of this town." The older doctor's fingers played with the handle on his coffee cup. "We had five more patients come in last night."

"Where did you put them all?" Nelson knew from the quick tour Dr. Bachman had given him last night that there weren't that many beds in the tiny clinic attached to his home.

Dr. Bachman shrugged. "That's the problem. The men are on pallets in my exam room. The one woman is on the settee in the parlor. And the *kinder*, the children, are on the floor there, too."

"Not ideal, but what else is there?" Nelson couldn't help wondering why this town only had a small clinic. From what Harold and Dr. Bachman had told him, quite a large rural community relied on Dr. Bachman's medical care. There used to be a larger hospital, but it had been abandoned in favor of a smaller clinic. The old hospital building now housed a mercantile.

Dr. Bachman took a large sip of coffee then speared Nelson with his dark chocolate gaze. "We ask Mildred if we can use the Sunday house." He paused, contemplating his next words. "And we need her nursing skills."

"But—" Nelson heard Mildred's words from last night echoing through his head.

"I know." Dr. Bachman nodded sharply. "She's done nursing. But there's no way around it. We need her." Another nod. "And that's where you come in, my boy."

"Me?" Nelson's eyebrows rose.

"*Ja.* You persuade her to be a nurse a little longer, so she can care for patients at the Sunday house."

"Why me?"

Dr. Bachman's eyes twinkled with mischief. "Because you are young, good-looking, and persuasive."

What a joke! He'd virtually run away from Arlington to get out from under his father's insistence he join the family practice. Nothing he said, persuasive or otherwise, changed his father's thinking. And now this man wanted him to use his nonexistent power of persuasion on Mildred?

Dr. Bachman nodded again, confirming his words, and stood. "Right after we eat some breakfast, you go and persuade her, ja?"

Nein. But one look at the man's face convinced him not to express it. The matter was already settled. "Ja."

After a small but substantial breakfast of pumpernickel and ham, and a quick round to see the patients with Dr. Bachman, Nelson found himself standing outside the tiny house they had escorted Mildred to the night before.

In the light of day, he compared the Zimmermann Sunday house with those close by. This one had a lean-to added onto the back, making it larger than most. Still, Nelson wasn't sure it would be big enough to house more than a few patients. And how would they keep everything sanitary? Field hospitals were bad enough, and these houses looked pretty basic without the modern amenities of indoor plumbing.

He edged to the side of the house and located an outhouse

on the back of the property. He grimaced. This didn't look too promising. However, he'd committed to recruiting both Mildred and her family's Sunday house. Dillydallying out here on the walk wouldn't get the job done.

Taking a calming breath, Nelson climbed the two steps to the small porch and knocked on the door.

"Come in," Mildred's soft alto called out.

Come in? She didn't even know who was outside. Surely she locked the door. Nelson hesitated then put his hand to the handle just as it turned.

He snatched his hand back as though it were on fire and gazed at Mildred's beautiful face.

"Good morning, Dr. Winters."

"Uh. . ." All words rushed from his mind.

Pink rose in Mildred's cheeks, and he realized he was staring. *Say something, you idiot.* But still, words wouldn't come.

"Didn't you hear me say to come in?" Mildred motioned him into the room. But his feet had grown roots and anchored him to the porch.

"Uh, no, I mean, yes. . ."

Her smile stretched wider, deepening a dimple on her right cheek.

Nelson closed his eyes. What was he thinking? He was here on business, not pleasure. He would do well to remember Helena. Romance, love, wife, family—all were out of his reach now. Helena and the constant ache in his leg had taken care of that.

Nelson cleared his throat and opened his eyes. "Your uncle sent me to talk to you."

Mildred held the door wider. "Okay, but could we do it inside? It's chilly out there. Besides, you can sit down in here."

All his mother's teaching on propriety and what society expected of a gentleman did not include what to do in a small town set in the hill country of Texas. But he hesitated only a moment longer. She was right. He'd be more comfortable sitting, out of the chilly air.

He followed her in the door and eased it shut behind him. Habit had him looking for a lock on the door to click in place. . .but his fingers searched in vain.

Mildred laughed, a pleasing sound. "Where are you from? A big city is my guess."

What did that have to do with no locks on doors? "Arlington, Virginia. Right outside Washington, DC."

"Well, city boy, we don't lock doors around here." She shrugged and motioned to a small settee for him to sit. "There's no need. We all know each other."

But they didn't know him. He eased himself down on the settee, loosening his coat as he sat. The room was furnished with beautiful wood pieces—a pie safe near the wood cookstove, a lovely mantelpiece surrounding a small fireplace, the settee, a wood rocker.

A door near the cookstove had to lead to the lean-to he'd seen outside.

Mildred's amused voice broke into his perusal of the small living area. "Does the room pass muster, Dr. Winters?" Her eyes twinkled as provocatively as her uncle's had earlier.

He quirked his lips into a smile of appreciation. "Yes. It's lovely. The furniture is very unique. That rocking chair, especially. It's similar to the one in my room at the doctor's."

"It should be." She laughed. "My father built all the furniture. It's what he does."

"But I thought your parents were farmers."

Mildred shook her head. "My father is the oldest son, so when his father died, he inherited the farm. But he was already an established carpenter and furniture maker. They needed a bigger home, so they moved out to the farm where Father now has his workshop. My uncle George, Father's brother, farms the land."

"So, why is this called a Sunday house?"

"When the town's founders came to Fredericksburg from the old country, they settled outside of town. But they didn't want to miss church services, so they built these small houses for the weekends. They would come into town to get supplies on Saturday and then stay overnight, go to church on Sunday, and return to their ranches and farms Sunday afternoon." She shrugged. "At first they all looked alike—one room with a sleeping loft for the kinder. The stairs are outside so as not to take up room inside. Eventually most of them had rooms added on and indoor plumbing installed. Gas lighting replaced kerosene lamps, and now electric lighting is starting to replace the gas."

Nelson's mind grasped onto one of the improvements. "Indoor plumbing? You have it here?"

"Yes, of course." She motioned toward the back of the house. "Father built the lean-to for his first workshop, but today it's a bedroom with a small bathroom partitioned out of it." She stood. "Do you want to see it?"

"Uh, sure." He knew his mother would be cringing at all the "improprieties," but she wasn't here, and this was a different world.

They stepped into a cozy room with a bed, wardrobe, and nightstand. To the right, a door led into a small bathroom containing a sink, a claw-foot tub, and a toilet. All sparkling clean.

Dr. Bachman's idea made more sense now. All he had to do was propose it.

Mildred stood to the side of the bathroom door watching him. He carefully pivoted and led the way back into the main room. "Very nice. Your uncle was talking about the Sunday house this morning."

Mildred reached for a coffee cup on the shelf above the stove. "Really? Why?" She motioned him to a chair at the table then picked up the coffeepot off the back of the stove. "Would you like some coffee?"

"Yes, please. Just black is fine." He settled into the chair and wondered how to ease into his task.

"So what did Uncle Will have to say about the house?" Mildred gave him the coffee then sat next to him, cradling her own cup.

"He would like to use it as an overflow clinic."

"Why?" Mildred's piercing gaze drove the words from his mind again. "What's happened?"

"Five more influenza patients came to the clinic last night. And more arrived just as I was leaving to talk to you. There simply isn't more room."

Her mouth tightened as she took in the implications of

his words. "Is it really that bad?" At his nod, she asked, "Who would care for them?"

Nelson swallowed hard. This was the tricky part. "You."

"Oh no." Mildred set her cup down hard and started to rise.

Nelson put his hand over hers, and she sank back into her chair. "I know what you said last night, but I don't think either of us knew the extent of the influenza here."

She hadn't removed her hand from under his, and he allowed his thumb to caress the soft skin. She still wore her nursing uniform—judging from the size of her small pack, she probably had no other clothes with her. He didn't say anything more, letting her process her uncle's plan while he memorized her features. As if he needed to, judging by the picture in his mind all night and into this morning. He knew he shouldn't even entertain the thoughts being in her presence inspired, but he was unable to check them.

Finally, her chocolate-brown gaze met his and then flicked around the room before settling on him again. "Okay. But we'll have to rearrange this room. Henry can help us."

A flash of jealousy caught his heart. "Henry?"

"My brother. I called out to the farm this morning. He's driving the Model T in to get me." She flashed a small smile, so quick he almost missed it. "At least that was the plan."

Her gaze dropped to their clasped hands. She gently removed her hand, reached for their cups, and stood. "How many do you think we can care for here?"

Chapter 3

Mildred stretched to a full standing position and reached to touch the low ceiling of the Sunday house. Her back ached from bending over the patients in her care. She glanced around the small front room at the beds lined along the right and left walls—five on each side—with a narrow aisle between the feet leading from the kitchen to the front door. A sense of satisfaction rose within her, and she allowed herself to bask in it for a moment.

For the last three days, she'd been busy with the twenty-four-hour care her patients needed, snatching small naps when nothing else demanded her attention. Uncle Will and Nelson—um, Dr. Winters—needed more help, but the demand of the influenza epidemic extended across the country. Even with the doctors and nurses returning from the war, there still weren't enough people to fight this home-front battle.

Mildred eased the front door open and stepped onto the porch, pulling down the mask covering her nose and mouth. Drawing in deep breaths of fresh air, she sank into one of two rocking chairs and absently stroked the silky-smooth wood arms. Her father made these chairs for her mother shortly after they were married. Back when his woodworking barely had enough income to support a wife and three young orphaned cousins. God honored Papa's commitment to fulfilling the purpose He'd intended for him, and now the business continued to thrive, in spite of war and economic hardship.

A flood of grief for *what could have been* washed through Mildred's thoughts, and she laid her head against the high back of the chair, closing her eyes. Harold was dead. It was hard to believe she'd never see him again. She'd planned to return to the farm until her wedding and then settle into married life. But Uncle Will's plea for help couldn't be ignored. So she'd only seen her parents and siblings a brief few minutes on Sunday when they stopped by the Sunday house after church.

Tears seeped out from under her eyelids and slid down her cheeks.

"Are you okay, Millie?"

Mildred startled and opened her eyes. "Clarice!" Her best friend and cousin perched on the bottom step to the porch. "Uncle George told me you were in San Antone."

Clarice hopped up the stairs and held her arms out for a hug. Mildred rose and returned the embrace then held her petite cousin away from her to gaze at her sweet face.

Clarice was her opposite in almost every way: short to Mildred's tall; fair-haired to her own chestnut bob; vivacious and outgoing to her quiet shyness. Mildred couldn't imagine life without Clarice in it.

Pulling her into another hug, Clarice asked again, "Are you okay?"

Mildred released her friend and sank back into the rocker,

indicating the other for Clarice to sit. Fingering the strings to her mask dangling around her neck, she said, "Harold's dead, Clarice."

"Oh honey, I know. Mama told me."

Clarice reached over and covered Mildred's hand with her own, bringing to mind Nelson's touch a few days before. Harold's touch never ignited a fire deep within her like Nelson's did, and try as she might, she couldn't erase that sensation from her mind.

"I am sorry." Clarice gave a final squeeze and let go. "I know you're missing him."

Mildred nodded.

Clarice sat quietly for a moment, but in true Clarice-like fashion, she couldn't stay silent for long. "So who's taking care of the patients while you're out here?"

"No one. Everyone is resting, and Nelson is over at the clinic with Uncle W—"

"Nelson?" Clarice's eyes lit up even more. "Is he the new doctor Mama mentioned?" She leaned forward and lowered her voice. "Is he as handsome as Evie says he is?"

Mildred squashed the unexpected stab of jealousy at hearing Clarice's younger sister's description of Dr. Winters. Accurate, though. It was her first thought of him a week ago. "Evie's right on that count." She smiled.

"So, what's he like otherwise?" Clarice practically bounced in her chair.

Mildred laughed. "Why should you care? What would Thomas say?"

Clarice shrugged. "Just because I'm getting married in

twelve days—but who's counting?—isn't a reason not to scope out a good man for my best friend."

Mildred's humor evaporated.

Clarice slapped her forehead then reached over and covered Mildred's hand with her own. "I know you're grieving, but Millie. . ."

Mildred sighed and squeezed Clarice's hand. "Go ahead. Spit it out."

"Well, it's just that you and Harold were really good friends, and I know you planned to marry him after the war, but"—Clarice scrunched her pretty little nose—"you know."

Mildred shook her head. "No, I don't know. Not until you tell me, silly."

Clarice took a deep breath. "Okay. You and Harold never had the spark between you. . .you know, like Thomas and me. I mean, I simply melt every time he holds my hand or kisses me. You and Harold were always so. . .um, businesslike when you were together. Not really in love." She let go of Mildred's hand. "Oh, I don't know. I'm afraid I'm not being very clear."

Mildred pulled her lips into a wry smile. "Only too clear, dear cousin."

"I probably said too much." Clarice grimaced. "I'm sorry."

"Don't be. You've said nothing more than what I've already thought." She was sorry Harold was dead. She'd even shed tears. But no matter how she tried, she couldn't conjure up the grief she imagined she should have for the man she expected to marry. Only regret at her own actions. If only she hadn't written that last letter. . .

"Okay then." Clarice's eyes danced again. "What's Dr. Winters like?"

Mildred turned her gaze down the street—toward downtown where Nelson was—as though conjuring him up in her mind. Not that she had to. She shook her head in disgust. What was wrong with her? She couldn't be in love with a man she just met. Even if she had spent more time with him in the last week than would normally be considered proper. Their patients were usually their only chaperones.

Their patients. How long had she been out here? She looked at her watch. "Oh goodness. I only meant to come out here for a quick breath of air." She stood. "I've got to check on the patients and get a meal started."

Clarice stood with her. "I actually came to help you for a bit, and here we sit. . .talking." She pulled a mask from her skirt pocket, looped the strings behind her ears, and tied it into place. "Tell me what you need me to do."

Relief surged through her at her cousin's request. For the first time, Mildred noticed Clarice was dressed in a serviceable gray skirt and white shirtwaist. Almost as severe as her own nurse's garb.

"Are you sure you want to risk it with such a short time before your wedding?"

Clarice fluttered her hands at Mildred's question. "Pooh! I've been helping Dr. Bachman off and on all fall. I'm fine. So quit arguing and tell me what to do."

Mildred shrugged and led the way inside. She knew better than to try to stop Clarice when she had a mind to do something. "First, let's get you an apron to protect your clothes." She headed toward the cabinet next to the stove. Clarice shut the door quietly behind her then followed. Mildred pulled a fresh apron off the middle shelf and handed it to Clarice.

"Where do you wash?" Clarice tied the apron and held her hands up like a doctor preparing for surgery.

Mildred smiled and pointed to the sink on the other side of the stove. "We have running water there, but the water isn't always hot enough. So use some from the kettle on the stove." She lifted a jar from the ledge above the sink. "And Nel—um, Dr. Winters wants us to use the carbolic acid solution to sterilize our hands. Like this."

Setting the jar on the edge of the sink, Mildred turned the spigot for the hot water, lathered her hands with lye soap, and rinsed them in the bowl Clarice filled with hot water from the kettle. Then she poured a little of the solution into her palm and worked it over her hands and up her forearms before rinsing them again.

Clarice nodded her understanding and went through the process as Mildred dried her hands on a clean towel. Coughs and wheezes and the occasional moan punctuated the silence, and her heart stirred once again, thankful for the ability the Lord had given her to ease pain and suffering.

"Is it time for medications?" Clarice's low voice cut into her thoughts, and Mildred turned toward the table. The plain wood kitchen table had been transformed into a laboratory worthy of the finest training hospitals in the East. She smiled, seeing Nelson bent over the petri dishes and medicine components far into the night.

"Nel—Dr. Winters believes in newer methods of treating the influenza." She reached for a green bottle that contained a smelly goo and held it up for Clarice to see. "This Vicks Vapo-Rub helps ease the tightness in their chests from the cough, though Dr. Winters says it does little else."

She motioned Clarice to follow her, and they stopped by the closest bed to the kitchen. "You know Johnny Zuckerman, right?" She waited for Clarice's nod, watching Johnny's gaze dart back and forth between the two of them. "Is it okay for Miss Clarice to help you, Johnny?"

He grinned slightly and nodded a yes. Then coughed.

"Cover your mouth when you cough, please." Even to her own ears, the words sounded rote—spoken without thinking. But Johnny flashed an apology with his eyes as he raised his hand to his mouth.

Mildred handed the jar to Clarice then pulled the sheet and blanket covering Johnny down to his waist. Under his nightshirt, she had placed a padding of cloth on his chest. When she lifted it, the sharp scent of wintergreen wafted to her nose.

"Everyone has a compress like this on their chests." Mildred looked around the room. "You can add another layer of the Vapo Rub and replace the compress."

Clarice nodded.

"Women and children are on this side." Mildred waved toward the other four beds stretching away from Johnny's bed. Then she nodded to the beds across the small aisle, which ran down the middle of the room. "Men are over there."

Not all the beds had occupants. Some had improved

enough to go home. Those beds lay bare of sheets or blankets. After administering aspirin to each patient, she and Clarice would make the beds ready for new patients. Unfortunately they never stood empty for long, and sadly the epidemic didn't look like it was letting go of its grip on Fredericksburg anytime soon.

Sighing, Mildred turned to the table to prepare the next round of medications.

Chapter 4

Nelson rubbed his eyes and then stretched his arms above his head. Silence reigned in the Sunday house as the patients eased into sleep, some deep and healing, others uneasy, still struggling to breathe. He really should take a quick walk around the house to stretch his aching leg. Absently he rubbed the scarring around his wound, wondering if he could talk Mildred into joining him.

He glanced toward the closed door into the lean-to where she had disappeared a few minutes before. Earlier that day, she attended her cousin's wedding, serving as maid of honor, and she'd returned even more subdued than usual. Was she thinking of Harold and their plans for a future? Plans that died with Harold. Plans he had helped destroy.

Sighing, Nelson turned back to the petri dishes and his handwritten notes lying on the table before him. Speculating on Mildred's broken dreams wouldn't get the report to the Public Health Service.

Much as he would like to pursue Mildred, comfort her, hold her in his arms, she would no doubt reject him.

As Helena had done.

Not for the first time he wondered why he had never caught on to her shallow character. Images of Helena as he'd last seen her refused to be squashed. Nelson squeezed his eyes shut, allowing the scene to play again in his mind.

That bright fall day in October, when the doctors told him he'd never walk unassisted or without pain, was the day he lost Helena. Though if he were honest with himself, Helena had been pulling away ever since the navy sent him home for further treatment at the military hospital in DC.

Though she still wore the extravagant ring she'd insisted on when their betrothal was announced before the war, she barely found time for him. Then her grandmother's death in Rochester, New York, took her away for a while. Finally, Nelson received word that Helena and her family had returned and they were receiving visitors. But when Nelson dutifully presented himself, she acted as though he were the last person she wanted to see. And even Nelson's ardor, much as he hated to admit it, had waned.

He'd expressed his regrets over her grandmother's death, but she shrugged it off. *"It's for the best. Grandmama was old."*

Hard. Cold. Bullets of ice pelting his mind. The woman shooting them was not the Helena he knew.

Though she sat in a wingchair to one side of her sitting room fireplace, she didn't offer for him to sit. Only his mother's strict social training kept him upright. "You still have that stupid cane. Isn't it about time you throw it away?" The scorn dripping from her words sizzled into his heart.

"I can't."

Her eyebrows rose into sharp peaks. "Can't? Or won't?" She stood and paced the area between her chair and the door. "I never knew you to back down in the face of a challenge."

"And I'm not backing down now." Nelson placed his hand on

the back of the chair Helena vacated, willing her to sit again. "The muscles are too badly damaged. I'll never be able to walk without a limp. . .or the cane."

That brought her to a standstill right in front of him. She eyed him warily. "Is this a play on my sympathy? Because if it is, I warn you, I'll not put up with it."

He reached for her hand, but instead she jerked the cane from his other hand and threw it across the room. It crashed into an expensive vase, splintering the vessel, before coming to land in the debris.

Involuntarily he took a step or two across the room to retrieve it. And his leg buckled under him, sending him to the floor.

Helena laughed—a high, shrill sound with a touch of hysteria in it. But her words drove themselves into his heart with as much force as the bullet that shattered his leg.

"Surely you don't expect me to marry you now!"

He couldn't answer as he struggled to a sitting position.

Neither did she wait for him to respond. She went on speaking in that bone-piercing pitch. "Look at you! You can't even stand without that horrible cane." A sneer twisted her lips as she yanked the ring from her finger and threw it at him. "I could never love a man who is less than perfect. No matter how rich he is."

It hit him square on the forehead, and he could feel the blood trickle down his nose. He put his hand to the small cut and winced, then picked the monstrosity off the floor.

She turned away. "I'm not willing to be shut up with an invalid the rest of my life."

Helena slammed the door on her way out, leaving him to drag himself across the room to his cane. Using the table the vase recently occupied, he pushed himself to a standing position. Once he stabilized, he concentrated on getting out of the room and the house where he was no longer welcome, leaving his dreams in the rubble of the vase.

A soft hand touched his shoulder, pulling him out of his memories, and he looked up into Mildred's face. A question he hadn't heard puckered her forehead.

He blinked. "I'm sorry. Did you say something?"

"I asked if you were okay." Removing her hand, she sat down in the chair next to his. "You looked like you were a million miles away. . .and not in a good place either."

The compassion in her voice soothed his troubled mind, and he smiled. "Neither so far away or as bad as I once thought." Though the sting of Helena's rejection still pricked, it wasn't the heart-stabbing wrench he remembered. Much of that had to do with Mildred's gentle acceptance of his deformity. "I thought you'd gone to bed. You seemed rather tired after the wedding."

Mildred's lips turned up, but the smile didn't go all the way to her eyes. "I was, but more because it wasn't the double wedding Clarice and I had always planned—her and Thomas, me and Harold." She sighed and looked over at the beds lining the walls. "I'd rather be out here than alone with my thoughts." Pulling the sheaf of papers to her, she went on, "Do you need me to help record your notes?"

His heart warmed. Her melodic voice was low, quiet, so as not to disturb any of the sleepers. She was always thinking of others.

"But it's late." She stared into the dim room. Then she

pulled her chocolate gaze back to him. "You look like you could use some sleep."

He massaged his forehead and temples and rolled his shoulders. "It's just a headache." Brought on by reliving his memories, no doubt. "I really need to finish this report before going to bed."

She reached for the pen lying beside the microscope. "You dictate. I'll write. Then you're going to bed." Her voice was firm, her gaze penetrating.

Heat rose to his cheeks under her scrutiny. Would she interpret it as fever? A cough tickled the back of his throat, and he reached for his coffee cup.

Her eyebrows rose. "We can't have you getting sick, too."

Chapter 5

Mildred looked down at Nelson lying in one of the patient beds. She might have avoided the nightmare of the last three days if she'd insisted he go to bed when he admitted to the headache. With his stethoscope extending from his ears, Uncle Will sat beside Nelson on the bed, listening to his heart and lungs.

Finally he pulled back. "It sounds like you're on the mend, my boy." He patted the younger man's shoulder then stood.

Mildred let out a sigh of relief. "Thank God."

Nelson touched her hand. "Yes. Thank Him."

Tears burned her eyes, and she turned to the stove to hide them. What was wrong with her? Except for a few tears, she still hadn't cried over Harold, but she couldn't keep the tears away as she nursed Nelson. She wiped her hands on the towel she'd soaked in the carbolic acid solution, and thought about Nelson's rapid descent into the illness that had killed so many.

While they had worked on Nelson's report for the Public Health Service, he reached for another petri dish to examine under the microscope and brushed her arm. He protested when she pulled a thermometer from the jar of alcohol and forced it between his teeth.

His fever raged at 104. She promptly put him in the closest available bed. . .on the women's side. No matter. They had rigged curtains to surround each bed for privacy. So she kept his pulled, except for the side that faced the kitchen.

Not many patients remained in the Sunday house, so she was free to focus most of her attention on Nelson. Thankful for the telephone her father had installed two years before, she used it to call Uncle Will. He'd come immediately and together they fought Nelson's copious nosebleeds and racking cough.

Now that the initial danger had passed, she would classify that day—the day she'd planned to marry Harold alongside Clarice and Thomas—at the top of her worst-times list. It confirmed what she'd suspected ever since arriving home—God didn't hear her prayers anymore. He'd allowed Harold to die, robbing her of her dreams of being a wife.

"Look at Nelson, My child."

The almost audible voice startled her. Had Uncle Will spoken to her? She turned from the stove where she stirred the savory chicken noodle soup she'd started earlier. But Uncle Will sat on Johnny's bed, laughing at something the boy said.

Nelson lay propped against a mound of pillows, his eyes closed. Though still pale and a little blue around his lips, he was definitely on the mend. A testimony of his own treatment methods, yes. But an answer to her prayers? Nelson's falling ill on her almost-wedding day rankled. No, she wasn't ready to accept that God heard her prayers.

Mildred turned back to the soup, gave it one more stir, and reached for the bowls. "Lunchtime." She spoke over her shoulder, catching her uncle's eye.

He stood, squeezed Johnny's shoulder, and stopped by Nelson's bed. "Well, my boy, God is good to spare your life. Now eat. We need you working."

Nelson quirked his lips and nodded but didn't speak.

Uncle Will came up behind her and placed a gentle hand on her shoulder. "Do you need help, my dear?"

Mildred shook her head. "No, Clarice will be here any minute to help me get lunch out." She nodded at the table. "Sit down. I'll get you a bowl of soup before you leave."

"How long. . .have I been. . .sick?" Nelson's voice, though low naturally, rasped from coughing.

"This is the fourth day." An eternity. After serving Uncle Will, Mildred set a bowl of the steaming broth on the stand next to Nelson's bed then went to the table to retrieve a chair. She would feed him. Clarice could take care of the rest.

Nelson swallowed. "Didn't. . .realize. . ." His words trailed off in a paroxysm of coughing.

Mildred frowned. "Don't try to talk. I won't be able to get any food into you at this rate."

Uncle Will laughed. "Better listen to her, Nelson. A woman needs to fill her man's stomach. It's the way to the heart, you know."

"Uncle Will!" Fire burned her cheeks.

Still chuckling, the old rogue raised his hand in farewell as he walked down the aisle between beds to the front door. He stopped to let Clarice in before he closed the door behind him.

Mildred set the bowl back on the stand and marveled that nothing spilled. The way her hands shook. . . Of course it was only a reaction to seeing Clarice back from her wedding trip, not a result of her uncle's words. Her man, indeed!

Clarice's gasp scattered her thoughts and she jerked to a stand, whirling to face her cousin.

"Nelson?" Clarice's gaze took in Nelson, the curtain shielding him from the other patients, and the soup bowl on the stand. "What happened?"

"He—"

"Influenza." Nelson shrugged and attempted a weak smile. "Didn't know"—he coughed—"you were back from..."

Mildred handed him a clean rag to spit into and pressed his shoulders back down on the pillow then gave her cousin a hug. "How was the trip?"

"Wonderful." The words came out on a sigh, and her face radiated her joy.

Mildred looped her arm through Clarice's, pulling her fully into the kitchen area. "I'll be back in a minute, Nelson." She looked his way but couldn't bring herself to look him in the eye. Her cheeks still burned. Maybe she should take care of the other patients and let Clarice feed him his lunch.

Clarice freed her arm, shrugged off her fashionable outer wrap, and hung it on a hook near the lean-to door then turned to the sink. "As soon as I wash up, I'll get lunch out to the others. Doesn't look like there are as many here."

Mildred shook her head. "There aren't. Most everyone has gone home to convalesce." In fact, only two out of the dozens of patients she'd cared for under Nelson's tutelage died. He said the disease had advanced too far in them to be affected by any kind of treatment.

"So go, before his soup gets cold." Clarice made shooing motions before grabbing a bowl and filling it with Mildred's soup.

"But—"

Mildred slid a glance over to Nelson, and her eyes collided with his. A hint of amusement in the depths of his steely blue eyes rekindled the fire in her belly. She turned away and lowered her voice. "I was going to let you feed Nelson. I can take care of the others."

"Now why would you do that?" Clarice, making no attempt to hide her astonishment, paused ladling soup into the bowls. "I'm fully capable—"

Flustered, Mildred stammered, "I—didn't mean to—" She stopped. Why was everyone pushing her toward Nelson?

Shoulders slumping, she turned back to Nelson's bed and the soup bowl waiting on the stand.

"Is my presence upsetting you?"

She met his gaze briefly before allowing it to skitter away.

"I—no—uh, yes—" Brilliant. That should make him feel better. She swallowed and tried again. "Sorry. No."

He studied her face. "No, what?"

"No, your presence doesn't upset me. In fact, I'm"—she stopped, not sure how to describe her feelings now that he was on the mend—"relieved you're getting better."

Nelson said nothing, but his intense gaze probing deep into her soul did nothing to settle her shaking hand. What was wrong with her? None of her other patients made her quiver with pleasure deep within her, setting every nerve end in her body tingling.

Mildred took another shaky breath, willed her hands to stop shaking, and without another word spooned some soup into Nelson's mouth.

Chapter 6

When Nelson woke, Mildred sat next to his bed, crocheting. Or knitting. He could never tell the difference. Taking advantage of her absorption in her work, he studied her. An occupation he found quite enjoyable.

Her calm spirit wrapped around his, enveloping him with peace. Not passive. Her mind was too quick and intelligent. Over the last couple of months, through the worst of the influenza epidemic, he'd thanked the Lord many times for giving him a nurse who rarely allowed impatience or a ruffled spirit to show to the people in her care. Even when he knew she was exhausted, she calmly pursued her duties, never rushing.

A shadow passed over Mildred's face as she started a new row. What troubled her thoughts, he couldn't imagine. She was much what he'd expected from Harold's descriptions and the portions of her letters he'd read aloud to those who would listen. What Harold hadn't mentioned was her sharp mind, her understated sense of humor, and her ability to laugh at herself.

Except when it came to his "new-fangled" methods of treating the disease. He smiled at the memory. When he first told her what medicines he wanted dispensed, how much, and how often, she'd dug in her heels, certain all her patients would die under his care. Until the evening he'd forgotten to put away his notes on the research he'd been doing for the Public Health Service.

Shortly after they set up the Sunday house for patients, Nelson moved into the upstairs loft, accessible only by the steep staircase attached to the outside wall. One evening a few days later, Nelson had come downstairs to check on the patients and to get the notes he'd left on the kitchen table. When he walked into the main room, he found Mildred reading the pages. Her concentration was so complete, he checked on his patients before disturbing her.

"What do you think?"

Startled brown eyes stared up at him. "Oh, I'm so sorry." She dropped the papers onto the tabletop and rose.

Amusement tickled the corners of his mouth. "For what? Reading my reports?"

Her cheeks sported a lovely shade of pink, leaving him breathless. "I didn't mean to snoop."

"I wouldn't have left them out if it were something I wanted to keep private." He pulled out the chair across from her and sat. "Sit with me a moment. Please."

She hesitated. "But the patients. . ."

"Are fine." His eyebrows rose, challenging her to comply with his request. "I want to hear your opinion."

"Oh." She sank into the chair and met his gaze. "On your research?"

"Yes." He resisted the urge to squirm under her intense scrutiny, as if he were a blob in a petri plate under the microscope.

"In my experience, doctors aren't interested in their nurses' opinions. They want blind obedience." Then the edges of her mouth quirked up and her eyes sparkled. "Except Uncle Will."

When she paused, he held his breath.

"And now you."

The rush of pleasure at being put into the same category as her beloved uncle swamped his mind, blocking any coherent thought.

"After reading your notes everything makes sense. I mean"— she waved a hand at the patients—"you've introduced some interesting methods of treating the influenza. Some things I've never heard of or considered." She stopped and chuckled. "And I've been the silly hen who thinks the sky is falling if we try something new when the old ways aren't working."

He laughed out loud at her analogy. "Go on."

"Well, your methods are born out of your research. I understand why you insisted we follow your somewhat unorthodox treatments. And why they're working—" She broke off, looking dazed.

He couldn't wipe the huge grin off his face. She got it. What would it be like to share his life with a woman like her? One who truly shared in his work?

The next day he moved all his research downstairs and set up his lab on the kitchen table. And she proved to be an able assistant with that as well. He'd never had a better research partner.

Now, Nelson could keep his mouth shut no longer. "A penny for your thoughts?" He kept his voice low for the other sleeping patients, but the words still rasped his sore throat.

Mildred startled, dropping the yarn and hook into her lap. "Oh." The pink rose in her cheeks, making her even more beautiful in his eyes. He shut his eyes against the thought.

When had he gotten so sappy about a woman? Never before. Certainly not with Helena, though maybe he should have.

"How long have you been awake?" Mildred's low voice broke into those unproductive thoughts. "Do you want something to drink?"

"Hot tea? Or coffee?" He hoped the hot liquid would clear some of the raspiness in the back of his throat. He reached out a hand when she started to rise, stopping her. "Tea, I think. If the water is hot."

She glanced at the stove a few feet from his bed. "The coffee is hot and somewhat fresh. Uncle Will was here a bit ago. I made some fresh for him. And the water is hot. Just need to steep the tea, add some honey."

He smiled, delighting in her nervous babble.

Mildred caught his smile and looked away. "I'm babbling." She stood and laid her work on the chair. Hopefully that meant she planned to sit with him a little longer. "I'm sorry. I'll get your tea."

While the tea steeped, Mildred checked on the other patients. When she came back around his curtain, he asked, "How many are here?"

She carefully poured him a cup of tea she'd sweetened with honey and put it on the table beside him. "Besides you, three. Mrs. Klus, Pastor Gloeckner, and Johnny." While she spoke she fluffed the pillows behind him and helped him sit up against them. Then she handed him the teacup. "Johnny and Pastor Gloeckner should be well enough to finish convalescing at home."

"And Mrs. Klus?" She was more at ease talking about her

patients. "How is she? Didn't she come in the day I got sick?"

Mildred picked up the yarn and hook and sat back down. "Yes. She'll be here a couple more days." She refused to make eye contact with him, busying herself with her handwork.

His time was also limited. It wouldn't be right for him to stay at the Sunday house, even in the loft, if there were no patients. Truthfully, he'd be better off in his own room at Dr. Bachman's, away from Mildred's distracting presence.

He snorted. Who was he fooling? She had invaded his thoughts from the moment he met her. Time to change the subject. "So what about that penny for your thoughts?"

Mildred shot a quick glance at him and back to her knitting. Or crocheting. But she didn't reply.

"At least tell me what you're doing. Knitting? Crochet?"

She quirked a smile. "You have a mother and a sister, and you don't know the difference?" The bantering tone matched his own.

"Nope. They only do embroidery."

"Well, at least you know that much." She held up the scarf she was making and showed him the hook. "Crocheting uses a hook. Usually just one." She set them in her lap and rooted in a cloth bag at her feet. She pulled out two long sticks and waved them in his face. "Knitting uses two needles."

"Those are needles?" He studied the two pointed shafts of wood. "Doesn't look like any kind of needle I've ever seen. Where's the eye?"

She laughed, low and melodic. The sound sent shivers of delight to the pit of his stomach. "No eyes. They aren't sewing needles."

"They aren't suturing needles either. Can you imagine sewing up a cut with a needle like that?"

"Knitting uses the sticks to make loops and draw the yarn through them." She reached into the bag again and pulled out another piece of yarn work.

He really didn't care which was which. He only wanted to keep her talking. To keep her near him. Forever.

Mildred held up the yarn patch for his inspection. "This is knitting." She reached for the other, lacier, much larger piece. "This is crocheting."

"So I can tell the difference by how lacy a piece is?"

"Not really." She flashed him a cheeky grin. "Knitting can be lacy, too." She looked down at the smaller piece. "But I'm not very good at knitting, so I usually choose the denser patterns for that. And crocheting can be dense, too, depending on the stitch I choose to use." She looked back at him.

"In other words, it depends on whether you're using a hook"—he pointed to hers—"or n–needles." He stumbled a bit over the word. Still didn't look like any needle he'd ever seen.

Mildred nodded approval, put the knitting away, and picked up the crocheting.

Nelson wasn't fooled. She still hadn't revealed her thoughts in answer to his first question. Determined to get it out of her one way or another, he looked forward to the verbal sparring match. What better time than now to probe into Mildred's thoughts?

But she beat him to it. "Who's Helena?"

He stared. "How do you know about Helena?"

"You had a pretty high fever that first night, and. . ."

Great. "I was delirious, obviously." But since he entertained thoughts of Mildred as his wife, it was much better to learn now whether she would reject him for the same reason. "She was my fiancée."

She met his gaze, studying him. "Was?"

He nodded. "She consented to become my wife after the war. But when I came home wounded. . ." He grimaced. "Then I learned I would always be somewhat crippled, would always have to use the cane to walk. When she found out. . ." He swallowed hard.

"She rejected you because of your war wound?" Mildred's voice rose. She stared at him, wide-eyed. "Why, it's a badge of honor in itself."

His heart warmed. He decided to exorcise Helena, once and for all, from his thoughts. "The actual medal appealed to her more."

"You received a medal? Which one?" Mildred laid down her crocheting and focused all her attention on him.

"The Silver Star."

Her eyes narrowed. "What kind of woman wouldn't want to marry a man of honor, recognized for valor by his country?" She spoke so softly, he leaned forward to hear her. "And recognized by God for his faithfulness."

Shame threatened to smother blossoming hope, and he rubbed his wound. "But I failed God. . .lost my faith."

She gazed at him steadily. "No faith? Then who has prayed with every patient he's seen the last two months? Who prays before eating a meal? Who speaks of Christ to his patients—and to me—and tells of His compassion and love for those who were sick and hungry and. . .lame?" Her voice broke and she swallowed. Her lips set in a thin line, yet respect and loyalty shone in her chocolate eyes, wrapping him in their sweet goodness.

How he loved her—her passion, her loyalty, her commitment to duty and serving others. "But—" Dread boiled in his gut, and he drew in a shaky breath. She had to know the worst about him. "I killed my best friend, your fiancé."

Chapter 7

Harold?" Mildred couldn't believe she'd heard Nelson right. "My Harold?"

Pain radiated from his blue eyes before he hooded them. His fingers plucked at the blanket covering his lap. "Yes." The word came out in a whisper.

"But he died of the Spanish influenza." Mildred couldn't grasp what Nelson meant. He was already home, convalescing from his wounded leg, well before Harold died. "I—I don't understand." Her voice faded to an almost inaudible whisper, and her fingers choked the yarn ball in her lap.

Still, he heard her. But he hesitated. Then he motioned her closer. She dragged the chair forward a few inches, until her knees dug into the bedside table leg.

"Sit here instead." Nelson patted the bed beside him.

Her heart rate sped up. That close? But she pushed her chair out of the way and sat beside him on the bed. She realized then that she still had a death grip on the yarn, so she reached for the bag and emptied her hands.

Immediately she regretted her action. What was she to do with her hands now? She clasped them together and stared at them, not wanting to make eye contact with Nelson. She needed to hear what he said, not distracted by the way his penetrating stare seemed to read her like a book.

She risked a glance and saw that Nelson's eyes were closed again, his lips moving in a silent prayer. Bowing her own head, she breathed her own petition, fully expecting no answer in return. *Oh Father, help.*

"Listen to him, My child."

Mildred's eyes popped open. That voice again. Was it only that morning she'd heard it the first time?

Was that You, Lord?

Nelson's hand covered her clenched fists, drawing her eyes to meet his own. She didn't try to remove her hands from his comforting grasp. It calmed her spirit, warming her from the icy pit in the depths of her stomach all the way to her heart.

"Do you really want to hear this?" Nelson's gaze intensified as he sought his answer in her eyes.

Mildred's nod was more of a jerk. "Yes. Tell me."

"Did Harold ever tell you of the Meuse-Argonne Offensive in September?"

Mildred nodded. "He was sure he would have died if it hadn't been for his best friend. . ." Nels. That was the name he'd written. "Nels? You?"

Nelson closed his eyes against the pain of hearing Harold's nickname for him. "Yes." He let loose a low, bitter laugh and gripped her fists a little tighter.

Mildred loosened one fist, turned her hand palm up, and twined her fingers through his. Surely she felt the electric shock that bolted through his heart. When he dared to look at her again, memories clouded her vision. She said,

"Harold always shortened names."

"Millie?"

Her laugh sounded almost as bitter as his had. "Or Mills." She winced. "I hated that one, and he knew it. For some reason it amused him to see how many ways he could shorten a name."

"Especially when the owner of the name protested."

"But Harold was alive after that battle. I mean, he wrote me afterward."

Nelson shuddered. It wasn't a memory he wanted to dwell on, even if his leg served as a constant reminder of his sin. "His unit was ordered to flank the front line of attack, and to stand ready to charge when the command was given. But their commanding officer was shot and unconscious."

Mildred's fingers tightened around his. Oh, how he would love to raise her hand to his lips. But now was not the time to romance her.

"I was part of the attending medical unit, and when we got the message about the lieutenant, I was sent in to get him out. I had combat training, as well as battlefield medical training." He swallowed. "I worked my way to the front lines without too much trouble. I was armed, of course."

Staring at the wall opposite him, Nelson could recall in vivid detail the horror of that mission. "When I found them, the lieutenant was dead. The rest of the unit had gone to earth in some nearby foxholes—dug by the Germans. But Harold spotted me checking on the lieutenant, and he ordered his unit to retreat." Tears streamed down his face. "I shouted, 'No,' but they didn't hear me. The Jerries opened fire and mowed down the lot of them."

Mildred gasped. "But Harold?"

"I tackled him, sending him back into the foxhole. And took his bullet." He motioned to his leg.

"But how is that killing him?"

"Not then." Nelson felt his chest tightening. Lung spasms. He needed to finish his story before the cough returned.

"We waited for dark. Harold took off his uniform jacket and pressed it against the wound, slowing down the blood flow. If he hadn't, I probably would have died from blood loss." He sighed. "That would have been best in the end."

"How can you say that?" Mildred demanded. "You saved his life."

"In order to take it away from him in the end." More tears trickled down his face, but he didn't try to remove them. "Harold was second-in-command. His orders were to continue the charge if his commanding officer went down. When we got back, I had to report his giving the order to retreat that killed his unit and wounded me." He swallowed hard. "His failure to follow through resulted in the loss of many lives and nearly cost us the battle. He was facing a court-martial."

Mildred's eyes widened and he looked away. He didn't want to see the condemnation he knew he deserved in her eyes.

"That's still not killing him." Her grip on his numb fingers relaxed a little, and they tingled as the blood flow increased.

"I didn't realize his cowardice would result in his going AWOL."

She gasped. "AWOL?"

He nodded. "One more death sentence if he was caught." What was he trying to do? Alienate her completely? He expected her any moment to snatch her hand away from his.

But she didn't.

He could feel her eyes on him, but he refused to meet her gaze. He had to finish this. Then he could sink back into the rising fever and encroaching pneumonia.

"I never saw him again. Didn't know what happened to him until Dr. Bachman told me about your telegram."

Mildred shifted on the bed and brought her other hand up to cup his whiskery cheek. "Those were his choices, Nelson. Not yours. You only did what was your duty."

Nelson shook his head fretfully. How could she be so compassionate when he killed her husband-to-be? She would never be his. She would never—

He heard her gasp of alarm and felt her snatch her hand out of his grip before he sank back into the blessed darkness.

Please, God, take me home.

Chapter 8

Clarice squeezed Mildred's hand as Uncle Will leaned over Nelson, once again listening to his heart and lungs. The toll of the last twenty-four hours caught up to her, and she clung tightly to Clarice's grasp. Nelson's relapse after telling his story shook her more than the news of Harold's death.

She hadn't had time to examine why. Nelson's fever, which had hovered around 104 all the previous night and that morning, finally broke around midafternoon. She hadn't even thought to get a message to Uncle Will, until he stopped in that morning to check on the patients.

He'd been the one to get Clarice to come care for Mrs. Klus, after he sent Johnny Zuckerman and dear Pastor Gloekner home. The pastor had prayed over Nelson before he left. And then Uncle Will had helped her nurse Nelson. Even though Nelson's temp had come down, he hadn't regained consciousness.

Was God going to take him, too? Despite his confession last evening, she didn't want to let him go. Not with the guilt he carried over Harold's death. Guilt she knew was misplaced. He had relapsed before she could tell him about her last letter to Harold. The guilt was all hers, not Nelson's, and she longed to tell him.

Uncle Will straightened. "He'll do."

Relief surged through her, weakening her knees.

"Careful, honey." Clarice patted her hand.

Mildred caught the meaningful look Clarice and Uncle Will exchanged, and the starch returned to her legs. As she pulled away from Clarice, Uncle Will turned back to Nelson.

Clarice grasped her wrist and tugged her toward the front door. But Mildred refused to budge. "Is there something I can do for him, Uncle Will?"

The fatigue lines in his face gentled when he looked up at her. "Take a break."

"But—"

"Doctor's orders, liebchen." He waved his arms toward the door. "The best thing you can do for your young man is get some fresh air and rest, or you will be the next to join your patients."

When Clarice tugged again, Mildred followed. But it felt as though she moved through quicksand. Outside, the sun shone brightly in a cloudless sky. Mildred sank down into a rocking chair and took in a deep breath.

Clarice took the other rocker. "What an absolutely gorgeous day!" She tipped her head against the back of the chair and took a deep breath.

"Just what the doctor ordered?" Mildred couldn't resist the opportunity to tease her cousin.

Clarice grinned. "You heard what he said. Besides, we haven't had a chance to chat since before the wedding." She winked. "And you obviously have some talking to do, girlie."

"I do?" Mildred knew better than to act as though she

didn't understand Clarice, but her relief brought out her ornery streak. "How was the wedding trip?"

Clarice twisted her features in mock despair. "Don't think you're getting away with that approach."

Mildred's lips turned up at the corners in spite of herself, and she laid her head back and closed her eyes. The sun was bright and the air crisp. Perfect for someone who had stayed inside too long. She closed her eyes. "Well?"

Clarice exhaled loudly. "It was *wunderbar*."

"That good, huh?" Mildred opened one eye and scrutinized her cousin. She only used German to express the highest form of approval.

Clarice's face glowed with contentment and happiness. Mildred's heart twisted and she closed her eye. But the pain she'd expected from the loss of her dreams didn't come.

"Better than good." Clarice giggled. "You'll understand when you have your turn."

Mildred's eyes shot open. "My turn at what?" A wedding trip? "In case it escaped your notice, Harold and my dreams of marriage and wedding trips and children are finished. Kaput."

Clarice arched her eyebrows. "Somehow I don't think the man in the bed in there would say so."

The heat rose in Mildred's cheeks.

"And neither do you really believe it." Clarice laid a deliciously cool hand over Mildred's fiery cheek. "Honey, ignore it all you want. It doesn't change the truth. I only pray you wake up and recognize it before you push it—and him—away."

Clarice broke the connection and Mildred stared into the distance. Surely Clarice was mistaken. Not about her feelings.

She'd known for a few days that she'd fallen for Nelson Winters—hard. But he could never love her back. Not with Helena's name still on his lips. Besides, whatever Clarice said to the contrary, she'd loved Harold.

"I'm not saying you didn't love Harold."

Mildred switched her gaze to her cousin who had the uncanny knack of reading her mind. "I did. I mean, I still do."

"Really? Then tell me, who comes to mind when you think of marriage? Even more, who were you thinking of at my wedding? The day you were to have married Harold?"

Mildred, unable to tear her gaze away from Clarice's knowing eye, desperately wanted to say Harold. But it would be a lie. So she pressed her lips together and said nothing.

"Uh-huh. Just what I thought."

Mildred rolled her eyes and sat back.

"Don't roll your eyes at me, girlie." Clarice smirked. "You never loved Harold more than a brother. You fancied yourself in love with him, and you would have married him, too. You believed it was your duty because that's what everyone expected. But you would have been miserable." She put her hand on Mildred's. "Honey, you have to know. . ."

"Know what?" Mildred forced herself to look Clarice in the eye.

"I prayed every day you were away that the Lord would open your eyes before you married Harold."

"So you prayed him dead?" Clarice's prayers felt like betrayal. Bitterness rose in her like bile, burning her throat.

"Of course not!" Clarice sat up straight. "What are you talking about?"

"You prayed for God to remove Harold from my life. And he died. How can you say you didn't pray him dead? What about me? What about my dreams?" The words spewed from her mouth and flowed over her like hot lava. Yet she found it impossible to stop the eruption.

"I loved Harold. More than a brother. I would have made him a good wife. Yet you prayed him dead." Hot tears flowed over her cheeks. "I thought you loved me."

Clarice stood next to Mildred's chair. She laid a hand on her shoulder, but Mildred shrugged it off, knowing how Clarice would respond. Without a word or a backward glance, Clarice went down the steps, onto the sidewalk. Back to her precious Thomas.

Leaving Mildred to smolder. Why couldn't she keep her mouth shut? Her own words had robbed her of all she held dear.

The door to the Sunday house opened behind her, and Mildred stood to go inside. But Uncle Will blocked the door.

"Liebchen." He stretched his arms toward her. She walked into them and burst into tears against his broad shoulder. His arms wrapped around her, he stood like the rock she needed as she allowed the remorse to drain from her heart.

Remorse for her words to Clarice. Remorse for her last letter to Harold. Remorse for the love she might have had with Nelson but now lay in ruins before it got a chance to build.

All because of words. Her words.

Chapter 9

Mildred woke to silence. Blessed silence. The lean-to's door stood ajar, open to the empty main room.

Uncle Will had sent Mrs. Klus home the day after Mildred's outburst, and then he moved Nelson back to the clinic and his room there. Although Nelson protested having to go the two blocks in a wheelchair, Uncle Will's stubbornness had overruled. Mildred smiled at the memory.

Uncle Will, sensing her discomfort at having to face her patients after her awful explosion, sent her to bed and called for another volunteer to do night duty at the Sunday house. The number of flu patients had decreased to just a handful at the clinic, and Mildred was no longer needed.

She rose from bed, washed her face in the sink in her miniscule bathroom, and dressed. Today her brother Henry was coming to help dismantle the beds and cots and take down the curtains they'd placed between the beds. She would have the Sunday house back in order before the end of the day.

Then what? She could move out to the farm with her family again. But her spirit was restless. They didn't need her either. Maybe she would stay in the Sunday house and work somewhere.

She knew Uncle Will would be glad to have her continue

nursing for him. But now it would be too awkward having to work alongside Nelson.

As she went about preparing a small breakfast of oatmeal and toast, her cheeks burned when she remembered realizing Nelson was awake. She'd caught his gaze for just a moment but long enough to see the compassion in his eyes. Along with the pain.

Her oatmeal ready, Mildred sat at the table, said a quick prayer of thanks, and ate. Or attempted to. Like everything else she'd tried to eat the last couple of days, it tasted like the sawdust that carpeted her father's workroom. She choked down a few bites before pushing the bowl away. Even the toast slathered with her mama's delicious plum jelly was tasteless.

Mildred dumped her uneaten cereal and toast into the slop bucket by the stove and set the dishes on the counter by the sink. She'd wash them up later.

Right now, she needed to get to Clarice's before her courage failed her. It wouldn't be the first time in their long-time friendship that she'd had to apologize. She also knew from experience that Clarice would wait her out. Mildred would have to go to her.

She looked at the time on her watch. Her late start guaranteed she'd find Clarice at home.

Only she wasn't. No one answered the door when Mildred knocked on Clarice's door fifteen minutes later. She walked around the house, thinking Clarice might be hanging clothes. But no one stirred.

Surely Clarice was shopping and would return soon.

Mildred found a bench on the flagstone area and sat. She breathed deeply the balmy air, her back resting against the house.

Spring was just around the corner, but already Mildred could smell jonquils and the agarita bushes by Clarice's porch bore tiny white and pink petals. It wouldn't be long before her favorite bluebonnets were in bloom. Now that her nursing time was over, she could spend time in the wild-flower field her mother had planted so many years ago. There might be a few early bluebonnets already peeking through the grass.

Glancing at the time, Mildred stood, looking both ways along the block. Henry would be at the house soon.

Deciding to take the longer route back to her house, Mildred strolled toward downtown. Maybe she would run into Clarice coming back from shopping.

Mildred greeted several townspeople shopping downtown but still saw no sign of Clarice. She walked by the clinic and thought about stopping to visit with Uncle Will a few moments. But knowing Nelson would be there, too, kept her feet moving.

What a mess her words had created.

As she rounded the corner to her own street, she saw the Model T parked in front of the house and Henry sitting on the porch.

Someone was with him, but she couldn't see whom, since he sat back in the shadows. Her heart raced. Something about him made her think of Nelson. . .again. Truth be told, he was rarely far from her thoughts. But she couldn't imagine any reason he would seek out her company now.

Still, she couldn't stop her heart bursting into song when she turned onto her house's front walk. It was Nelson, watching her approach.

Henry didn't bother with the stairs but bounded up to her and planted a loud smooch on her cheek before she could fend him off. His exuberant approach to life, so different from her own, always brought a smile to her face.

"What are you doing out here, lazy boy?" Looping her arm through his, she forced him to walk her sedately onto the porch.

"Lazy?" He guffawed. "Where have you been? We were waiting for you to supervise the work."

"We?" Mildred smiled a welcome to Nelson. "Surely you're not well enough to—to—" She waved her hand indicating the work. Mercy goodness. Why did words always fail her around this man? Or turn her into a babbling fool?

"Oh but I am." His intense blue eyes twinkled, and he made a small bow toward her. "Just awaiting your command."

Fire burst in her cheeks and, flustered, she turned to open the door. "You don't need me to get started. Why didn't you go on in?"

Henry pushed past her and entered the house first. "I just got here. Dr. Winters, uh, Nelson was already here."

"Why?" Mildred looked over her shoulder at Nelson, who motioned her to enter before him.

"I came to see you." His voice was soft and low, for her hearing only, and her unruly heart leaped into her throat.

"Me?" It came out as a squeak. "Why would you do that?"

She fumbled with the button on her cardigan, and her neck tingled when he put his hand up, ready to help her remove it.

She turned to take the sweater from him, and his gaze trapped her again. Something she couldn't read lurked in the depths.

He cleared his throat. "We hadn't seen you at the clinic the last few days. So I came to see if you were well."

"A house call from my doctor then?" Pushing away her disappointment, she turned away and laid her wrap over the arms of a nearby wingchair.

"No. Not a house call." He paused then laid his hand on her arm, turning her toward him. "Liebchen." The endearment was almost inaudible. "Look at me."

Henry, the beds, the temporary clinic—all vanished from her mind when she met his gaze. "I came to see *you*. To see if you would take a walk with me this afternoon."

She couldn't speak, so she nodded. He wanted to see her. To walk with him. To spend time with him. Her heart burst into a symphony of praise. He didn't abhor her.

"So where were you, sis?" Henry's voice broke into the silent conversation flowing between her and Nelson. She turned toward her brother.

"What?" She swallowed. "Oh. I went to see Clarice, but she wasn't home."

"You shoulda waited for me. She's helping Aunt Leisel. Uncle George has the Spanish influenza."

Dismay clenched her stomach. "Oh no! Is it bad?"

"Naw. He's on the mend now." Henry pulled the mattress off the bed nearest the door. "But Clarice went to help her mom with the younger kids." Another mattress hit the floor.

Mildred's stomach slowly relaxed. "Maybe I should go out to check on them." She glanced at Nelson, who nodded. "How are you transporting these things, Henry? It all goes back to the clinic."

"Yes. That's why I brought the wagon instead of the Model T."

How had she missed the wagon? She stooped to look out the low window. "That's not Papa's automobile?"

"That's your Uncle Will's." Nelson spoke behind her.

"Uncle Will has a Model T?"

"Oh yeah." Henry piled another mattress with the others by the still-open door.

"I believe he said he got it shortly after you left for the war." Nelson sounded amused. "Says he thought it would make the house calls outside of town easier."

Henry paused in pulling a bed apart. "Only he can't figure out how to fix it when something goes wrong." He laughed.

Mildred smiled. Sounded like Uncle Will. Uncomfortable with modern conveniences. "But you can, I assume?" She looked at Nelson.

"Yes." He shrugged and bent to help Henry with the bed deconstruction.

Was there anything the man couldn't do? "Do you want all your lab things to go with the beds?" The paraphernalia still littered her kitchen table, though she'd pushed it together to make a space for her meals. "And the medicines in the cabinet?"

Her father had built a cabinet into the main room wall

next to the fireplace. It had served well as the medicine closet the last three months.

Nelson straightened and stretched his back. He grimaced. "Let's move the medicine back to the clinic. But would it be okay to store the lab stuff here for a while longer?"

"Of course." Mildred looked at the growing stack of bed parts. "We need to start getting some of this out of here, don't you think?"

Henry started for the door. "I'll bring the wagon and horses around." He slammed the back door shut behind him.

Of course. She'd forgotten about the old watering trough at the barn on the back edge of the lot.

Mildred grabbed her cardigan from the chair then headed into the lean-to. She had an empty box stored under the bed she could use for the medicine bottles.

When she came back into the main room, Nelson had shifted some of the mattresses onto the porch. Mildred could see the wagon backed up to the porch and Henry pulling a mattress into the wagon bed. That should keep them busy for a while.

She turned to the cabinet, placing the box on a low table nearby, and started removing the bottles and other medicine-related items. The one part of nursing she really enjoyed was preparing the medicines. It fascinated her how different chemicals and herbs worked together to treat various illnesses and ailments.

Before she'd gone to Europe, she had started a study on the various medicinal qualities of herbs and other plants. She knew many doctors had no use for "medicine women," preferring to rely on new discoveries. But she believed there was a use for both. Maybe she could take up that study again, now that she was no longer needed for nursing.

As she packed the last of the jars into the box, she looked around the room now stripped of hospital beds and nightstands. They would have to get the other furniture in from the barn where they were stored.

She carried the box to the door, intending to give it to Nelson to put in the Model T, and found the furniture crammed onto her porch and front lawn.

"Do you want everything back where we had it before?" Henry paused next to a large buffet.

"That will be fine." Mildred moved out of the way and let the men move the furniture back into place. She would get the doilies and dresser scarves out later, when she was alone.

Once they were done, Henry jumped into the wagon seat and took up the reins. "I'll meet you over at the clinic, Nelson."

"Be there shortly." He waved Henry off then turned to Mildred. "Henry says the jonquils are already blooming in the wildflower field your mother planted."

"Oh good. I thought I smelled some over at Clarice's." Maybe tomorrow she would ask Uncle Will for the use of the car, go see Clarice and her aunt and uncle, and stop by the field.

"Would you like to take a drive this afternoon instead of a walk?" Nelson stood in front of her, clutching his hat. "I'd love to see your favorite place."

A sudden shyness descended between them, almost as tangible as a curtain. Mildred took a deep breath and tried to dispel the awkwardness. "I'd like that." She smiled. "Very much."

Chapter 10

Nelson watched Mildred out of the corner of his eye, managing to keep one eye on the road. More like a cow path. He hoped no other vehicle—wagon or automobile—met them. There was no place to go, except into the ditch that ran on either side of the road. And he didn't want that, especially not at ten miles per hour, the fastest he dared to go.

They didn't speak. The rumble of the motor overpowered all sounds. But as the distance from town increased, Mildred's facial features relaxed until a small, contented smile rested on her lips. Peace rolled off her, bathing him in its blessed calm. He loved discovering there were depths to her that delighted him, though he wasn't sure why it should.

Helena hated the country. As soon as the thought wriggled through his mind, he squashed it. Why did he continue to compare the two women when there was no comparison? He knew he was well rid of Helena, but she crawled into his thoughts at inopportune moments.

Banishing Helena from his mind, he intended to enjoy this day with Mildred. Sweet, quiet, calm Mildred. Even the fiery explosion he overheard last week didn't scare him away. Her feisty spirit brought a grin to his face.

When she told Henry this morning that she'd gone to

see Clarice, he'd rejoiced that she was trying to make amends with her best friend. He knew the ties between them were strong and that Mildred's love for her family ran deeper than most.

Intent on his thoughts, he startled when Mildred's hand rested on his arm for a brief moment. She pointed ahead. A wagon pulled by two huge draft horses rounded the curve in front of them. He braked until the speedometer showed three miles per hour.

But he still didn't see a way out. Casting in his mind for a turnout he might have missed, he realized he'd been so preoccupied with his thoughts that he hadn't taken in much of the countryside.

Mildred touched his arm again and pointed to a grassy area to the side of the road a few yards ahead. He nodded to show his understanding and directed the steering lever in that direction. But as the automobile pulled out of the ruts, the right front tire blew, jerking the lever out of his hand and sending the vehicle back into the rut.

The car ground to a halt a few feet short of the turnout. The farmer with the wagon stopped his horses, and for a moment the two men stared at each other.

"Papa!" Mildred fumbled with the door handle.

Nelson reached across her and opened the door. Mildred leaped onto the grassy verge and ran toward the wagon.

The older man, his tanned, leathery face wreathed in smiles, jumped down to meet her. He caught his daughter up and twirled her around as if she were a young child.

Nelson slid awkwardly across the seat and exited the

passenger door. His usual method of jumping in and out of the automobile over the stationary driver's door was impossible now with his leg. Grasping the cane from behind the seat, Nelson balanced himself before trying to navigate over the uneven ground. He maneuvered to the front of the car and choked the engine.

"Papa." Mildred's sweet voice sounded clear in the sudden quiet. "Come meet Nels—uh, Dr. Winters." She grabbed the older man's hands and pulled him toward Nelson.

Hank Zimmermann stood an inch or two taller than Mildred and had the upper body musculature of a man who wasn't afraid of hard work. The hand that rested on Mildred's shoulder was scarred, and the grip of welcome on Nelson's outstretched hand was strong yet gentle.

"Pleased to meet you, sir."

"And I, you." The older man studied Nelson for a moment or two then nodded. "Young Henry speaks nothing but good of you. As does my wife's uncle Will."

"They are kind." Nelson basked in the secondhand praise and wondered anew at the ready acceptance that characterized all the members of Mildred's family. It was as if they didn't see the cane, his limp.

"Papa, would Clyde and Sam be able to pull the Model T to the turnout?"

Mr. Zimmermann turned toward his wagon. "Sure they can." He reached the horses. "What about it, boys? Ready to take on Uncle Will's automobile?"

The horse closest to Mr. Zimmermann whickered and nuzzled his shoulder as the older man undid the traces. Once they were loosed from the wagon, he led them forward, turned them around, and backed them to the automobile. Nelson eased himself across the passenger seat and positioned himself behind the wheel, pulling the gear lever out of gear.

After harnessing the horses to the front axle of the Model T, Mr. Zimmermann took the reins and gave his horses the command to pull. In short order, and with very little strain that Nelson could detect on the part of the horses, the car came to a stop on the grassy verge, out of the way of the wagon.

Nelson crawled back out of the car. While Mr. Zimmermann and Mildred loosed the horses, Nelson examined the ruined tire and thanked the Lord he'd thought to put a few spares in the trunk.

Well, it wouldn't take long to fix and they would soon be on their way.

Nelson pulled out a spare tire and tried to roll it toward the front of the car. But he hadn't counted on his gimpy leg and the cane. The task proved much more difficult than he'd remembered.

"Here, let me help." Mildred's strong, capable fingers wrapped around the thin rubber tube and carried it to the front of the car.

Nelson's shoulders slumped. Helena was right. He was useless with his injury. A burden on everyone around him. A large, work-worn hand landed on his shoulder, and Nelson looked into the bold-featured face of Mildred's father.

"Son, God never intended for anyone to go it alone. In fact, you have it better than most of us."

Nelson quirked an eyebrow. "How so?"

"You have a tangible reminder to depend on God and the people with whom He surrounds us." He nodded toward Mildred, who had equipped herself with the necessary tools and was very capably changing the tire. "The sooner you allow her to help you, the better off you'll be. She doesn't easily take no for an answer." He grinned. "Just like her mother."

"I heard you, Papa." Mildred winked at her father. Then she grabbed the tools and restored them to the trunk.

With a final slap on Nelson's shoulder and a quick hug for his daughter, Mr. Zimmermann climbed into the wagon seat and took up the reins. "Better get to the river and load up the wood I cut last week." The horses started forward. "Bring the good doctor to supper, sweetie, since you're out this way. It will be a treat for your mama."

Mildred smiled up at him. "I was planning to." She raised her hand in farewell and watched until the team disappeared over the next swell in the road.

Nelson stood beside the open car door, waiting. But Mildred turned away from him and waded out into the fragrant and colorful sea of grass and flowers edging the road.

"Come on, Nelson. I want to show you something."

He shut the automobile door. "What about the wildflowers?"

She grinned and waved her arm across the field. "Right here."

She waited for him to come alongside her, then looped her arm through his and guided him along a narrow footpath he'd not seen from the road.

His heart sang as Mildred pressed in closer and gave him the support he needed to negotiate the rough path with his injured leg. He inhaled the fragrance of the flowers and her hair as her head brushed his shoulder. Not for the first time he wished she could care for him as he did for her. He'd fallen fast and hard.

Mildred stopped to point at a gazebo perched on a foundation of rock in the center of the field. "Here. This is my favorite part."

She moved quickly away from him, and his eyes followed her movements as she stepped from one clump of flowers to the next. She reached down to stroke the petals, breathing deeply of the rich aroma.

When she reached the gazebo in the center, she paused on the bottom step and looked back at him, grinning. "What are you waiting for? We can sit in here."

He moved toward her, leaning heavily on the cane. Then he felt her hand on his arm as it slid down to grasp his free hand. Her father was right. Mildred made a very good partner. With her, he felt whole again.

She led him up the steps and sat next to him on the bench that lined the outside latticework of the building. Absently rubbing his leg, he took in his surroundings.

The wide wood planks of the floor matched the lattice-work of the low walls. Overhead, perched on long spindles stretching toward the sky, a cedar-shingled roof protected them from the sun. The craftsmanship was superb. "Your father built this?"

"Yes. He built it for his and Mama's wedding. I often

dreamed of it during the war." Mildred's voice was hushed, reverent. She made a jerking motion with her free hand. "It's so peaceful. A piece of heaven on earth." Her laugh matched her voice, and she looked at their linked hands. "Sounds kind of silly put that way."

"Not at all." Nelson wished he'd had a place like this to take his mind away from the horrors of war. "A shelter. A refuge from the storm."

Mildred met his eyes, her own shining. "Exactly."

"Your mother planted the seeds?" Nelson was intrigued. "What kind of flowers are these? The blue ones—I've never seen them before."

"Those are Texas bluebonnets. Wait another couple of weeks and the whole field will be blanketed with them. Then there's the Indian paintbrush. Jonquils. Primroses." She pointed to different plants as she said their names. "Mama and her students planted them. She was the town's teacher and planned a day outing near the end of school. Papa drove them out here in wagons. They brought a picnic lunch and the seeds. But before Papa could get back to pick them up, a storm overtook them. By the time Papa found Mama, she was unconscious from a fall. Papa says she scared him so bad that when she finally woke in the clinic, he proposed."

Nelson scanned the sky for storm clouds and laughed at himself. Had he hoped for similar circumstances? He looked down at Mildred's hand, still encased in his. Sure, Mildred patiently assisted him, instinctively understanding when he needed support and when he could manage on his own. But even if she loved him, it would quickly wear thin, and she would soon tire of caring for a cripple.

Galloping hoofbeats pulled Nelson from his troubled thoughts. Mildred jerked her hand out of his and stood at the top of the steps, the better to see the road. He laid his hand on her shoulder as he came up behind her, and she raised hers to cover his.

As the rider came into view, he glanced their way and checked the horse's forward motion. "Millie!" He got the horse under control and trotted the animal through the field, careless of the flowers he trampled.

"Ernie! What's wr—"

"Oh Millie." The boy gulped back a sob. "First Mama. . . then Henry. . . sick. . ."

The color drained from Mildred's face. But she stiffened her back and pitched herself at the horse's bridle.

"Off." Her voice was sharp with command.

"But—"

"No!" She barely waited for Ernest to jump down before flying onto the horse's back. "Come with Nelson."

Chapter 11

Mildred sank into the rocker next to Mama's bed and listened to her labored breathing. How quickly the day had disintegrated into horror. Both Mama and Henry struck down with the Spanish influenza.

Her worst nightmare come true.

She'd allowed herself to think her family was safe, now that the epidemic had slowed in town. Allowed herself to take a day off. Allowed herself to hope Nelson would take a hint from the story she'd told of her parents in that lovely, romantic wildflower field.

She let out a soft snort. As if Nelson would even consider her as a suitable mate. But still she'd hoped. Foolish woman.

Leaning her head back against the rocker, she closed her eyes, letting her thoughts run over the events of the afternoon. After Ernest's interruption of the idyllic afternoon, she arrived at the farm mere minutes before Nelson and her youngest brother. Nelson helped her get Mama and Henry into their beds. Her box with all the medicines was still in the jump seat of the Model T, so she'd wasted no time in getting the proper medications started. A few petri dishes she'd slipped into the box now contained sputum so Nelson could try to isolate a bacteria.

Mildred's heart clenched. The onset was so sudden. But Nelson seemed to think if they made it through the night, they would be out of danger. It would be a long night.

He'd gone back to town to return Uncle Will's automobile. She hoped he'd be back in the morning. Papa and Ernest finally agreed to settle in the front room—Papa on the sofa, Ernest on a pallet on the floor. Much better than having them both pacing between the sickrooms. Her younger sister, Klara, tended to Henry, sponging his hot skin, trying to get his fever to break.

Mildred pushed herself off the rocker and laid a hand on her mother's forehead. Still much too warm. She reached for the washcloth in the basin on the bedside table and started the sponging routine once again.

What would she do without her mother? She wished she could send for Clarice, but she was busy nursing her own family. Besides, Mildred still hadn't apologized.

Please, God, spare Mama. And Henry. Please. But she didn't hold out much hope.

Harold died after her letter containing harsh words for his lack of attention, for the furloughs he'd taken—with other women. She closed her eyes against the pain of that betrayal. It had taken the surprise out of Nelson's revelation of Harold's cowardice. Why had Harold even bothered to telegraph her about coming home and his change of plans?

Then she'd spoken harsh words to Clarice last week, and now her precious mama and brother were near death's door. A verse from her childhood floated into her mind. *"If I regard iniquity in my heart, the Lord will not hear me."* It was her punishment for not controlling her tongue.

"But God isn't like that." Nelson's words from a late-night discussion over the petri dishes on her kitchen table drifted back to her. *"He doesn't exact vengeance on His children. He extends love, grace, and mercy."*

A longing to know this God of whom Nelson spoke—so different from the judgmental, wrathful God she knew—welled up and threatened to drown her in the impossibility of it. Her parents had taught her of the God Nelson talked about, but the war and its aftermath caused her to doubt the truth as they all saw it.

"No man is expected to bear difficulty alone. God allows these things to cause us to depend on Him." Her father's voice from that afternoon was so clear, she glanced at the door, half expecting to see him standing there.

Had she misunderstood God? Had she somehow missed Him in the horrors of the war? *Who are You, God?*

Mama moved restlessly then coughed, a deep, tight sound that told Mildred the influenza was digging its ugly claws into her mother's lungs. She redoubled her efforts to lower the excessively high temperature, wondering if Henry was responding better for Klara. She would need to check on them soon.

Nelson stepped into the kitchen and met Dr. Bachman. "Ah, you have returned." The doctor's gaze sharpened. "What is wrong?"

Nelson eased down into a chair, and Dr. Bachman placed

a plate of scrambled eggs, toast, and bacon on the table. The aroma caused his stomach to rumble, and for the first time realized they had not gotten their promised supper.

"Mrs. Zimmermann and Henry both contracted the Spanish flu." He raised a quick thank-You to the Lord for the food then shoveled the first bite into his mouth.

"Amelia?" Dr. Bachman sat heavily across from him. "When?"

"This afternoon." He knew the older doctor wanted a full report, but his stomach was more insistent at the moment.

As if understanding, Dr. Bachman waited until Nelson pushed away his empty plate. "Did you come back for medicine?"

Nelson shook his head. "Mildred put the medicine from the Sunday house in the car this morning. I didn't unload it before taking her for a drive. So she has all she needs." He took a long swallow of the coffee Dr. Bachman poured for him. "Mildred will call later to report on their condition."

The doctor nodded then reached to the desk behind him and grabbed a distinctive Western Union telegram envelope. "This came this afternoon." His voice sounded tired, resigned. "I hope it isn't bad news."

But it would be, of course. Nelson ripped the envelope open and pulled out the message.

COME HOME. NEED YOU. SPANISH INFLUENZA
RAMPANT. HELENA ILL. CHARLES.

Nelson squeezed his eyes shut, wishing he didn't have to

obey his brother's summons. But it was no use. Duty called.

"What is it, son?" Dr. Bachman's compassion reached into his heart, soothing his troubled thoughts.

"I'm needed at home. The influenza is still raging there." Nelson's fists clenched. Oh, how he wanted to stay.

"I see." Dr. Bachman rose. "When will you leave?"

Nelson stood, too, and met the kind doctor's eyes. "On the first train going East in the morning." At the doctor's nod, he turned toward his room. "I need to pack."

A light knock on her parents' bedroom door roused Mildred from her doze. Fear clutched her heart, and she reached out to touch her mother's hand. Warm, but not hot. Then she heard the breathy rasp in her mother's throat, and she relaxed.

The knock sounded again. "Yes, come in." Her father wouldn't knock. Had Nelson come back? Her heart raced and she stood to greet him.

But the words died before she spoke as the expected tall outline morphed into one much shorter. And feminine.

"Clarice!" Mildred kept her voice low, not wanting to agitate her mother. "What—"

"I heard about Aunt Amelia and came as soon as I could."

"But your father?"

"Is fine. Recovering."

"Then why—I mean, after my—" Mildred shut her eyes. Why couldn't she apologize without stumbling over her words? They were fluent enough other times.

170

Clarice wrapped her arms around Mildred's waist and squeezed tight. "You need me. I came. You would have done the same for me."

Only she hadn't. She'd allowed Henry to convince her everything was fine.

"What about Thomas?"

Clarice released her and stepped back. "He told me to come." She pushed her light shawl off her shoulders, tossed it onto a small table under the window, and headed for the washbasin. "What do you need me to do? Who's caring for Henry?"

"Klara. I'm sure she'd welcome your help." Mildred watched her in a daze. "How did you find out? Nelson?"

"Nelson? No. Haven't seen him. I thought he'd be here."

Mildred handed Clarice a clean towel. "He returned Uncle Will's automobile. But he said he'd be back in the morning."

"That's fine then." Clarice laid the towel beside the washbasin. "Where's Henry?"

"Upstairs." Mildred started to follow Clarice out of the room, but Clarice put up her hand.

"No. Stay with your mama." She quirked a little grin. "I know what to do."

Mildred responded with a smile of her own. "I know." She leaned down for another quick hug. "Thanks, Clarice." God must be listening after all.

Returning to her mother's bedside, Mildred picked up the stethoscope—the one Nelson left—and listened intently to Mama's lungs. Were they a little clearer than when she listened last? Or was it wishful thinking? She rested the back of her hand against her mother's forehead and cheeks. But they remained cool. The fever had broken.

The bedroom door opened again, but Mildred didn't turn.

"How is she, liebchen?"

"Uncle Will?" She looked behind him for Nelson, but the doorway remained empty. "Mama's past the worst of it, I think."

"And Henry?" Her uncle placed his bag on the bed near her mother's feet.

"Klara was still sponging him down the last time I checked. Clarice is with him now."

"Then I will check him first." Her uncle turned to leave.

"Uncle Will. Wait." Mildred peered hopefully over her uncle's shoulder. "Where is Nelson? Didn't he come with you?"

Uncle's Will's shoulders slumped. "He's on the train going home." He held out a paper. "This came for him last evening."

Mildred moved closer to the gas lamp next to the door as Uncle Will slipped out of the room. As she read, two words seared her mind: *Helena ill.*

Chapter 12

Mildred crossed the road, skirted the turnout, and stopped a few feet into the wildflower field. Bluebonnets vied with primroses and Indian paintbrush as they crowded the dance floor of green foliage and grasses. Everywhere she looked the flowers bent their fragrant petals in the gentle April breeze in a graceful country-dance of bowing and scraping.

She closed her eyes and took in deep drafts of the fragrant air. Mama would have loved to come with her, but Mildred needed to be alone. Besides, Mama hadn't fully recovered from her near brush with death. Which was why Mildred was still on the farm. Caring for her father and younger siblings kept her busy from first light until well past sunset.

Today Ernie and Klara were on a school outing until after supper. Henry was busy with Papa in the furniture workshop. So Mildred took advantage of the break in routine and walked to the field.

She reached into her skirt pocket and pulled out the ragged yellow paper with the message that had called Nelson home. Four long weeks ago. Then, she thought he was beginning to care for her.

But one telegram bearing Helena's name took him

away. And she hadn't heard from him once. Mildred's heart clenched against the familiar ache, and she buried the paper out of sight again. When she got back home, she would put it in the burn barrel. Not that it mattered. The contents were etched into her memory.

Mildred picked her way along the narrow path, wading through the bluebonnets that spread their petals in a purply blue canopy. She stopped several times, reaching down to pinch off dead flowers, making room for more to grow in their stead.

Since that awful night at her mother's bedside, Mildred was learning to take delight in the many ways God showered her with His mercy and grace. He had heard her desperate prayer when all she could do was lean on Him. First Clarice came, without being asked, and then Uncle Will came to aid her.

The Lord even allowed Nelson to stay long enough to see that his patients were stable before going to get Uncle Will. Then Papa and Uncle Will were the towers of strength she needed when she learned Nelson was gone.

But why hadn't he written? Not even to Uncle Will. She could understand Nelson not wanting to write to her. After all, he went back to his Helena. They were probably engaged again and planning their fancy June wedding. But he could have let Uncle Will know what his plans were. She hadn't thought he could be so rude, so uncaring. That wasn't the man she thought she knew. And loved.

Mildred climbed the stairs of the gazebo and gazed toward the river. *Father, why can't I let Nelson go? What purpose does it serve for me to keep dwelling on him? Please, please take my love for him away.* Her decision to follow the God of love Nelson believed in brought her more peace than she'd thought possible. And she reveled in the intimacy of prayer. Still, she didn't understand why He hadn't answered this particular prayer.

A flash of red in the trees near the river caught her attention. Low, just above the blue carpet that continued past the edge of the wooded area. Curious, she left the gazebo and made her way toward the river.

Like a homing pigeon, she tracked her way through the flowers until she saw the object. A man's tie?

She reached to free the fabric from the low branch that had snagged it. Not just any man's tie. She recognized the small blue pattern.

"Nelson?" They'd gotten no farther than the gazebo the last time he was here. Besides, he wasn't wearing his red tie that day.

Crushing the fabric in her fist, Mildred allowed her gaze to dart across the field again. No one there. She turned back to peer into the undergrowth in the trees leading down to the water's edge.

"Father God, what's going on?" This was Nelson's tie. She had no doubt. But what was it doing here?

Shrugging, she turned away from the river and smacked into a man's hard, broad chest. A man who grunted at the impact and wrapped his arms around her, keeping her pinned to him.

Too stunned to fight off the liberties the man was taking,

Mildred inhaled the spicy tang of Nelson's cologne. *Wait.*

She twisted and gazed up into his face. The familiar blue gaze radiated joy and love, and Nelson held her as though he would never let her go.

She closed her eyes, sure that when she opened them he would vanish. Instead she felt the rumble of laughter roll from his chest.

"Nelson?" She jerked from the comfort of his arms. "How—how—despicable—" How dare he laugh at her? He went running back to his Helena. He shouldn't have been holding her in the first place.

"Despicable?" Another shout of laughter echoed through the trees.

Mildred pulled her gaze away from his mouth, along with the thoughts of what it would be like to be kissed with those lips. Ugh! Now who was despicable?

Tears started to her eyes, but she furiously blinked them back. "Why are you here? So you can gloat over your good fortune?"

Confusion clouded the joy still radiating from his eyes. "What?"

She ripped the paper from her pocket and shook it in his face. "Your precious Helena." Her voice made the woman's name sound dirty and twisted, like the crumpled paper in her hand.

Nelson gently grabbed her fist and released the paper. Keeping her hand captured in his, he smoothed out the telegram. A line appeared between his eyes. "Where did you get this?"

"You left it behind in your hurry to get to your ladylove." Her words pelted him like stones, but they didn't carry the bitterness he'd expected. Or deserved.

He honestly couldn't remember what he'd done with the telegram. But he never expected to find it Mildred's possession. Why she'd kept it...

His lips trembled with suppressed mirth. How predictable, yet so contradictory, she was. And he loved every aspect of her complicated being.

He knew he'd have his work cut out for him in order to win her back. She had every right to be angry. He'd wanted to see her last night as soon as he arrived, but Uncle Will advised against it. Not until the older man had prepared Mildred for the shock. But Nelson couldn't resist spending more time in the wildflower field, recalling the short time they'd spent together there before their worlds fell apart.

Then, little Ernest's news derailed the words of love he'd worked up the courage to speak. So when she strolled into the field this afternoon, he praised God for smoothing the way before him. He wasn't about to waste any more time.

He crumpled the ragged paper and tossed it toward the river. She followed the yellow ball with her eyes until it plopped into the water and disappeared.

He wrapped his arm around her waist. "The cat got your tongue?"

Her lips firmed into a thin line. He pulled her tight against his side and tilted her head toward him. "Mildred, sweetheart, look at me. Please."

Relief flowed through him when she finally raised her gaze to his. Questions, reproach, and something else warred in her eyes. Love? For him?

"I didn't go home because of Helena. How could I when my heart was here?"

"Then why?"

"My brother never, ever asked for my help before. Although his wife, Charlotte, was instrumental in getting navy nurses into the field hospitals in Europe, he never approved of my going to war. Even as a medic."

Nelson tucked Mildred's head under his chin, and she nestled against him, but she didn't relax.

"In fact, it was because of him I decided to accept your uncle's invitation to join him here. I had no plans to return to Virginia for any length of time." He paused. "And I still don't. Fredericksburg is my home."

"But why didn't you write?" The anguish in her tone wrenched his heart.

"I did. Long, long letters every night, describing my days, my nights, working and longing for you. I even wrote to Dr. Bachman telling him when I planned to return."

She pulled back and pinned him with her gaze. "But we..."

He sighed. "Two evenings ago, I discovered them in my mother's desk."

"What?" Disbelief and indignation poured out from her. "Your mother took your letters out of the mail?"

"Yes." Once again he felt the sharp pang of disbelief.

His own mother. "Almost every day I asked if any mail had come for me." He shook his head. "Every day the answer was the same. I could understand why you might not want to answer"—he ignored her protest—"but hearing nothing from your uncle bothered me. He'd always been so prompt to reply before."

"So how did you find out?" She snuggled back against him again.

"When I said I was going to check with the post office about the missing mail, Mother finally admitted her interference." Until then, he had no idea that she sided with his brother about Nelson's going to war. Plus she nagged him unmercifully about repairing his relationship with Helena. It would be a long time before he could trust her. If ever.

"Anyway, you can read the letters later. I decided to special-deliver them. But before that, I have something to ask you."

"Hmmm?"

"Can you ever forgive me for killing Harold?"

Mildred jerked away from him. "What? Are you on that again?"

He tottered at her sudden movement and reached for her. But she stepped away and handed him the cane he'd placed against the twisted mesquite next to the path.

"Nelson, you're not the only one who had harsh words with Harold. I found out"—she whirled away from him as her voice cracked. "He—he said, promised, he would spend his last furlough with me."

Nelson touched her shoulder, but she shrugged him off.

She wiped tears from her face with the back of her hand. "He spent his leave with. . ." She gulped in a breath and finally turned back to him. "With another girl." Her mouth twisted into a wry smile. "I'm sure you can imagine that last letter I wrote."

He could, but it made him smile, not shudder. "Maybe he didn't get it before he fell ill."

She gave a short laugh. "I hoped that, too, until I got all of his personal items. The letter was there, opened and well read. He even made notes for his reply." She groaned. "He was going to tell me about you. Said we'd make a good match if you ever got your head on straight about Helena."

Amazement sizzled up his spine and seized his brain. Words failed him.

"Come." Mildred motioned him to follow her. "You need to sit."

No, he didn't. His plans didn't call for sitting, but he followed her to the gazebo. When she sat, she patted the seat beside her. Instead, he leaned his cane against the bench and knelt in front of her.

Her eyes widened when he gathered her hands into his.

"Mildred, when we were here before, certain events— God's timing—prevented me from speaking my love for you. I didn't go home because of Helena. I couldn't when I loved you. In fact, I never saw her." His bad leg protested and he shifted his weight. "After this last month, I knew that I never want to be separated from you again. You complete me as no other thing or person ever has. Please say you care about me. . .at least enough to consider marrying me."

She slipped off the bench and knelt in front of him. "Yes, yes, yes!" She pulled her hands from his and wrapped her arms around his neck. "I love you, Nelson. More than I can say." Her eyes radiated the truth of her words.

His eyes drifted down to her lips that begged to be kissed.

He needed no second invitation as he wrapped his arms around her and sealed their love with a kiss that exceeded his expectations.

Marjorie Vawter is a professional freelance editor who proofreads and edits for CBA publishers, edits for individual clients, and writes. An avid reader, she also judges for several prestigious awards in the inspirational marketplace, and she serves as conference director's assistant for the Colorado and Greater Philadelphia Christian Writers Conferences. She has published several articles and numerous devotionals, many of them in Barbour publications. Mom to two adult children and a daughter-in-love, Marjorie lives with her husband, Roger, and cat, Sinatra, in the Ozarks of southwest Missouri. You may visit her at www.marjorievawter.com.

LETTERS
FROM HOME

by Lynette Sowell

Dedication

To Connie, Margie, and Eileen – thanks for grafting me
into "the posse" as we developed our stories together.
It was a joy to research with you as we drifted
from one time period to another.

To those from the "Greatest Generation," example
of tenacity and courage to all who've come after you.
Truly these were your finest hours.

A big thank you to the Pioneer Museum in Fredericksburg
for answering questions during our research trip
to your sweet town.

*My people will live in peaceful dwelling places,
in secure homes, in undisturbed places of rest.*
ISAIAH 32:18 NIV

Chapter 1

C 'mon, Trudy! C'mon!" Eric Meier tugged on his sister's arm. "We're going to miss the parade! We can find a good spot to watch if we hurry."

"Hold your horses. I'm right here with you." Trudy didn't mean to drag her feet, because part of her wanted to see the parade and hear the band and some of the Hollywood performers passing through Fredericksburg. Listening on the radio wasn't the same thing, or reading about it in a magazine. Little Fredericksburg wasn't a regular stop for many Texas visitors. Not until their own Chester Nimitz had risen to the top ranks of the navy to show the world that even from landlocked Fredericksburg, someone could go on to do great things.

But today Trudy felt closer to forty-one than twenty-one. Her legs felt like lead weights, her muscles tired from working at the beehives until sundown yesterday. She fought away the fatigue, clutched the Brownie camera that hung from a strap around her neck, and tried to be positive. Maybe today she'd get some good shots. Of course, she'd need to order more photo paper, something at a premium during these lean years.

She paused at her parents' bedroom door. "Mama?" She

heard nothing, so she pushed the door open a few inches. Her mother's low snore filtered through the space. It was best she let her sleep, all worn out from her volunteer work at the hospital. She'd arrived home early that morning.

The front door banged. "Tru–dy! Come *on!*"

Trudy shook her head and closed the door. Eric could tear all over the countryside on his bicycle, yet for some reason he couldn't make it to town without her presence at his side? "I'm coming, Eric."

The May morning sun promised a toasty afternoon. If she had her way, she'd bicycle down to the creek with a book, a pen, and her camera. She'd sit under her favorite live oak tree and watch the wind blow the puffy clouds across the sky. The favorite tree would remind her of Kurt and the promise they'd made to each other under its branches.

Trudy blinked at the momentary pain and let it pass. She closed the front door to the house behind her, as if that could close off the memory. Today, she'd definitely win the bike "race" to town that Eric always tried to egg her to join.

"They have a midget submarine, you know." Eric's voice jolted her. He bent over to check the chain on his bicycle. "All the way from Japan. I wonder if we can touch it."

"I'm sure you'll make it your mission to find out if you can." *Thank You, Lord, that Eric can keep his childlike wonder, even during the war, even with Father away.* It seemed like everyone gave something up once their country had entered the war. A lifetime of days had ticked away since December 7, 1941, a little less than eighteen months ago.

Soon they were off, down the winding road that led into

town. Trudy could close her eyes and feel each curve in the road, anticipate each landmark, no matter how minor. The sameness should comfort her, but instead it itched her like a wool scarf that her grandmother had made.

Trudy thought of the ring that still lay inside the jewelry box on her dressing table. Kurt had released her from her promise to marry him after he returned from the war, before his last letter. . .

He deserved someone who'd be by his side at the peach farm owned by his family, someone who was satisfied with Fredericksburg, with the small-town routine. Once, she'd shared with him her wild dream of seeing the world. Kurt had blinked and asked, "Why?"

Less than a month later, his orders came and he shipped out, leaving her behind. Jealousy fought against fear inside her.

The town hadn't changed much since her childhood. She caught sight of the first few homes on the outside of town, a snug row of Sunday homes, the middle one owned by her family. Her *oma* had lived there until her passing over the late winter. Trudy slowed down. If things were different, she'd ask her mother if she could stay in the house by herself and have a measure of independence. Of course, her help was needed most at home.

Next door was the Zimmermann family's home. How she'd loved Sundays growing up in Fredericksburg, all the comings and goings and visiting. And the food. *Oma, I miss you, and every time I see the house, it reminds me of what we've all lost.*

Eric left her literally in his dust. He rang the bell on his bicycle and the jubilant sound joined with the sounds of celebration ahead of them on Main Street. The war bond tour had descended on Fredericksburg. It wouldn't surprise her if nearly the whole town assembled along Main Street.

Instead of following Eric, Trudy moved off the road and circled back. She might as well leave her bicycle parked at the Sunday house. She could negotiate any crowd on foot, where a bicycle might get in the way.

"You're just in time for the parade." Her longtime friend Kathe exited the Zimmermann family's Sunday house. Kathe Zimmermann, soon to be Kathe Mueller, grinned.

"Eric made sure." Trudy tried to pop her kickstand down, but the contraption stuck so she leaned the bicycle against the house, just past the porch. "So how are you? I've been such a poor bridesmaid, and I should be helping you prepare for the wedding."

"You've done plenty," Kathe said as she linked her arm through Trudy's. "Peter and I are keeping things simple, especially now. But my cake is going to be made with white sugar, not brown, and have gobs of buttercream frosting."

The thought of a rich, creamy wedding cake with plenty of frosting made Trudy's sweet tooth ache a little. "I'm so happy for both of you."

"Thanks." Her friend's expression fell. "I know this must be hard for you, with Kurt. . ."

Trudy shrugged. "It's all right. Like I said, I'm happy for both of you. The fact that Peter survived, came home to you, and now you get to have your happy ending, I'm just glad someone else is finding some joy in the middle of all this."

She didn't have to mention the Wagner twins who'd perished and now lay buried in a Fredericksburg cemetery. The war had cost Fredericksburg so much already, even with their favorite son, Chester Nimitz, commander in chief over the Pacific theater.

Kathe hugged her. "Thank you. I'm praying you'll have your happy ending, too."

"I hope so, someday." A lump swelled in Trudy's throat. *Gertrude Meier, I see now why you wish to travel the world and see life beyond Fredericksburg. That has never been my desire, and I release you to find your way. Lord willing, once this war is over and you have traveled, maybe we will find our way back to each other again.* Trudy shoved the letter's words away, burned into her memory. "Let's go. I wonder if Mitzie Harmon looks the same in person as she does in the movies."

Kathe laughed and the sound propelled Trudy back to more innocent times, to childhood. She echoed the laugh as they ambled the rest of the way to Main Street.

Bradley Payne stepped off the bus, the dust of Main Street Fredericksburg swirling around him. He slung his duffel bag over his shoulder. The bag contained all his worldly goods—well, everything that he'd been toting since leaving Washington, DC, just over three weeks ago.

He adjusted the brim of his hat as he scanned the street lined with people, its buildings resembling something out of a Wild West show combined with European charm he'd seen in Germany. Fredericksburg. Home of his father's family, the family he never knew. *Father, why did you leave the family who accepted you and took you in?*

Bradley continued to the Nimitz Hotel, a curious-looking, three-story structure on the corner of Main Street and North Washington. A flag flew from the roof, the building resembling a ship. Charles, the old man who'd built the hotel, was once a sea captain. Ironic that he'd build a hotel like this far from the ocean.

Ironic that Bradley's travels should take him here as he and his fellow journalists followed the war bond tour that stopped in the hometown of Admiral Nimitz. Chester Nimitz, grandson of the man who built the Nimitz Hotel, was born right here in a small Texas town hundreds of miles from any body of water large enough to float a battleship, yet he'd risen through the ranks after graduating from the United States Naval Academy to achieve the highest-ranking position in the Pacific theater. Hopefully, Bradley would find someone well acquainted with the Nimitz family, as Chester hadn't been back to Fredericksburg in quite some time.

Growing up in the family's hotel, Nimitz had likely seen a myriad of people pass through its doors. If anyone new came to town, the Nimitz family would know.

Nimitz had grown up without a father, who passed away before Chester was born. At least Nimitz's father hadn't deserted him and he'd had the love and support of his extended family during his childhood. Admittedly, Bradley had had the love of his mother who told him to love his father and pray for him.

A long-ignored bitterness oozed from Bradley's soul

in sharp contrast to the merry tune played by the band on the town square. This was no way to meet the town he'd be exploring during the tour. This was no way to find his story. *Help, Lord,* Bradley prayed silently as he ambled in the direction of the music. The town square lay just past Adams Street, opposite the library and the courthouse.

His editor, Frank McAffrey, had clamored during the entire trip about finding the story everywhere he went. "*Letters from the Homefront is one of our readers' favorite columns. So don't disappoint them,*" Frank had said before Bradley left.

No one ever disappointed Frank McAffrey and kept their job long, or at all. Plus, there were too many other journalists wanting to write for *This American Life*. Bradley had worked hard to get this position, and even harder to convince Frank that following the war bond tour would bring an even more personal touch to his column.

Find the story, find the story, he reminded himself as he studied faces in the crowd. Wherever the tour had gone, they'd encountered a similar atmosphere, yet with a character unique to the people of the local area.

The voices of the crowd rang out in laughter at Mac Mackenzie, the traveling comic's antics on the makeshift stage festooned in red, white, and blue. Bradley allowed himself to remain at the edges of the crowd, close enough to observe but not so close that he'd miss something if not having the eyes of an outsider.

Then he saw a pair of young women that grabbed his attention. A proverbial willowy blond with eyes the color of the waters of the Mediterranean. Now, she was a looker. She chatted with her friend, pushing wayward strands of hair over one ear. But her cool, tall figure didn't keep his attention.

Instead, he focused on her friend, a brunette with dark honey tones in her hair, eyes the color of amber. She bit her full lower lip with her teeth, holding up her camera, her eyes narrowed while she studied the scene through her lens. Her tall skinny friend giggled at the comedian and bumped her shorter friend's elbow.

The brunette murmured something and shook her head, then laughed, lowering the camera. Her gaze traveled across the square and locked with his. She'd caught him staring, and he refused to look away.

A half grin quirked in his direction, and she lifted the camera and pointed it at him.

Chapter 2

Y ou took his picture?" Kathe glanced at Trudy. "I can't believe it."

"He was staring at us, like he knew what we were thinking." Trudy wound the film in her camera until she felt the familiar click. What on earth had compelled her to snap a picture of the man? Okay, he was handsome enough. He could stand beside any of the silver screen heartthrobs and hold his own. He definitely wasn't from Fredericksburg.

"Now he's coming this way."

"So's your Tante Elsie." Trudy nodded toward Kathe's aunt. "She can set him straight."

"Ha. She can set anybody straight." Kate smiled.

"Girls, hasn't it been a wonderful show?" asked Tante Elsie.

"You couldn't go all the way to Austin to see a finer one at the Paramount," said Trudy.

"Good afternoon." A rich baritone voice tugged Trudy's attention away from the older woman.

Trudy turned to face the man she'd brazenly snapped a photograph of less than two minutes before. The townspeople were used to her bicycling around town during her free moments, photographing this and that, waiting for the correct light conditions. But to photograph a complete stranger?

She felt Kathe's elbow in her ribs. "G–good afternoon, Mr.—"

"Ah, so you're going to ask my name, now that you've taken my photograph?" His smile made a bolt of heat shoot through her insides.

"It's only proper that I can identify my subject." She felt a grin tug at the corners of her mouth.

"Bradley Payne." He removed his hat and nodded.

"Trudy Meier." She extended her hand. "And this is my friend Kathe Zimmermann, and her aunt, Miss Elsie Zimmerman."

Mr. Payne hesitated a fraction of a second before putting his hat back on. "Zimmermann, you say. . ." Then he cleared his throat and continued. "It's a pleasure to meet you all while I'm visiting your fine town. I'm here following the tour."

"I assumed as much, since I didn't recognize you." Trudy clutched her camera in front of her.

"You must take some time and get to know our town." Tante Elsie was studying him thoughtfully. "You know that Admiral Nimitz, commander of the entire Pacific theater, comes from Fredericksburg."

Trudy glanced at the older woman. Was that a tear in her eye? She met Kathe's gaze. Kathe shrugged.

"That I do, Miss Zimmermann." He looked at Trudy again with those dark eyes of his. "I actually work for *This American Life* magazine."

"You do?" Trudy's heart beat even faster. "I try to buy it when I can." The name Bradley Payne should have seemed familiar to her, as much as she read the magazine cover to cover.

"That's swell. It's always fun to meet a reader." He eyed her dangling camera. "I take it then you're a camera buff?"

"Yes, yes I am." She clutched her Brownie again. "One day I'd like to get a better camera, but for now, this one does fine." Now she felt like a nincompoop for taking his photograph. He was probably a seasoned traveler, working for such a renowned national magazine.

"Do you do your own developing?"

"I do. My closet doubles as a darkroom, and it works fine as long as my little brother doesn't come charging in." Her cheeks flamed.

"Excuse me," Kathe interjected. "I see Peter's mother over across the way, and I need to ask her a question about the wedding rehearsal."

Sure. Leave her here, floundering as she tried to untangle her snarl. This would teach her to be impulsive. Truly, she would never try anything so foolhardy again.

"We'll see you soon," Tante Elsie said, looking from Mr. Payne to Trudy, then back to Mr. Payne again. "Where are you staying while you're in town, Mr. Payne?"

"At the Nimitz Hotel, of course. Only for tonight, I think. The troupe is moving on in the morning."

"Well, should you need to stay in Fredericksburg longer, you might inquire to see if one of the local Sunday houses is available." Tante Elsie placed her hand on Kathe's arm. "Let's see about talking to Mrs. Mueller."

Trudy watched them leave. Now, how to extricate herself from the conversation. "I hope you enjoy your visit."

"What's a Sunday house?"

"It's a weekend home, here in town," Trudy explained. "Those of us who live on farms outside town, our families built them years ago so we didn't have to travel back and forth on the weekend to do business and go to church. They're generally quite tiny. It's easier to drive back and forth to town now that we have cars. But we've kept our houses. Sometimes now they're rented out, or our grandparents move into them to be closer to town. That's where Miss Zimmermann lives now."

"Ah, I see." Mr. Payne glanced around the town square as the crowd filtered away. "Did you know they're having another performance tonight at the high school?"

"I do. But I only came to see the one today." Trudy bit her lip as reality bit into her. "I'll be needed back at home tonight."

He nodded. "Do...do you know if there is a Sunday house close by that I might rent for a time? The tour will be moving on, but I think I might stay for a while." He slung his jacket over one shoulder.

Trudy thought fast. She'd wanted to escape the conversation, the feelings swirling inside her at merely talking to this handsome stranger, but times were tough and she knew her family's coffers could use the money. "My family has one. It's empty right now. How...how long were you planning to stay?"

"I–I'm not sure. A week or two?" His expression was unreadable.

"We charge twenty dollars for a week, one dollar a day extra if you want us to provide a food basket." She hadn't consulted Mother, but the house had been empty since Oma's passing. Other families rented out their empty homes, why not the Meiers? The food basket was an impulse as well. First, snapping photographs, then renting out the Sunday house. What was with her?

"That's fair enough." He nodded at her, the shadow of his hat brim slanting across his face. "I'll want a food basket, too. I'll be spending my time writing, not hunting down meals."

"All right then, Mr. Payne. It's a deal." She extended her hand and they shook again, their grip lingering. Her breath caught in her throat. Now she needed to explain to her mother what she'd done.

"Deal." Mr. Payne released her hand. "How will I know which house?"

"I—I can meet you with a key at the Nimitz Hotel when you check out tomorrow, and show you the way."

"I'll see you at noon." He smiled again. "And, call me Bradley."

"I'll see you, Bradley." Trudy fled in the direction of the library.

The sun had set on Fredericksburg, not long after 9:00 p.m. That was a switch for Bradley, who was used to the sun setting earlier in the Northeast. He ambled along Main Street, the quiet soaking into him.

Tante Elsie Zimmermann. Tante Elsie. His aunt. Only on his deathbed had his father talked about the kindness shown to him as a child by his cousin and his wife, Hank and Amelia. Hank was his father's cousin, but with the age difference, he'd addressed them as aunt and uncle. He'd left home as soon as he was grown and hadn't looked back. Father never allowed anyone to fill the empty space yawning inside him after his parents' death. As a child, he'd moved on, but as he'd grown older, he'd started questioning the family's love for him. Micah Delaney Zimmermann's scars from nearly being sent to an orphanage by his own grandfather—Hank's father—had never healed. Consequently, Bradley had a close bond with his mother, who had been an only child and had no family close by. The pen name, Payne, came from his mother's side of the family.

He supposed he should introduce himself fully to Tante Elsie and the rest of the family. Would the Zimmermanns acknowledge him as family?

He entered the lobby of the Nimitz and found Heinrich, the concierge, at the desk. "Mr. Payne, I have that line to Washington D.C. you needed."

"Thank you very much." Bradley accepted the telephone receiver from Heinrich. "Frank, are you there?"

"You're calling me from Texas? This had better be good." Frank's voice held an edge to it. "It's after 10:00 p.m. here."

"I want to stay in Fredericksburg for a while instead of heading west with the rest of the group."

"You'd better have a good reason."

"I want to show a different slant, letters from home, but from the hometown of Admiral Nimitz. I want to get to know its people. You know most of them are German. I think they'll have a unique perspective of the war."

"You don't say. Well, I'll give you a week to begin with. Get me some good stories."

"Thank you, sir. I won't let you down."

"Of course you won't. I'll send Briggs to meet the group in New Mexico and we'll see how it goes."

"I'll wire a story to you in a week."

"Have it wired by Friday."

Three days. Bradley sucked in a breath. "You'll have it."

He hung up the phone and glanced at Heinrich. "Thank you, sir."

"You're very welcome, Mr. Payne."

Bradley nodded then strolled out of the lobby and out again into the Texas night. His mind drifted back to Trudy Meier and her funny little camera. She'd been so earnest, and he saw a glimmer of the same curiosity that he had as a writer. She stood on the fringes, like he did, and watched. He understood that.

She liked him, too. Pretty girls were a nice distraction, but that was it. A distraction. Maybe someday, he'd settle down when he met the right girl. Not that he had a family to bring her home to, with Father and now his beloved mother gone.

He'd watched from the edges for most of his life, having worked his way out of high school and then through college, making his mother proud. Most of the other boys had had money. He had a scholarship and hard work. Even there at university, he'd felt on the outside.

But now here he was in Fredericksburg. His father had told him years ago that he was related to Hank and Amelia Zimmermann in Texas, that they'd adopted him after his parents had died. Here he had a pile of family, and all he had to do was make himself known. He realized that Trudy's tall skinny friend was even a cousin of his.

The thoughts swirled in his head. What did he want, here in Fredericksburg? He wasn't sure. But knowing he had a scrap of family here, well, he had to see where this trail led him. Spending some time with Trudy Meier wouldn't be unpleasant, either. Maybe she had someone off fighting in the war. It wouldn't surprise him if she did. He'd follow that trail, too, if only out of his journalist's sense of curiosity, nothing more.

Chapter 3

Trudy parked her bicycle at the front of the Nimitz Hotel and popped the kickstand in place. She was on time to meet Bradley, but she'd had to hurry. Her mother hadn't been terribly pleased about renting their Sunday house to a stranger. Trudy agreed to accept the responsibility if anything went awry. Which, of course, it wouldn't. She'd spent the morning at the house, sweeping and scrubbing and airing the place out. The mustiness was gone, at least. It would be a tragedy if the scent of Oma's lavender disappeared forever. Now the Sunday house was ready for its first tenant. Mother couldn't argue with the extra income Mr. Payne would bring them.

Bradley. One of the last things he'd said was his first name, Bradley. She tried not to fuss over the wisps of hair that pulled out of her headband. Headband. Like a schoolgirl. She stuffed away the thought. She needn't worry about what Mr. Payne thought of her. It was a business transaction with a visitor to town. She knew nothing about the man. But dreams of travel and everything he'd seen followed her home.

Trudy yawned. She'd sat up too late, poring over her old issues of *This American Life*, with its photos of adventures throughout the country. A few articles from Bradley Payne. His head shot looked glamorous, half a grin spread on his face and his jacket slung on his shoulder, as if he'd just returned from a fabulous trip. Now, here he was in tiny Fredericksburg.

"Here I am, Miss Trudy Meier. It *is* miss, or. . . ?"

"Yes, it's miss." So he wondered if she was married. . .but that meant nothing. "But just Trudy is fine."

"You don't seem like a 'just' anyone."

She found no response that would make sense and tried not to stammer as she said, "I—I have the key here, although you shouldn't need to worry about keeping the house locked. We watch out for each other here." Heat rushed through her face.

"That's nice to hear." He shifted a duffel bag on one shoulder. "Lead away."

Trudy nudged her bike's kickstand up into place and pulled it away from one of the pillars. "It's not far, just down a side street and almost at the southern edge of town."

"Have you lived here all your life?"

"Yes, all my life. My parents have a farm, and we keep bees and grow peaches like a lot of people around here do. My father is away, in France the last we heard. I have a younger brother who's twelve and I try to keep him out of trouble as best I can." Her mouth was running along at a steady pace, like the train that chugged into Fredericksburg regularly from Austin.

"So how did you get interested in photography?" Like a gentleman, he slowed his pace to match hers.

"My father. . .he brought home *National Geographic* magazine, and the pictures were so beautiful. Then I got to go on a trip to see Ansel Adams photography in a gallery in Dallas. I knew I wanted to take pictures of anything and everything." Her cheeks flamed. Her photos weren't of any exotic or dramatic subjects, though.

"Of course, you had to try. Did you take photographs when you were in high school?"

"Yes, I did. We even had a small club. I was the president. Everyone else took it for kicks, but. . ." She didn't tell many people she wanted to be a photographer, more than portraits of families and children.

"I'd like to see some of your photographs sometime. I've shot some photos for the magazine before."

"Really? I'd love some pointers. But I know you're here to work."

"I won't be working all the time." His grin made the temperature shoot up at least ten more degrees. *Oh dear. Slow down. He's here now, but he'll be gone soon enough.* She had grown up knowing Kurt Schuler and had loved him once, probably still loved him a little, but the feelings clamoring for attention inside her, well, she'd never experienced these with Kurt.

"All right, then. I'll bring my portfolio." She suddenly felt shy again as she led him down the street. Two more blocks and they'd be at the house. Time to ask him some questions of her own. "So, why Fredericksburg for your magazine?"

"Why anywhere? For one thing, there's Nimitz. What kind of atmosphere did he grow up in that made him the leader he is now? That answer is here in Fredericksburg. Plus, like many small American towns, your town has given a lot."

She nodded. "That it has. . ." The twins. Kurt. Plus

dozens of other fathers, sons, husbands, away without any word of when they would return.

"And then there's the obvious. Most of the town is German. Has that affected the way you're treated, here in Texas?"

"Ah, now that's always a good question." She paused, pondering how best to answer him. She never thought being of German descent would be a problem, but as the war escalated, it didn't seem to matter to some people that her own people were fighting for the right side. "Well, there are some who won't do business with us. But we've been pretty self-sufficient here."

Bradley nodded. "I've seen lots of small gardens in town."

"Yes, the idea of having a victory garden is nothing new to us. We've always grown what we needed." Funny. He'd changed the conversation back to Fredericksburg, away from himself. They approached the first in the small row of houses. Tante Elsie sat on the porch in her rocking chair, fanning herself, a jar of cool tea beside her foot.

"Hello, you two," Tante Elsie called out.

"Hello, Tante Elsie." Trudy smiled at the woman. She treasured the friendship with the Zimmermanns even more now that her own oma had passed on. Even Tante Elsie was almost like an oma to Kathe, with her own grandmother passed away.

"Miss Zimmermann." Bradley tipped his hat to Tante Elsie, an elegant gesture. "We're going to be neighbors for a while." There was something refined about him, yet somewhat unpolished. Trudy glimpsed a dark shade of stubble on his chin. She envisioned him hunched over a typewriter, clacking away at the keys into the night, rubbing his chin as he thought of the right word.

"Ah, so I see." There was a sparkle in the woman's eye. "I'm sure the Meiers will take good care of you."

Trudy dreaded the familiar sensation of blush. She tried to act normally, as if walking with Bradley Payne were something she did every day. She pulled the sack from her bicycle basket. "All right, there's not much to show you here." She balanced the sack on one hip and unlocked the door to the house. "We only kept this locked since it's been empty, but now that you're here, you can leave it unlocked."

She stepped into the familiar space, now clean and swept. The one room contained a narrow bed in one corner, covered. Her dusty sneakers thudded on the wooden floor. Oma's braided rag rug made a circle in the center of the room.

Bradley entered behind her and moved to shut the front door.

"No, please leave it open." Trudy stepped toward him. "It's better that way. People won't, um, talk. . .about us being alone in here, behind a closed door."

A half grin appeared on his lips. "Okay, you've got it. Door open. Nobody talks."

"So," she said, placing the sack on the square wooden table, "in that small cupboard in the corner, you'll find some bowls and cups. The woodstove works, but you likely won't need it. I've brought a few things for you. My mother's biscuits and a jar of peach preserves, as well as a jar of honey. Plus a sandwich. I hope that will do. I can bring more biscuits by tomorrow, plus some of mother's chicken potpie."

"Sounds tasty. This will be fine for now. I have to write, and I don't eat much when I'm on deadline." He paused, the breeze from outside swirling into the small space and lifting the front of his hair. "There's something else I'd like you to bring, though. I'd hoped you would today."

"What's that?"

"Bring some of your photographs. I'd like to see them."

She almost smacked her forehead. "Oh, I did. They're in the sack, in a folder." She pulled it out. Mr. Greiner at the newspaper office didn't care much for her photographs. Maybe Bradley wouldn't either.

He accepted the folder from her and opened it. "The light's not very good in here. I'm heading outside. C'mon."

She followed him and settled onto the swing beside him. The friendly, almost intimate seating arrangement made her heart flutter. That, and the fact her heart was shown through the photos.

"This is beautiful." Bradley held up the print she'd made of a field of bluebonnets and Indian paintbrush, sweeping up to an old barn that filled the sky. She'd lain on her stomach, shooting uphill to get that shot. "When did you take it?"

"That was this spring, in April. I wish you could see the colors."

"You have an eye for composition, and contrast. The lightness of the flowers, with the barn looming at the top of the background." Bradley moved to the next print.

Her throat caught. Oma's hands, kneading out bread dough, the sun slanting into the window. Then a photograph of the schoolchildren of Fredericksburg, linked arm in arm in front of their scrap collection piles, proudly celebrating what they'd done to support the war effort.

"What's this?" Bradley asked. "A scrap king and queen?"

"Sounds silly, but they had a contest at the high school for who could bring in the most scrap metal." Trudy shrugged. "It was newsworthy. Mr. Greiner even bought that photograph for the newspaper."

"Nice job. You're a pro." Admiration filled his voice. Or was that her wishful thinking?

She looked up at him and met his gaze. No, not wishful thinking. "I'm not a real professional."

"You were paid for your work. And that"—he poked her arm—"makes you a pro."

"I sort of always dreamed of being a real photographer, traveling and taking pictures," she admitted. "My former teacher told me I should open a studio and take portraits. But—"

"But you don't want that."

"No, I don't."

He smiled. "I understand. I'd rather be traveling and writing than staying in one place."

"What about your family?"

"My. . .my father left when I was young. He was in and out of my life. A year ago, my mother passed away. I was an only child." A shadow passed across his eyes.

"I'm sorry. What about grandparents, or cousins?" She placed her hand on his arm. "Surely you're not completely alone."

"No, not completely." The shadow grew darker in his eyes. "Well, Miss Trudy, I hope you'll bring me more photographs. Or maybe, we could go for a walk sometime. I'd like to see more of Fredericksburg and it would be nice to see it through a local's eyes."

She nodded slowly. Whatever secrets he held, he was welcome to hold them. "I'm developing a roll from yesterday. I can bring those prints. The good ones, anyway. Sometimes I get some duds."

"I'd like that, Trudy Meier." The shadow in his eyes disappeared with his smile.

"Tomorrow then, Bradley Payne." She returned the grin.

The sun slipped toward the horizon and Bradley watched the shadow of the porch railing stretch longer and longer. He sat at the simple wooden table, writing out his thoughts on the last evening's show.

The small borough of Fredericksburg...

He crossed out *borough* and wrote *town* above it.

The small town of Fredericksburg welcomed the war bond tour with a greeting as big as the Lone Star State.

Not bad. He thought of the Japanese Ha-19 midget submarine they'd wheeled down Main Street, a reminder of the proverbial last straw that had catapulted the United

States into the thick of the Second World War.

> With the ocean many hours away, the Japanese
> Ha-19 midget submarine spurred the people into action,
> to give to a cause that lies thousands of miles away,
> where many of their men are serving in harm's way.

Not *spurred.* These people didn't need to be spurred. The town, over seventy miles west of the capital city of Austin, might be far from any typical civilization, but it wasn't immune or isolated from the effects of war. He circled the word. He'd find the right one before he wired his story to Frank.

His thoughts drifted to Trudy. She'd started to pry, gently, and he didn't blame her. He'd quizzed her about her family and the town. Of course she was curious about him. Something about her was comforting, familiar. Maybe it was the photographs, the common wanderlust they shared. He could see it in her eyes.

"Hello there, young Mr. Payne," a voice called out.

Bradley snapped his attention toward the porch. He wasn't a betting man, but a hunch told him it was Miss Zimmermann come calling. He set down his pen and left his papers on the table.

Sure enough, the woman stood beside the single step that led onto the porch. "Miss Zimmermann."

She regarded him with sharp eyes. "I see you've settled in."

"That I have. I'm very grateful to the Meiers for renting me the house while I'm here."

"You look like someone I know, only that was many, many years ago. He left the day he turned eighteen, broke all our hearts." She leaned on her cane as she helped herself onto the porch. "You're the spittin' image of my little brother, Micah Delaney. Our sister, Joy, is going to become a grandmother any day now."

He swallowed around a lump. "Wow, you don't say. It's funny how that happens."

"Becoming a grandparent, or you resembling my brother?"

He wanted to squirm under her look. He'd encountered tough interview subjects, but seldom had found himself under someone else's spotlight.

"Miss Zimmermann," he heard himself say, "I believe you're my aunt. Micah Delaney was my father."

"Of course he was," Tante Elsie whispered. "Was, you say?"

"He. . .he passed away two years ago. But he told me about all of you before he died."

His aunt sank onto the porch swing. "I'm glad he did." She patted the seat beside her. "Sit, sit. We have a lot to talk about."

Bradley complied, not sure what else to add to the conversation.

"Well, you have a large family here, and I know they will all be glad to hear about you. Micah, your father, was the youngest of the three of us. But what you don't know is that our adoptive mother and father had three more children after they took us in. Kathe is Lily's daughter. We lost Lily to sickness and Kathe's father is away fighting, so I've been keeping an eye on her. Kathe and your new friend Trudy are thick as thieves, best friends since they were in pigtails."

"I noticed that the other day."

"We're having a wedding soon, in June, at my parents' house. Your grandfather, Hank, is still alive, too."

Bradley's throat caught. Grandfather. "I'm looking forward to meeting him." So much to take in. He knew his father had family, but to have ignored them for so many years. Bradley realized how much he'd missed out on. *Father, if you'd only told me years ago. . . .*

Tante Elsie patted his arm. "So. Tell me about you. You're a writer. How did you decide to do that?"

"I always wrote from the time I was a kid. Then after high school, I studied journalism at the university in Ohio, where I grew up. Then I got a stringer job in Washington, DC, reporting. A friend helped me get an assignment for *This American Life* magazine and the rest is history."

"What? That's it? Is there a ladylove, someone special waiting for you back in the capital of our country?" She gave him a sideways glance.

"No, no one."

"Why not?"

"Time. It takes time to know someone, time I don't have. Writing sort of takes over everything, and some women don't understand that." Bradley shrugged. He'd been up past midnight, writing out his first piece in longhand, then walking, bleary-eyed, in the morning to the mercantile to wire his story.

"It sounds like it's *time* for you to slow down." Tante Elsie smiled at him. "You're not here by accident. Of course the war bond tour brought you here. But it's your choice to stay and take some time with your family. I think it's a good one. And who knows what can happen in a few weeks?"

He waited for a comment, linking him with Trudy Meier, but none came. "You're right, who knows?"

Chapter 4

The light hanging from a hook inside Trudy's closet glowed red. The aroma of photo processing chemicals filled Trudy's nostrils, and she tried not to sneeze.

"C'mon..." She placed the photo paper into the chemical bath and waited for the exposure to take place. A series of photos hung to dry from a narrow width of clothesline stretched from one side of the closet to the other. She'd clipped each of them to a hanger and in turn hooked the hanger from the line.

The photo of the small Japanese submarine looked pretty swell. Eric would love it. She'd definitely make another copy of the photograph for him, if her chemicals held out. The newest photo image in the chemical bath emerged from the blank paper. A sunlit crowd on the town square, with everyone facing toward the bandstand. Everyone except Bradley Payne.

His smile came to life, lit by the summer sun, the shadow from his hat brim shading one of his eyes. Charming, friendly, curious. Holding secrets. Did she dare ferret them out?

Mr. Payne's assignment here was a temporary one, so what did it matter? A sadness lurked deep in his eyes. Was it her job to help him? Maybe that was someone else's task.

Her mother warned her of strangers, that people weren't always what they seemed. Wolves in sheep's clothing prowled, looking for unsuspecting lambs to devour, or so she'd been told. Trudy would admit that she wasn't worldly wise. But she wasn't quick to trust strangers, either.

Yet there was something in Bradley's eyes, despite how he tried to push people away.

Dear Lord, we've all been through so much. We can use some hope, some joy. It's hard to believe sometimes that You're in control when the news talks about the insanity of war. Trudy slammed the brakes on her thoughts, especially the ones surrounding her doubts. It seemed, though, no matter how much anyone prayed and believed, the longed-for answers didn't come.

Bradley's image shimmered beneath the surface of developer. There. The photo was done. She snatched it out with her tongs then slid it into the water tray. After a rinse, she hung the photo to dry like its companions.

She clung to the faith she'd had since childhood, but as a grown woman, the answers of childhood didn't satisfy her as much. *Some answers I can live with, that's all I ask. And how can I help someone like Bradley Payne, when I don't have answers for myself?*

"Trudy!" Eric bellowed outside the closet door, the shrillness in his voice making her jump.

She bit her lip. "What is it? I'm only in the closet, not hard of hearing."

The door handle jiggled.

"Don't open the door, you'll ruin everything."

"Mama's home early. She's real tired. She wants to know if you picked the vegetables yet."

"No. Tell her I'll be right there." She sighed. Although, she had to admit that she found gardening relaxing. The first few vegetables were maturing now with an early onset of spring back in March.

"Don't be mad, Trudy."

"I'm not mad, Eric." She turned out the light and the closet filled with darkness. She reached with her toes to pull the towel away from the crack between the door and the wooden floor of her bedroom. She pushed the door open.

The room was empty. Evidently, Eric had scampered off to his next adventure. Oh, to be twelve again, when the biggest care was if your friend could come outside to play. She scolded herself. Eric didn't have it easy. A boy needed his father, and their father was an ocean away.

Trudy left her trays of developing solution in the closet and padded barefooted downstairs to find her mother in the kitchen.

"You're home early," she said.

Mother nodded. "They didn't need me today at the hospital. So I thought you and I could pick vegetables."

Of course this meant Mother wanted to talk. It seemed they all had battles with worries and cares since the war came to their doorstep. Within a few minutes, they both carried a basket to the back garden.

The first baby potatoes were ready, along with lettuce and tiny cucumbers. By summertime, they might have enough to put up jars of pickles. The soil felt cool to Trudy's feet as she squatted to pick some tomatoes.

"It's a good garden this year," Mother said. "Your father would be proud of us."

"I—I hope we get another letter soon," Trudy said aloud. "After what happened to Kurt, missing in action…" Missing. Not dead or wounded. But somewhere that no one knew about. And if someone did, they were likely the enemy.

"Are you sure you made the right decision, calling off the engagement?" Mother inspected the tops of the carrots, then passed them by.

"Yes. Not like it matters now."

"He might come back. Would you reconsider?"

"I don't think I would."

Her mother sighed. "Everything has changed. I never imagined this for our family. Here you are, twenty-one, halfway out our door. I just dread the thought of someone coming and taking you away…"

Trudy listened to the sound of the breeze whistling through the branches of the peach trees at the end of the garden. "I don't think anyone will take me away. But if I ever do leave, Fredericksburg will always be my home."

"I—I have a confession to make." Her mother retrieved a narrow envelope from her apron pocket. "Here. . .this is for you."

Trudy sat in the middle of the row of plants, not caring that her dungarees would get dirty. The return address was for *Texas Wildflowers* magazine. Back in April, she'd sent them a photograph of a field of bluebonnets, the Texas state flower.

Dear Miss Meier,

We find your photograph of the bluebonnet field of great interest to our magazine and intend to use it in our late summer issue. Please find a cheque for three dollars. We will also send you five complimentary copies of the summer 1943 issue of our magazine. If you have more photographs of our lovely wildflower landscape, we would like to see those as well.

Regards,
Terrence Irvine
Editor–in–chief
Texas Wildflowers

"When did this come in?" Three dollars. Someone paid her money for her photograph. Real cash money, once she brought the check to the bank.

"Last week." Mother dipped her head. "I'm afraid you're going to leave, go off hither and yon, taking photographs like you see in those magazines you love so much."

"Mother, I have no plans to leave just yet. This editor invited me to submit more photographs. He likes them. That doesn't mean I'm going to move to Austin or anything. They don't have wildflowers in the city, anyway." Trudy scrambled across the row of plants and hunkered down next to her mother, then embraced her.

"I'm sorry I hid it from you, and I'm sorry you're seeing me like this." Mother looked at the squash as she spoke. "I try to be strong for you, and your brother."

Trudy gave her a hug. "You don't have to be strong for me."

"I know you're all grown up. Just look at you, renting out our Sunday house. I'm not sure what your father will think about it. I'm not sure what I think about it." Mother wiped her brow with the back of her gloved hand. "To be sure, the extra money is nice, but—"

"But what?"

"Be careful, *schatze*. He's a reporter. I don't trust him."

"I'm careful, *Mutti*."

Bradley set his napkin on the table. "Thank you, or should I say, *danke*? I really don't know any German." The smiling faces that lined the dining room held no judgment of his lack of German. This little pocket of society was far from a large city, and its older residents held to their native language. But the younger people his age spoke little German, if any.

"That's all right," said his opa, Hank. He brushed off Bradley's apology with his wrinkled hand, callused from decades of woodworking.

The old man had cried when Tante Elsie introduced him as Micah's only son.

"My Amelia and I loved him as best we could. We built a family together, all of us." Opa shook his head, with the faintest of a tremor accenting his movement. "But my father was harsh. I'm sorry I didn't realize how deeply that affected Micah."

"Now Papa," Elsie interjected. "Don't apologize. Micah knew you loved him as a son. That should have more than made up for what your father tried to do."

Bradley didn't want to share with them about the last conversation he'd had with his father, so he held his tongue. If loose lips sank ships, the hurt that his late father's words could inflict would hurt many assembled at the Zimmermanns' home for supper.

He found himself the guest of honor, and although he was nowhere near a prodigal to this family, they'd killed the fatted calf and embraced Bradley as one of them. That, and there was cause for double celebration with the upcoming nuptials of his second cousin, Kathe, in several weeks.

"Will you still be with us?" Elsie asked.

"I–I'm not sure," Bradley managed to answer. "My job brought me here and is letting me stay on for several weeks. I'm writing a series of articles about Fredericksburg on the home front, actually."

"Please stay," said his cousin Kathe. "You are welcome at my wedding. We need a celebration around here, and having you here will add to it."

"I'll talk to my boss." He took a sip from his coffee cup. Never had he expected his writing journey to take him here.

"Have you ever been to Europe? Did you see any fighting?" asked one of his younger cousins—Walter, Bradley thought his name was.

"Yes, I was in Germany, briefly, as well as France and England. Then the war bond tour brought me here," said Bradley. "When my number came up, they sent me home because of my ear infections. I'm hard of hearing in one ear. They thought that was a liability, I guess."

"I'll be glad when the war ends," said Tante Elsie. "I know we all will."

A whistle echoed outside, followed by a call from a bullhorn in the street. "Lights out, lights out!"

Then, just like in many neighborhoods in many cities across the country, the younger Zimmermanns scampered around, turning light switches off and pulling down shades.

Bradley wasn't sure the little hamlet turning off all their lights and hunkering down would help the war effort, but maybe it made them all feel as if they were doing something instead of watching news reports.

"So, you're renting from the Meiers," Grandfather Hank stated.

"I am. I met Trudy right after the parade yesterday."

"I think she's quite taken with you," said Kathe.

"Kathe," Tante Elsie chided.

"Well, I haven't seen her like this, especially after Kurt." Kathe shook her head.

"What if he comes home? Then she has a choice to make." Tante Elsie rose from the table. "More coffee, anyone?"

"So she has someone, then." Bradley lifted his coffee cup. "I don't mind more coffee."

"No, not exactly." Kathe sighed. "Kurt is MIA, somewhere in France. He's been missing for three months now. His unit thinks he's been captured."

"That's horrible." It definitely gave a personal edge to the news. "His poor family. . ."

"So, I bet you'll want to know more about Fredericksburg's favorite son," said Hank. "I knew the old captain well, Chester's grandfather, Charles."

"You did?" Bradley pulled his notepad from his pocket.

"Put that thing away. Tonight's just for listening, not for working." Hank waved his pointer finger at Bradley.

"Yes, sir." Bradley tucked the notepad away, trying not to smile at the older man's gesture. So this was how it felt, being part of a family.

Chapter 5

G ood afternoon," Trudy called into the Sunday house where Bradley sat at the table, pen in hand. She shifted the folder under one arm and tried not to drop the basket she carried in the other hand.

He looked up and a smile spread across his face. "Good afternoon."

"Here's some chicken potpie my mother made." Trudy set the basket on the table.

"A wonderful smell"—Bradley leaned toward the basket, where the pie lay inside, wrapped in a cloth napkin. "I haven't had homemade potpie in. . .a very long time. I miss my mother's cooking."

"Did your mother cook a lot?"

"She did. She was the best. Even though it was just her and I for a long time." Bradley corked the inkwell and set down his pen. "My father left when I was nine. He still came around, though."

"I–I'm sorry." The conversation had taken a more personal turn, but this was what she'd hoped for. Something about him made her want to learn more.

The shadow passed from his face when he looked up at her again. "Enough about that. Did you bring more pictures?"

"That I did. They're the last roll I shot, including the

parade and war bond show." She pulled the photographs from an old school binder. "Here..."

Bradley thumbed through the set, nodding as he did so. "Good shots. You might want to up the exposure on the one with the midget submarine. A few of the details are lost."

"Okay." She knew she had much more to learn about photography.

"Do you have plans today?"

"I always have something to do, especially with Father gone. We manage as best we can."

"Will you take me around town and introduce me to people? I want to get a good picture of life here during World War II." The intensity of his tone compelled her to look him straight in the eye.

"I can, today." Spending the afternoon with Bradley? Her heart raced.

"Do you have your camera? Maybe I can see if my editor could use some of your images."

"I always have my camera with me." She was on her last roll of film and didn't know where she'd find some cash for more. Unless that editor of Bradley's would pay for photos.

"Perfect." He stood, picking up a slim notepad. "Where shall we go first?"

"You said that people look differently at us because we're German. We have nothing to do with the actions of that insane man and the people who blindly follow him. People need to see what we've given." Her throat caught. "You need to meet the Wagners. They had twin sons, both killed in the service and both buried in a Fredericksburg cemetery. Mr.

Wagner runs the soda shop in town, and Mrs. Wagner is a seamstress."

"We'll go there, then." He followed her out into the sunlight.

As they left the Wagners' home, Bradley fought the emotions rising inside. Trudy dabbed at her eyes with a handkerchief that she slipped into her pocket. "I don't know what to say," was all he could manage.

"I know." Trudy nodded. She gripped her camera strap, her fingers trembling. "I take my brother to get a soda, and it's hard to watch Mr. Wagner. I can see the memories in his eyes, remembering how his own boys were the same age as Eric once."

He touched her elbow, and she released her hand's grip on the strap and allowed him to take her hand. "May I?"

She studied their hands, fingers interlocked, and nodded. "Can I take you somewhere?"

"All right. Lead the way."

"I want to show you a place of beauty here. It's where I shot some of the pictures you've already seen." Her hands were soft, her fingertips having the tiniest bit of callus from working with chemicals.

He needed to tell her about his ties to the town, that one day he'd be back. Instead, he let her talk, pointing out the landmarks from the creek, to where she completed high school, to the historic school building where her mother and grandmother went to school.

"Here we are," she said, leading him under the shade of a trio of oak trees. "These are live oaks, probably at least one hundred years old."

The trees had massive trunks, so thick that Bradley could wrap his arms around only half of a trunk. Their thick, gnarled branches spread wide before reaching up to the sky. "These are something else. They're not as tall as the redwoods in California, but just as majestic in their own way."

"I'm glad you understand, not being from around here and all."

"Actually, I've been wanting to tell you something." He took her hand again. "It turns out, I do have ties to Fredericksburg. My father, Micah Delaney, is related to your friends, the Zimmermanns."

"Really? You're part of their family then?"

He loved watching a smile bloom on her face. "Yes. He was Tante Elsie's younger brother." Bradley explained about his father leaving Fredericksburg and never returning, then about his parents' untimely deaths.

"I'm so sorry, Bradley." She covered his hand with her other hand. "Your father was so alone, and he had people here who loved him all along."

"His loss, and I wish he'd realized that before it was too late." Bradley shrugged. "I wasn't sure what the Zimmermanns would think, but they've been very accepting. Aunt Elsie recognized me right away, it turns out."

Trudy had a musical laugh. "I'm certain she did." Her eyes held a curious light, with the breeze catching the ends of her hair.

"I haven't felt so at home since. . .ever." His throat tightened and he pulled Trudy close, and kissed her. The rosewater scent she wore surrounded him, and the remainders of the soda they'd drunk at the Wagners' shop were sweet on her lips. She molded perfectly against him. It was as if they'd known each other far longer than two days.

Then she pulled back, giving a little gasp. "Bradley, we hardly know each other."

"Maybe we know each other better than you want to admit. As far as the day-to-day things go, those are things we can easily learn about each other."

"But—"

"Is it Kurt? Well, I'm not Kurt. I'm sorry about what happened to him, and I hope they find him." He allowed himself to touch her chin and raise her gaze to meet his. "You can't let yourself be in limbo. The war will end, we'll start moving on with our lives, and where will you be? I'm thankful and blessed to have a job that somehow makes a difference in people's lives. You have a wonderful talent as well. Are you going to let yourself stay here?"

"Who told you about Kurt?" Trudy stepped back and crossed her arms over her chest. "I should have been the one to tell you. Not someone else."

"So you do have feelings for me."

"Of course I do. I've felt it from the moment we met, and it frightened me. There's so much uncertainty in life right now, I don't see adding to it." Her brow furrowed, and she lowered her arms to fiddle with her camera strap.

"Even without war, life is still uncertain. That's where

trusting God comes in." Unspeakable relief washed over him. She cared for him. She'd felt it, too, that instant connection that neither of them were expecting or looking for.

Trudy nodded. "Of course it does. Without my faith in God, I wouldn't have hope."

"Well, then. Have faith that whatever's happening between us will have a happy ending."

One corner of her mouth twitched. "I'll try." But her eyes held an uncertain expression.

Chapter 6

Trudy couldn't avoid Bradley over the next two weeks. She wanted to know him better, as he'd said. Everyday things were easy to learn about someone else. Likes, dislikes, little annoying or endearing habits.

What she'd intended to be a weekly ritual turned into an everyday happening. She would bring Bradley food, intending to drop it off and leave. She'd tote along either biscuits or rolls from her mother, or leftover meat or something for Bradley to make himself a sandwich. Instead of her heading straight back to the farm, she and Bradley would end up walking the streets of Fredericksburg, occasionally running into yet another friend or a distant cousin of his.

The day before Kathe's wedding, Bradley was grinning when Trudy arrived at the Sunday house. A brown paper-wrapped parcel sat on the table, addressed to him in care of the Nimitz Hotel. "Look what I have here. I was hoping it would arrive."

Trudy studied the parcel, securely tied with string. "A package. Good. You mentioned the other day about waiting for something to arrive."

He tapped the brown paper. "Go ahead, open it. It's for you."

"For me?" She worked at untying the string, which didn't work, so Bradley worked at it with his pocketknife. The paper unfolded to reveal a book, cover side down. She turned the book over.

Photography Fundamentals and Beyond: A Professional's Primer.

"Bradley—" He understood her. It wasn't a romantic gift, by any definition of the word. Any fellow could buy a girl flowers or chocolates, but this, this was personal. "I studied what I could, but I always had to return the photography book to the library."

"Well, now this copy is yours forever." He took her hand and squeezed it.

"Thank you, thank you so much."

"I think you could be a professional photographer, and not just portraits. You could work anywhere."

"It means a lot to have someone believe in me like this, especially you." The air grew thick, just like it did weeks before under the live oak trees.

"I do." He raised her hand to his lips and kissed it.

The memory of his gift followed her through a sleepless night until the following afternoon, when she stood inside her cousin Kathe's bedroom, where the temperature soared with early June heat. Kathe stood in front of a small circular fan, moving as it oscillated.

"I'm melting, Trudy. Oh, why, why didn't Peter and I wait until autumn to marry?" Kathe frowned, but Trudy laughed in spite of her own somber thoughts. "And here you are, my maid of honor, laughing at me."

"It's too late to turn back now," Trudy said. "Besides, Peter is well enough to get married."

Kathe nodded. "He's going to walk me during the recessional—oh dear, I can't cry. Not yet." She fanned her face and glanced at Trudy. "Okay, you. 'Fess up. What's going on with you and my handsome, young journalist cousin from Washington? You've been seen around town nearly every day."

"I don't know. I wish I knew. But"—Trudy shivered at the memory—"he kissed me once."

"No. Scandalous, and him so new in town." Kathe's eyes were wide, but she followed the fish-eyed expression with a smile.

"Don't act shocked." Trudy studied her friend's face. "Wait. Did you tell him about Kurt? Because the other day, he brought up Kurt and knew what happened."

"Um…well, we sort of all did, the first night he had supper with us." Kathe started moving back and forth in front of the fan again.

"I wanted to be the one to tell him. . . ." Trudy sank onto the bed. She should have told him herself, but she hadn't wanted to press the issue as if she were trying to prove to him that she was "available." She picked up the pink gown, simple, with an A-line skirt. The idea of getting into her maid-of-honor gown wasn't pleasant. Although the gown was beautiful and lovingly sewn by Tante Elsie, she'd melt just like Kathe would.

"I'm sorry. Bradley wanted to know, and it all just sort of came out."

A soft knock sounded at the door. "Are you almost ready?

The guests have almost all assembled in the backyard," said Tante Elsie.

"Almost," Kathe called out. Then she continued in a lower tone. "You're not mad at me?"

"Of course not. We—he and I—well, we agreed to continue getting to know each other."

"Why don't you look happy about it?"

Trudy stood and ran her fingers over the fabric of her dress. "For one thing, he's going to leave. That's a given fact. He can't write about Fredericksburg forever and his boss wants him to move on eventually. And another thing, how do I know that this isn't moving so fast? He makes me feel. . ."

"Like you're flying on air, like you've been running for a day and can't catch your breath?" Kathe asked.

"Something like that. . .yet I look at my parents, and I don't think I've ever seen them like that." Trudy frowned. "I don't want to chase some dream that will only leave me heartbroken in the end."

"I'm sure your parents felt that way about each other, as did mine," Kathe said. "We've just never seen them young and in love. Everyone starts somewhere."

"You're right." Trudy nodded.

Kathe took her dress from the hanger and held it up to herself, studying her reflection in the mirror. "I prayed long and hard about Peter. He'd come home injured, and I knew that now was the time for us to marry. But I wanted to be sure that it wasn't just me going all 'hearts and flowers' over the whole thing. One morning I woke up and I just. . . knew. . .beyond a doubt, that Peter was the man for me and I was ready to do everything I could to have a good marriage. And, here we are."

"Here you are." Trudy smiled at Kathe. "Let me help you get dressed. We need to get you downstairs so you can have that long-delayed wedding."

Silently, she added, *Lord, show me the way. . .*

Bradley watched as Trudy glided down the grassy lawn of the Zimmermanns' main house. Her hair swept up into a pile of curls on her head. Her light pink dress skimmed her knees with a wide skirt, and her bouquet of fresh flowers from the garden made a pretty contrast.

Her eyes met his, and a faint blush swept down her neck and toward her shoulders. What a two weeks it had been since taking up temporary residence in Fredericksburg. His first set of columns had won praises from Frank. That had earned him more time here.

But time here would be coming to an end, regardless of how much Bradley tried to prolong it.

"There's a war going on, Payne," Frank had told him. *"I appreciate the fact you've brought a human interest angle to the stories about Fredericksburg and your family, but our readers always want something fresh and new. If it starts to get stale, I'm pulling you out of there for your own good."*

"I understand, Frank," Bradley had said.

That conversation came roaring back into his memory as he watched Trudy pass by where he stood. He'd found a treasure here in this Texas town, a treasure of family and the promise of more with Trudy.

The minister asked them to rise as Kathe Zimmermann walked toward the outdoor altar. She leaned on Hank's arm. She made a beautiful bride, her dress simple yet just as elegant as any Bradley had seen in his travels. His grandfather gave him a slight nod as they passed.

Grandfather. Opa. *Thank You, Lord. Please don't let me make the mistake my father did by pushing people away and running from people who love me.* He didn't know how to act with a family. He was used to keeping his own hours, his own time and schedule, without anyone except his editor to give him a timetable for anything. Now people were asking for him, wanting to be involved in his life. He'd never found himself in a family gathering like this.

Kathe had asked if he wanted to read a scripture during the short ceremony. At first he declined, until his grandfather talked him into reconsidering. He could scarcely drag his gaze away from Trudy, who stood at her friend's side. If there was any indication that she had dreary thoughts about this not being her own wedding day, Bradley didn't see it. He did see the woman who'd stolen his heart. First, her talent and sense of adventure inspired him, but then he saw her love for her family and her town.

"And now, a few words from Paul's first letter to the Corinthians," said the minister. He nodded at Bradley, who rose from his chair and walked to the small arbor. He took the open book that the minister held, already turned to the correct passage.

He cleared his throat. "Though I speak with the tongues

of men and of angels. . ." The familiar poetic words of truth came from his lips. "Charity suffereth long, and is kind. . . beareth all things, believeth all things, endureth all things. . ."

He allowed himself a glance at Trudy, whose gaze held his for a millisecond before she lowered her focus to her bouquet. A blush swept over her features.

"When I was a child, I spake as a child, I understood as a child, I thought as a child: but when I became a man, I put away childish things. For now we see through a glass, darkly; but then face to face: now I know in part; but then shall I know even as also I am known. And now abideth faith, hope, charity, these three; but the greatest of these is charity."

Lord, help me, I'm in love with Trudy Meier.

The rest of the ceremony ticked by without his conscious thoughts directed at the newly married couple. This wasn't in his plans. What could he do now that his heart was held by a honey-haired photographer from a tiny Texas town? Certainly she talked about adventure and wanting to see the world. There were drawbacks. He knew them. Tough travel conditions, uncertain accommodations. There was occasionally some danger. He wasn't guaranteed a permanent position at the magazine. What if he ever found himself out of work, with a wife to take care of?

He knew Trudy's mother had expressed a few objections to the idea of her only daughter being paired with a freelance journalist. He didn't blame her. The practical part of him understood all too well. If it were his daughter, he'd want her tucked safely into the shelter of a town like Fredericksburg. But then, Trudy wasn't a child, but a grown woman capable of making adult decisions.

Someone nudged him. Opa Hank. "You going to hang back and not try to get a piece of wedding cake?"

"Huh?"

"You were anywhere but here, young man."

"Sorry. It was a nice ceremony. I'm honored that I was included."

"I know that the young Meier girl had your attention."

"Was it obvious?"

"Of course it was." His grandfather walked beside him in the direction of a long table filled with delectable dishes. Someone had baked a ham, another friend or family member had brought homemade sausage. Plenty of potatoes and garden vegetables. And—the cake.

"Hello." Trudy's voice came from somewhere off to the side, close to his right shoulder.

He turned to face her. "Hello, yourself. You look beautiful."

"Thank you." She colored at his words. "It was a lovely wedding, wasn't it? I'm glad you said yes to Kathe about reading the scripture. I know it meant a lot to her." Trudy waved off a fly, who'd developed an interest in her bouquet.

"It meant a lot to me, too. It'll be one of my favorite memories of Fredericksburg and meeting my family." He took a step closer to her.

"You sound as if you're leaving. . ." Trudy bit her lower lip.

"Eventually, I am." He tried not to put a damper on the day. "Okay, probably sooner than eventually. I knew I would be. . ." He didn't add, *and you did, too.* The pain in her eyes almost made him wince.

"I'd heard the rumors, but didn't want to believe them," a female voice said. Bradley didn't know the woman who'd come to stand beside them. She looked to be a few years younger than Aunt Elsie, and she glanced from Trudy, to him, then back Trudy again.

"What rumors do you mean, Mrs. Schuler?" Trudy asked.

"You've taken to running around town with this man who claims to be a Zimmermann, while my son—my only boy—is somewhere missing in Europe." The woman's eyes crackled with anger, but Bradley saw the fear inside them, too. One of his friends had gone missing after an air raid in London a year ago. No one had heard from him since. Sad, how life kept going even when someone's sudden absence left a gaping hole.

"I miss Kurt, too, and I wish he were here." Trudy stood her ground. The words she said sounded odd. How much did she really miss him? Bradley couldn't guess. Today wasn't the right place or time, but eventually they'd have to square off and face each other, all cards on the table, and both of them would see what the other held.

Chapter 7

Y**ou ready for bigger and better things, Payne?"** Frank's voice roared over the telephone line, the Wednesday following the wedding. "Genius, I tell you. Genius, profiling Nimitz and the town that helped him become the man he is now."

"I'm glad you're happy, Frank." Bradley had hunkered down, finishing the last of the series of articles featuring Admiral Chester Nimitz. A feeling like being stuck on the downward turn of a Ferris wheel entered his stomach. The day was coming when he'd be on his way, especially if he wanted to keep his job. Which, he did.

"I've got something coming up, something big that *This American Life* has never tried before. It's one of America's next frontiers, and if all goes well, I'll have you there in less than ten days."

"Ten days?" His own tone surprised him. Usually he was raring to go to the next assignment.

Trudy had barely stopped by the last several days, especially since the Zimmermanns had sent him home well stocked with leftovers from the wedding. He missed her. But considering the latest developments, maybe it was best this way. If she wasn't absolutely sure she could see herself having a traveling life—or even having a husband traveling much of the time like him.

Husband. . .him, a husband? He'd only been here for the story. . .and his family—

"Payne?"

"Yes, Frank?"

"Did you get what I just said? Because I have a feeling you didn't hear me."

"So, you can have me there in less than ten days?"

"Wind up the series. Get some photographs that we can use for a photo page, then hightail it up here to my office. We'll give readers enough to expect that your next setting will be something they've only seen in the news reels. You can cool your heels before you ship out again."

"I understand."

"Don't sound so glum. This is the chance of a lifetime."

"You're right." Bradley ended the call and set the phone back on its cradle.

"Are you okay, Mr. Payne?" asked the shopkeeper.

"Yes, yes I am. I'm going to be leaving sooner than I thought."

"Well, we've enjoyed having you in our fair town."

"Thank you, thank you. I've—I've enjoyed it as well." He slid some cash across the counter to help pay for the long-distance phone call. "I'll be back at some point, to see my grandfather and the rest of the family."

But back for Trudy—he wasn't a hundred percent certain of that. In a perfect world, he would come swooping back and they'd have themselves a grand reunion.

Trudy fumbled with the knife as she sliced the potatoes. Beef stew was the fanciest she could manage for a nice supper. She'd used garden tomatoes for the base and added fresh chopped vegetables from the garden. She'd bartered honey for a small end piece of beef from the butcher. Some people didn't want to buy the cast-off pieces, but others knew how to coax the toughness from the end pieces after cooking the meat for hours.

Bradley would enjoy this stew, or at least she hoped so. After the wedding, Trudy had done some long, hard thinking and praying. She loved Bradley, and it had hurt her the way Mrs. Schuler had talked to them. Yet she didn't want him to misunderstand about Kurt. She realized that loving Kurt had been a first love. She didn't think a first love had to be her only love.

Mrs. Schuler, to give the woman credit, had apologized after the Sunday service. *"I'm sorry for what I said to you at Kathe's wedding, Trudy. You and your family have been a great support to mine. Kurt told me in a letter as well that you both decided not to marry. It's just hard to see other people going on with their lives, when Kurt. . .when Kurt and his father and I have no chance to go on with ours."* Sobbing, she'd embraced Trudy and whispered in her ear, *"I know Kurt will always love you."*

Trudy hadn't known how to answer the woman and even now, had no answer. She'd mumbled that she would be praying for them. All of Fredericksburg did a lot of watching and praying, it seemed.

She gathered the diced potato from the cutting board and dropped it into the bubbling stew. Soon enough, the meal would be done. A fresh loaf of bread, wrapped in a dish towel, waited on the counter. Cookies would round out the meal.

Within thirty minutes, she'd tucked a ceramic covered pot of stew and the bread into the bicycle basket, plus her small battery-operated radio. It would be a clear night tonight, or at least she hoped so. Maybe they'd get a signal and listen to a show from Austin.

It was the least she could do for Bradley, especially after his gift of the beautiful photography book. The gift had touched her to the core. She'd spent her free time studying it, learning where she intuitively made good composition choices, and other places in her developing that she could improve upon. She bumped along the road on her bicycle, her blouse sticking to her back. It had been a silly idea to try to look fancy for him tonight, as if they were going out. As a reward, she'd be hot and sweaty by the time she arrived at the Sunday house.

Trudy pedaled along. The sight of the Sunday house's open door made her heart sing. Good. Bradley was home. Before long, the shadows would be stretching and the sun going down. As if he knew she was approaching on her bicycle, Bradley emerged from the house and squinted. A grin spread onto his face when he saw it was her.

"Hello there," he called out as she glided to a stop on the hard-packed dirt, dust swirling around her tires.

"Hi." She popped the kickstand down, got the bicycle

balanced, and pulled all the food from the bicycle basket. "I hope you're hungry."

"Just a little." He rubbed his stomach as he stepped off the porch. Bradley picked up the pot, while she gathered up the bread and the radio.

"It's beef stew, made with real beef," she said as she followed him into the house. The single, open room felt cozy. They left the front door open and the breeze drifted in.

"Real beef? I'm impressed." Bradley pushed aside a stack of papers and set the pot on the center of the table.

"I know we're in Texas, but our beef has been going elsewhere the past couple of years. And most of us don't ranch around here. We farm. However, I managed to secure some fresh meat." She smiled and patted the top of the pot. "And if you don't mind, I'm inviting myself to stay for supper."

"Of course you can stay." He pulled out a chair for her. "Please, sit down."

"Why thank you." Her heart sang. She knew he'd be leaving. He hadn't mentioned it lately, but his rent was paid up for one more week.

Bradley headed to the corner cupboard. "I must admit, I've missed you the past few days."

"I knew you had plenty of food after the wedding, when I saw Aunt Elsie packing a basket for you." Trudy removed the lid from the stew and inhaled. Hopefully, it was as good as her mother's.

"Here. I have bowls and spoons." He set one in front of her and kept one for himself. "Welcome to Payne's Café, madame."

"Why, thank you, Mr. Payne." She laughed. If only they could pretend there wasn't a war going on. She served them each a bowl of stew, then divvied up the bread.

"Oh Trudy. . ." Bradley reached for her hand. "I'm going to miss you."

"You're leaving soon, aren't you?"

He nodded. "I talked to my boss today. I'm wrapping up the series and heading back to Washington early next week."

She'd been preparing herself for this, but even so, the edges of her heart crumbled. She tried to smile. "We—we can keep in touch."

"Of course we can." Then he cleared his throat. "You know, I'll be back to see my family, when I can."

"But you don't know when that will be." She blinked to clear her burning eyes. No, she wouldn't let him see her tears. Not tonight. Tonight was supposed to be a night to remember.

"You're right, I don't. But you can be sure I'll be back to see my family, when I can."

"If you didn't have family here. . ."

"I'd still come back, somehow."

Trudy nodded. "I'm glad. But—"

"I can't ask you to wait for me, though. That's not fair to you."

"What if I want to wait for you?"

Bradley sighed. "Even after the war, I'll still travel a lot."

"I know." Trudy fumbled with the spoon beside her bowl.

He squeezed her hand. "I'll ask the blessing over our meal."

Trudy nodded and bowed her head.

"Lord, we thank You for this day. I thank You for this food. Bless the hands that prepared it, and strengthen us for Your service. Amen."

"Amen." Trudy pulled her hand away from his. "Here, maybe we can find some music to play for supper, and we can pretend we're somewhere exotic." She almost sounded like a child, acting out make-believe.

"That's a great idea."

The strains of "Taking a Chance on Love" filled the air, with only a hint of static. They ate their stew, talked, and laughed. Trudy imagined that tonight was all they had, and refused to let her mind ponder the fact that Bradley was leaving in four days.

All too soon, the stew was finished and the pot empty. The music kept playing. Thankfully, no news reports broke in to shatter the moment.

"It's probably cooler outside," Bradley said. He stood and gathered the bowls together before she had a chance to reach for them. "I'll clean this up later."

Bradley took her by the hand and led her outside. "Oh, my sweet Trudy. . .this is much harder than I thought it would be."

She wanted to tell him, *Take me with you, please*, but she kept silent. She wasn't going to beg, or plead. Instead, she said, "I know. I feel the same way. . .what are we going to do?"

He pulled her close into the circle of his arms and she responded in turn, listening to his heartbeat through his shirt.

"Would you come with me?"

Trudy opened her mouth, but the roar of a car's engine bit

through the twilight and made them both jerk apart. Trudy glanced toward the road. Her mother, behind the wheel of the family's car.

She honked the horn and the car ground to a halt. "Trudy! There you are." Her mother's tone made her stand bolt upright. Was it Father?

"What's wrong?"

Her mother leapt from the car. "Not wrong—Kurt's mother got a telegram. Kurt's been found, alive, and will be sent to a hospital in Washington in a few days."

Chapter 8

Trudy and her mother hurried, hurried, hurried down the corridor of the army hospital, the scent of antiseptic making Trudy's stomach turn. Kurt…asking for them. For her. Alive. What he must have been through. Of course she had to come. It was the least they could do. Exhaustion pricked her eyelids. They'd taken a train and had sat upright for three days in the car. She wished they'd had the money to get a sleeping car. But at least they were here, now, in the nation's capital.

Kurt's parents had fallen ill suddenly, too ill to travel, so they begged Trudy and her mother to go in their place. "If he can't see us, we know he'll want to see you."

Making the trip with Bradley helped. Neither she nor her mother had traveled this far before, and he made the process smooth. He attended to what they needed, whether it was securing a pillow or a blanket, and helped them connect to the right trains. They laughed when they could. Laughter was an antidote to the pain of war, to the constant reminders from the radio and newspapers. Even Mother relaxed, although she kept worrying that someone was going to steal her purse. That and if Eric was behaving for the Zimmermanns, who volunteered to let him stay with them.

From the taxi, Trudy glimpsed the Capitol building and Washington Monument as they made their way outside the city to the hospital. If her trip hadn't been so urgent, she'd have loved to stop and take photos.

"I'll see you to the hospital," Bradley had promised. He even accompanied them inside the hospital, inquiring at the desk about where to find Kurt. He followed them along the hallway like a silent shadow.

Trudy held his hand, regardless of her mother's opinion at the moment. She smiled at Bradley. "Thank you for everything." He replied by kissing her hand.

Now each step drew Trudy closer to Kurt. For a few moments, she remembered their childhood promises, their romance that seemed so perfect—to everyone else, but not her. What was romance or true love? She knew that bottle rockets and swooning didn't last. But weren't you supposed to feel something for the one you loved? Of course, she felt some affection for him.

But Kurt had never made her feel like Bradley did, like she was on the brink of some discovery or big adventure.

"They said he's in ward two," Mother whispered. Trudy nodded. A nurse passed them, efficient and neat in her crisp, white uniform and cap. Somewhere, a man sobbed about needing more medicine.

Oh Lord, please don't let that be Kurt. But then, she wished it wasn't anyone. This was the side of war she wanted to hide from, the reason she tried not to read the newspaper much, the reason she turned the radio off if it played anything but music. She glanced at her mother. The times her mother had volunteered at the hospital back in Texas. . .what had she witnessed? Trudy had never bothered to ask.

"Here we are," Mother said.

Trudy felt her feet seal themselves to the tile floor. "I—I don't know if I can go in."

"You can do this." Bradley slipped his arm around Trudy's shoulders. "I know you can."

"I—I want to go in by myself first," she said. The Schulers had been vague about his injuries, other than that he was malnourished and had had a fractured leg, and some facial lacerations.

"We'll be right here." Mother gave her a hug before she entered the ward.

Sunlight streamed through the large window at the end of the two rows of beds. Trudy tried not to stare, but some images still seared themselves into her eyes. Bandages, tubes, bruises. Which one was Kurt? It had been well over a year since he'd left Fredericksburg.

"Trudy." One of the figures spoke. But which one? She glanced from face to unfamiliar face. It had been so long, but how could she not recognize him?

One of the men cracked a grin at her. "I wish you were here to see me, doll." His left eye was covered with a bandage, but his right eye, a shade of robin's egg blue, winked at her.

"I—I'm sorry," was all she could stammer to the wounded soldier. She did pause at the foot of his bed and until she found her voice. "I hope you get well soon." Just because she was here to see Kurt didn't mean she had to ignore everyone else.

"Over here." A feeble, bony hand waved from the second bed from the end, then lowered to the starched white blankets.

Trudy willed herself to walk tile by tile to Kurt's bed and stop at the foot, by the arched metal frame of the footboard. She tried not to clamp her hand over her mouth or gasp when she saw him.

Kurt Schuler wasn't the young man she'd once known. Sunken cheeks, skin stretched taut over bones. His hand reminded her of a skeleton, covered with a layer of skin. Scars marred his once clear face. She remembered how she'd liked his strong jaw, his boyish shock of blond hair, now cropped close. Some had fallen out in patches, likely due to malnutrition. One leg was gone, with a stump left that didn't come close to matching the other side. All this she took in within a few seconds that ticked by one painful second after the other.

"Kurt, I—we've been so worried. . .all of us have been." A sob caught her throat. "I'm sorry. I wasn't going to cry. But I'm so happy you were found. . ."

He reached for her hand and she refused to let herself recoil at the boniness of its touch. "I counted every day I was captured. I think. After a while, I lost track. They fed me once a week, twice if they remembered."

"Well, you're here now, and all you have to think about is getting better." She swallowed hard. "My—my mother is here. We came because your family can't right now. . .soon, though. I needed to see you because of your last letter. I hope you got mine. . ."

"I did." She tried not to stare at his bruised face, the

stitches. Her fingers felt numb in the grasp of his hand.

"Trudy, I can't promise you much more than a simple life in Fredericksburg. But even with my leg gone, I plan to walk again. I'm going to farm like my father did. He promised me at least fifty acres of my own, with peach trees, and enough space to build a house and have room for a garden." Kurt sucked in a breath then started to cough.

"Kurt..."

"I know I released you from our engagement, because I knew we were both so young, but now, I can't help but ask again..." He coughed, then spoke in a clear voice that rang out through the ward. "Gertrude Meier, will you marry me?"

"I—I—" Trudy sighed. "Oh Kurt..."

Bradley had heard enough, standing in the hallway opposite Trudy's mother.

"I'm—I'm heading to my office now, Mrs. Meier. Do you think you'll be able to order a taxi to bring you to your hotel? Here." He slipped her some coins for the fare.

She nodded. "I can do that... Mr. Payne, I know you care for my daughter, and I know she cares for you. But right now, with Kurt coming home again, it will be very complicated for her."

He nodded. "I don't know when I'll be back." In fact, he knew he was doing the right thing by leaving for his office immediately. Part of him wanted to march into the ward and talk to the former prisoner of war, now found and returned home. But it wasn't the place or the time. Kurt Schuler wasn't the issue, either. Even without Kurt, they both had difficult decisions to make.

"I understand. It's probably best to give her some time." Mrs. Meier glanced into the ward. "I'll tell her for you."

Bradley tipped his hat to Mrs. Meier. "Thank you, ma'am."

With that, he walked away without a backward glance. Maybe this was a sign that Trudy and Kurt were meant to be together, and his own summertime affection for her had been merely a distraction. Either way, he knew she needed distance now, not two suitors pressing her, one of them barely alive.

Numbly, he took a cab back to the office and headed straight to see Frank.

"Payne, you did amazing work in Texas. I wasn't sure about letting you stay like that, but you captured the hearts of those people and shared them with us." Frank pumped his hand and clapped him on the back. "Phenomenal work. Pulitzer worthy, and I'm not pushing it to say that, either."

You captured the hearts of those people. No, it was his heart that had been captured. Bradley rubbed his stubbled chin. He'd barely been back, only dumped off his rucksack at his desk before speeding off to the hospital with the Meier ladies.

"Thank you, sir." He blew out a pent-up breath. "So, this next frontier. Where am I headed?"

"I hope you like coconuts and pineapple, because you're going to Hawaii." Frank clapped Bradley on the back as if he'd just won a prize. "The housing isn't fancy, but you'll have room to spread out. I want you to cover the Pacific angle of the war. Keep up on the news there. Lucky dog, writing from paradise."

But paradise didn't appeal to him without Trudy by his side.

Chapter 9

"Mother, I can't believe you let Bradley leave like that," Trudy said as they entered their hotel room. Small, but tidy. "I wanted to introduce him to Kurt."

"He said he needed to go to the office, and I agreed with him." Her mother set her handbag on the dresser.

"What did you tell him?"

"I told him you needed time."

"Oh Mother. I need to call him as soon as possible." Trudy found the telephone number for *This American Life* and dialed from the hotel room telephone. The efficient-sounding operator put her straight through to the editor-in-chief's office.

"Frank McAffrey's office," a woman said.

"I'm—I'm looking for one of your staff writers, Mr. Bradley Payne," said Trudy. "He's been in Texas, in my town actually, but is now back in Washington."

"Yes, he's been to the office, but he's not here at the moment."

Her hope deflated a little. "Is there a way I can leave a message for him, next time he comes by? I'm Trudy Meier, a photographer from Texas."

"You don't say." The lady rustled some papers. "Well, I'm

not sure when he'll come by again. We've sent him to Hawaii. He's going to lead our Pacific division for the rest of the war."

"I—I see. Thank you anyhow."

"If he calls, I'll tell him you asked about him."

"Thank you." Trudy ended the call. Hope deflated? No, this was hope dashed to pieces. She'd wanted to tell him about Kurt, that there wasn't going to be an engagement, or a wedding. Kurt had been disappointed, but she'd sat with him for hours, talking about the goings-on in Fredericksburg. She left him with a light in his eyes and a promise to always be his friend.

She turned from the phone to see her mother standing there. "Did you reach him?"

Trudy shook her head.

"Maybe it's for the best. You don't want a man who's the leaving kind. He ought to fight for you, to stay around long enough."

"But his job—"

"His job alone means no stability." Her mother hugged her in a warm embrace, but that didn't help ease the sore spot in her heart.

Bradley Payne was gone, and he wasn't coming back.

"I'm going to write every week, Tante Elsie," Bradley said to his aunt.

"I'll hold you to that promise." His voice was warm and soft. "I feel like I have my little brother back again."

"I'm glad I found the family I never knew I had for the

longest time." Bradley's throat caught. He wanted to ask about Trudy, but dared not. He'd thought that he'd found someone, someone who understood what it was like to have wings, yet someone who taught him the importance of having strong roots.

"You know, your Trudy isn't getting married."

"What?"

"No. Kurt will be home in Fredericksburg soon, but Trudy told him no, that she wouldn't marry him. I think some in town were hoping they would make a match of it after all."

"Trudy. . .not married."

Tante Elsie stood and hugged him. "Well, I know you came here just to tell me good-bye, but you do know the way to her house. Go, go after her, Bradley."

"Yes, ma'am." With that, Bradley left his family's Sunday house and stepped into the sunlight.

The small space of the Sunday house felt like a gaping hole that echoed with emptiness. Of course Bradley Payne had left. He'd gone on to his next story, his next big thing. Hawaii, imagine that. Briefly, Trudy had dreamed of traveling at his side as Mrs. Bradley Payne, photographing the world, yet always having Fredericksburg to return home to. He did have her address. Maybe he'd write, or send a postcard. Or something.

Trudy sank onto the bed, covered with her grandmother's quilt. "Oh Lord, I love him. So much. This came as a complete surprise to me, and even better, he's part of the Zimmermann family. . ."

She dashed away a tear. No time for tears. Now was a time to be strong, like her father had always encouraged her and Eric to be. Reality meant that sometimes things turned out, sometimes they didn't.

Enough of feeling sorry for herself. She stood, the floorboards creaking under her feet. She crossed a few steps and stopped at the table. Bradley had left pens and a bottle of ink behind. Trudy picked them up. He'd left that, plus she had a few photographs of them together. Sentimental girl. . . she allowed herself a sigh. She might as well head home.

A shadow blocked the sunlight. "Trudy—"

"Bradley." She dropped the pens and the bottle of ink, which rolled off the table. "You're—you're here? But you're supposed to be going to Hawaii."

"I am. I took a moment to stop here on the way. Out of my way, but I wanted to see Tante Elsie and Opa before I left."

"I'm sure she's happy you did." She wanted to tell him that there wasn't going to be a wedding, that she'd looked for him, and she wanted to ask him why he left that day at the hospital. But she didn't.

"My aunt told me something interesting, though." He stepped inside the Sunday house and closed the gap between them.

"What's that?"

"You're not getting married."

"No, I'm not." She shook her head. "Not to Kurt. He's a good man and has a long road to healing, but. . .but we called off the wedding before he went missing. He needs someone who'll be content to stay here, to be a farmer's wife. And, I'm not. . ."

A smile bloomed on his face, and Trudy wished she could capture the expression with her camera.

"I know it's been a fast summer for both of us, but when I met you, I felt like for the first time ever, I'd come home." Bradley took her hand. "You're beautiful, sweet, kind, and you have an adventurous spirit that pulls me along. I—I love you, and I want to spend the rest of my life with you, wherever God takes us."

"I love you, too."

He pulled her into his arms and kissed her until she was breathless. Surely, this was a dream. He released her, but still kept her in the circle of his arms. "I think we should talk to your mother."

"She'll be dubious. She thinks you're one who leaves."

"I left because of Kurt. I knew that you both had a lot to talk about, and he's been through a lot. But now that there's no Kurt. . ."

"You came back."

"I did. . .then when Tante Elsie told me you weren't getting married, I knew I had to find you." He frowned.

"What's wrong?"

"I need to be in Hawaii as soon as possible. Will you wait for me?"

Trudy shook her head. "No, I won't wait for you."

"What?"

"Because I'm coming with you, as Mrs. Bradley Payne." She kissed him back. Truly, he brought out her reckless side.

No proper woman proposed to a man.

"Is that a proposal, Miss Meier?" His eyes twinkled at her.

"Indeed it is, Mr. Payne."

"Actually, I'm thinking of going by Zimmermann."

Epilogue

Nine months later

Trudy would never tire of seeing the ocean, much as she missed the hill country of Texas, and the German accents of her people. The bluebonnets of spring were vivid in her memory. But she wished she could capture the blue of the ocean to show her parents. A letter arrived from Mother every week. She'd heard from Father, who was doing well, but long past ready to return home.

Please forgive me for making things so difficult for you and Bradley. A mother only wants to protect her child. One day, I am sure you will understand, her last letter had read.

Trudy snapped another photo of a palm tree at the edge of a sandy beach, then wound the film. For a wedding present, Bradley had given her a brand-new camera.

"Are you out of film?" Bradley asked.

She nodded. "I can't wait to see how these come out." They'd turned their pantry into a darkroom, much to her delight.

"Frank is pleased as punch with your photographs, as am I." There was talk of eventually bringing *This American Life* into a color print format, one day. There was also talk of Trudy Meier Zimmermann winning a photography award as well, but Trudy wasn't thinking of that overmuch these days.

"I'm thankful that I get to do what I love, and that you and I are together in such a beautiful place like this. Our apartment isn't much to speak of. . ." She didn't mean to sound as if she were complaining, because they were often out and about on their assignments together.

"I wish it were more. . ."

"But I love it because we're together." She smiled at her husband.

Bradley kissed the tip of her nose, then touched her stomach. "Have you felt the baby move?"

"Not yet." She smiled. "It's too early. I think. My mother would know." Sometimes homesickness struck Trudy in waves, but the wonder of discovering the world around her kept that at bay most of the time. Now, she felt sickness for a different reason. Bradley had been over the moon when she told him about the baby.

"Now it's my turn with surprises." Bradley held up an envelope.

"What's that?" She reached for it, and he whipped it away from her grasp, then handed it to her with a smile, the ocean breeze ruffling his dark hair.

Trudy opened the envelope. "Plane tickets? Where are we going?" Their first stop would be Los Angeles. She didn't page through the tickets after that.

"Washington, with a detour by Texas first. I know you've been missing your family." He wrapped his arms around her and she leaned into him as they looked out at the crashing waves.

"That I have. I enjoy reading their letters, but I would

love to visit before I can't travel anymore." A mother. She was going to be a mother.

He nodded. "That's what I thought. And I know just the place we can stay when we get there."

Trudy smiled up at her husband. "Our Sunday house will do just fine."

Lynette Sowell is an award-winning author with New England roots, but she makes her home in Central Texas with her husband and a herd of five cats. When she's not writing, she edits medical reports and chases down stories for the local newspaper.

A HINT OF
LAVENDER

by Eileen Key

Dedication

GOD is bedrock under my feet,
the castle in which I live, my rescuing knight.
2 SAMUEL 22:2 MSG

Special thanks to Rebecca Germany and
Tamela Hancock Murray for believing in my work.
Posse-crit partners, couldn't do without you.
Trevor, Eliana, and Samuel, Nana loves you.

For Matthew, a God-given gift, who is learning to live.
PROVERBS 3:5–6

Chapter 1

Fredericksburg, Texas
Present Day

Gravel spit from under the car's tires as it swung out of the parking lot onto the ribbon of highway away from the peach stand, enveloping Gwen Zimmermann in a cloud of dust. She brushed grit from her eyes, coughed, and leaned against the white wooden counter, bumping the small cashbox with her elbow. Only nine thirty this first day of June, and she already wished for a shower. Heat waves shimmered over the asphalt. The scrub oak and mesquite stood still in the brown fields across the road. Dust hung in the air like an oppressive vapor.

She tightened her scrunchie, moving her ponytail higher on the back of her neck, and flapped her T-shirt against her chest for a breeze. Now that school was out, she'd spend most of her time working at her parents' roadside peach stand— in the heat. She angled the small fan on the countertop toward her.

"Yep, Gwen, cancel those summer-school plans." Perspiration trickled down her forehead. She swiped it away with the back of her hand then shifted ripe peaches into small baskets to replace the ones the last customers purchased. The sweet aroma made her mouth water.

"Morning, Gwennie." Harold Zimmermann strode out from the small store behind the stand carrying a crate tucked against his belly. "Need to set these out." He shoved the box on the counter and lifted a jar, tilting the label in her direction. "Peach salsa. Tried this one yet?" He raised his gray bushy eyebrow.

"Nope. Is it good?" Gwen grinned at her father. He was always eager to showcase a new product from a local farmer. Buy local was her dad's slogan.

His brown eyes twinkled. "Has a kick to it, all right. Good old South Texas style, I'd say." He dusted his hands and surveyed the counters. "Get your mom to bring out a cracker tray and set up a new sampler."

"Outside?" Gwen considered the heat and the possibility of insects. "Sure that's a good idea?"

Her dad laughed. "Okay, maybe you're right. Again. Miss Cautious." He poked at a peach. "Time was we'd eat these straight from the tree, dirt under our fingernails, not a thought to germs." His eyebrows waggled. "But you want to keep things sterile."

"Daddy," Gwen singsonged. "Not sterile, just clean. Safe. No food poisoning." She watched her dad position more jars on an endcap. He looked pale beneath his tanned, wrinkled skin, broad shoulders stooped and customary denim shirt loose across his back. He seemed to have aged since her spring break. "You feeling okay?" She placed one hand on his arm.

"Hmm?" He swiped at his face with a handkerchief, pushing away a fine strand of gray hair until it stuck straight up. "I'm fine. A little tuckered, that's all." His brow wrinkled.

"I'm okay, darling girl. And so grateful you are home to help us. I miss you when you're gone."

Gwen laughed. "San Antonio is an hour away and I come home all the time. I haven't abandoned the orchard in lieu of school." Her heart sped up. That wasn't quite true. She didn't want to return to the orchard, she wanted something new. This summer she could've worked near the college and taken more hours, but her family needed her—money was tight— so she'd foregone the opportunity and come home. She eyed her dad. Did he appear jaundiced or was it the early morning light? "But cautious that I am, I'm thinking you need to see Doc Hawkins if you're tuckered out at this time of day."

"I'm fine." He waved a hand at her.

Standard Dad answer. Gwen watched him walk through the stand displays, rearranging a peach here, a tomato there. The drought had taken its toll on more than fruit and vegetables. He was definitely not himself. She needed to corral her mom and find out more.

A truck turned into the parking lot, kicking up more grit, and the driver honked the horn. Gwen smiled as the red pickup stopped, her brother behind the wheel. Rob parked and slid from the front seat. "Morning, y'all. Got a new batch to sort." He tugged a basket of peaches from over the tailgate and plopped them in front of his sister. "Something for you to do, Peach-girl."

Gwen's lips pursed and she propped her hands on her hips. She glared at her tall, younger brother. A streak of dirt ran down his cheek and his A&M T-shirt clung to his back. A lock of his curly, blond hair drooped over his forehead, outlining a cherubic face. "Do not call me that."

He laughed and went to his truck for another basket. "Whatever you say, sis." Rob returned to the stand and angled his head toward his father. "You okay, Dad?"

Harold sat on the edge of a bench, bent forward, his breath coming in short puffs. "You know, I don't think so."

Gwen raced to her father's side and gripped his trembling hand. Her heart banged against her ribs. "Rob, help me get him into your truck." She braced her father under one arm and helped him stand. Her brother grabbed his other arm and flung it across his shoulders. Neither spoke. Fear rumbled in Gwen's chest and her mouth dried out. They shuffled to the pickup and Harold clambered in the front seat. "Grab me a plastic sack," he wheezed. "Feel kinda punk."

Rob tugged a black garbage bag from behind the seat, handed it to his dad, and then crawled under the steering wheel as Gwen climbed in and shut the door. Her brother darted a glance at her, his mouth a grim line. He started the engine and pulled onto the highway. "Doc or Hill Country?"

Gwen gripped her father's clammy hand. "Hill Country Hospital. Step on it."

How could a day that had started out so exciting morph into such a mess? Clay Tanner braced himself against the side of Larry's SUV. His friend's insistence on a hospital visit was probably smart, but Clay dreaded the idea. He leaned forward and tried to put pressure on his left leg. Pain shot through him. He bit his lip at the deep throb in his knee. Okay, maybe a doctor was in order. He sighed and eyed the sight in front of him.

Enchanted Rock was just that, enchanting. A mound of weathered pink granite some four hundred feet high at its peak, a geologist's dream. He'd promised his parents pictures of everything his team explored, and now this—another disappointment. He jerked at a pocket on his cargo shorts to see if his cell was there.

"I've secured your gear with mine, and Professor Wurst will make sure it's not disturbed." Larry flipped his keys in the palm of his hand. "Let's get you medical attention." Larry opened the passenger door and Clay hitched forward to climb in.

"Man, I'm sorry—"

"Don't start that." Larry shut Clay's door and got behind the wheel. "We're a team, looking out for one another. If I was injured, you'd haul me into town, I presume." A crooked grin crossed his friend's sunburned face.

Clay nodded. "Suppose so." He refrained from crossing his ankles, fearing another jolt of pain. "Although I'd probably leave you hanging for a few hours while I completed my day's work."

"Yeah, right. You're so cold, bro." Larry exited the park and headed toward Fredericksburg. "Just glad you fell early on before we were far into the hike. I wouldn't want to carry your bulky body down a rock."

"Bulky? After P90 workouts?" Clay ran his hand across his chest. "This is pure muscle, my man."

Larry darted a glance at him. "In your dreams."

Clay chortled and settled against the seat, looking for a comfortable position. His long legs were crammed into the SUV's well beneath the glove box. Bending his knee was almost unbearable. He should've grabbed ice from the campsite before his descent. He stared out the window. What did it matter? He'd messed up this golden opportunity. Hiking beautiful countryside and receiving extra credit hours toward his graduate degree—what a perfect plan. He traced a finger along the window edge. Or really his father's plan since he'd paved the way with his longtime friend Professor Wurst from the University of Texas. Roger Tanner, archaeologist, had all the right connections in the world of rocks. Now this. The youngest son blowing such a chance.

The brown landscape offered little to capture his attention and he nearly dozed off to the hum of Larry murmuring into his cell phone. Within a few minutes, they reached the hospital. Larry pulled to the curb and parked. Clay shoved the door open, gritted his teeth, and angled his body around then swung his leg out.

"Dude, let me help you." Larry reached for Clay's elbow.

Clay jerked away but teetered on his right leg. He ducked his head in a nod and Larry grabbed his waist. "Appreciate that." He grasped Larry's shoulder and hobbled with him toward the hospital entrance. A bead of sweat formed on his upper lip. He dashed a hand across his face and inhaled sharply.

Inside, a blast of cold air scented with antiseptic greeted them. A smiling orderly pushed a wheelchair forward. Clay sank into it gratefully. The twinges of pain had fully developed into stabs under and around his kneecap. Worry threaded through his middle.

The young man pushed the wheelchair into a small waiting room and accepted Clay's insurance card. "A triage nurse will see you shortly."

Larry stood in front of Clay, shifting from one foot to the other. Clay massaged his leg. "Hey, go on back. You don't need to stay. It's going to take forever, I'm sure. Most ERs do."

"Can't just dump you and run," Larry said. His face told another story.

"Yeah, you can. Keep your cell turned on and I'll check in when I know something."

"You sure?" Larry frowned. "It's just—hospitals. . .and I have so much. . . Face it, Clay, hospitals creep me out."

Clay sighed. He knew the feeling. "Go on. Seriously."

Larry waved his phone. "This won't leave my side. I'll be back by four, anyway, to check on you." He grinned. "Find a pretty nurse. Don't waste your time." He headed to the exit.

"Yeah, right." With the swish of the doors, a desolate and familiar feeling crept through Clay. Loneliness.

"Mr. Tanner?" A gray-haired nurse stepped into view. "Let's see what's going on here."

After a short interview, she settled him on a gurney behind a green-and-yellow-striped curtain and left him alone to wait for a doctor. Clay stared at the ceiling tiles.

"You're certain it was not a heart attack?" A woman's strident tone carried through the room.

"Miss Zimmermann, I'll run more tests on your father, of course, but so far it looks like angina, not a heart attack."

A man's soothing voice carried across the small space. "He's responded to the nitroglycerin and is resting comfortably. I do want to keep him overnight to complete a battery of tests. He will be back from the CAT scan soon."

Clay heard a shuffle of feet then she spoke again. "Should we go to San Antonio? My mother is on her way."

Then doctor-speak, "I don't believe it's warranted—"

A curtain swished and crepe soles crossed the linoleum floor then he heard a heavy sob. Clay felt for the woman beside him. His grandfather's heart problems had kept his family on edge.

A sudden clatter and a sharp exclamation startled him. The curtains parted and a brown-haired woman's head appeared.

"Um, excuse me. I dropped my phone." She bent her knees and scurried to pick it up.

"No problem." Clay smiled at her. "Hope your dad gets better soon."

She straightened. He gazed at wide brown eyes, a spatter of freckles, and a frown.

"Sorry, miss. I just overheard the doctor—"

"That was a private conversation."

The girl's acerbic words made Clay flinch. He extended a hand. "I said I was sorry."

"Well." She whirled about and bumped into his gurney.

"Look out." Pain radiated up his leg. He shifted on the hard mattress and fought a wave of nausea. He clapped a hand over his eyes and settled against the pillow.

"Take a deep breath and blow it out."

Clay peeked between his fingers.

The woman stood by his bed. "Helps with the pain. Breathe in slowly then exhale completely." She waggled her hand in the air. "They teach that in birthing classes."

"I'm not pregnant." Clay dropped his hand to his side and took a shallow breath.

The woman leaned forward. "Deep breathing helps."

He wondered how many kids she had. Her ponytail drooped, her face was devoid of makeup, tears stained her cheeks, and a grimy film coated her forehead. Probably on welfare.

"Thanks for your concern." He closed his eyes and heard the swish of the curtain as it opened and shut. "Butt-in-ski."

The curtain jerked open again and she glared at him. "Well, excuuuuse me." Another swish and her pounding footsteps faded away.

Chapter 2

Professor Wurst shoved the wooden door open wide so Clay could maneuver into a small, musty-smelling living area. He inched forward on his crutches, the throb of his knee matching the stab of each crutch under his arm. A drop of perspiration trickled down his back.

"I'm glad for you to use our house." The professor brushed past him, set a small sack on the end table, and tugged an old sheet from a faded floral sofa. Dust danced in the air and Clay sneezed. "*Geusundheit.* Sit. Sit. Things here are not fancy, but they serve a purpose."

Clay dropped to the couch, set his crutches on the floor, and sighed. "I'm really grateful for a place to stay, Professor. Mighty kind of you." He peered around the small room, which was probably no more than ten feet wide. He could see all the way to the back door.

"This house is not used much. It was." The older man perched on a wooden stool and faced Clay. " 'Tis called a Sunday house and was in much use during my childhood." He chuckled and pointed to a loft. "Many nights I spent dreaming up there."

"A Sunday house?" Clay looked at the ladder rising to a loft. He raised a brow.

"Early Fredericksburg settlers lived far from town, and

church was their social life. They received a plot of ground to build a small place to spend Saturday night and go to church on Sunday." He waved his hand. "Thus the Sunday house. Small, inexpensive, furnished bare bones, but a place to lay your head and rest. My family owned a homestead many years ago and have since sold it. But we still maintain our little home." His eyes twinkled. "My sisters and I cannot bear to part with the memories that echo inside these walls." He sighed. "The stories they could tell." He clapped his hands on his thighs, rose, and turned on a fan. "But for you, Clay, it's a respite. I know you can't return to the campsite on crutches, and right now there's no one to drive you back to A&M. Here you'll be comfortable until it's time to return home."

A spring stabbed his backside and Clay shifted on the sofa. Comfortable was a relative word. "Thank you, sir, for your kindness."

Professor Wurst walked to the next room and talked over his shoulder. "In here is a small kitchen with a twin bed so you won't have to sleep on"—he pointed at the sofa—"*der plage*. The devil sofa. How I know it is the devil, you have to ask my wife." He laughed. "We have brought things into this century, so you'll find a microwave and a refrigerator. And indoor plumbing. I've left a message with my neighbor, Katherine Zimmermann, explaining the situation. She'll feed you." He rubbed his stomach. "I almost wish I could stay for some of Katie's dumplings." He brushed his hands together. "But I have students—"

"Yes sir. I'm sure I'll be fine." Clay lifted his cell phone. "If they have pizza delivery, it's no problem."

"Then I will leave you." The professor tapped the white sack on the end table by Clay. "Here's your prescription. I'd take the pain pills as directed for the first couple of days. Don't play heroic and tear anything else."

"No, sir. One ACL is enough for me." Clay rubbed the brace over his knee. "I'll be fine."

With a nod, the professor headed toward the door. "Take care, rest, and I'll be in touch soon."

As the door whooshed shut another round of dust motes filled the air, leaving Clay stuck in place. He ran his hand over his face and sighed. "Great. This is just great." He slid his leg up on the cushions and leaned back against the sofa's arm. He tapped the screen on his cell phone to Google his location. "What is there to do in this town? Can't stay cooped up here forever." He yawned and closed his eyes, the effects of the pain medication dragging him down. His phone slid to his chest.

"Mama, what do you need me to do?" Gwen toyed with a black plastic fork on the tabletop. The small bistro on Main Street buzzed with midday diners. The smell of fresh bread wafted through the air but wasn't enticing as it usually was. Worry tempered her appetite.

Hannah Zimmermann turned her red-rimmed eyes on her daughter, her face had been wan in the hospital's fluorescent lighting. "Gwen, what we need now is money." Her voice was tense. She held her hands out, palms up. "There's no other way to say it. I know you gave up school to help at the orchard, but that's work Rob can do. We need cash. Period. This hospital bill and medication will set us back—" Her brows drew together and she shook her head. "The drought's hit the orchard hard and we're already in the pink." Her lips turned up slightly. "Not quite in the red, but really close. And your daddy will worry himself into the grave after he hears the news."

Indeed the thought of her father on bed rest for a month or so made Gwen shiver. She'd never seen her father still. He buzzed with activity.

"Dr. Hawkins said he'd be fine but he did need to slow down. And he needs quiet and rest for a few weeks. How are we going to accomplish that?" Hannah dabbed her eyes with a napkin.

"Guess we can kidnap him." Gwen patted her mother's arm. "You two go to the beach."

"If only that would work. I'd go in a heartbeat." Hannah shook her head.

"You did marry the hardest head in the whole Zimmermann clan, Hannah. You knew that from the start." Katherine Zimmermann pulled out a chair from the table and sat down. She wiggled a cup of orange Jell-O in Hannah's face. "You need to eat a bite of something. This is light. Force it down."

Gwen smiled. "Aunt Katie, Daddy may be hardheaded, but you might reign for bossy."

"Gwendolyn." Hannah gasped.

Katie laughed. "You are so right, Gwennie. And not the first person to tell me so." She propped her elbows on the table. "Let's connive. I have some ideas and opinions, if you want to hear them. If not. . ." She sat straight up, folded her arms across her chest, and said, "I'll keep my mouth shut."

Gwen bit her lip. *As if.* Katie Zimmermann had never kept her opinions to herself.

Hannah opened the Jell-O, took a bite, and swallowed. She cradled the container in her hands and stared at her sister-in-law. "Tell me."

"I need help at the store. You need money, Hannah." Katie pointed at her niece. "Gwen is available to work for me. I can loan you what you need, and she'll work it off."

Gwen's stomach seized. Indentured servant? She closed her eyes for a second.

"Don't worry, honey." Katie patted her hand. "I'll create a paycheck for you, too." She stared into her niece's eyes. "This is the only way my brother will accept help. He's never going to stand for a 'handout' and you know it. If he feels the money's being earned—"

"He'll let me work." Gwen nodded. Summer school had evaporated, would working off a debt to her aunt eat up the fall semester? But what choice did she have? "What time would you like me to report tomorrow?"

Katie laughed. "First let's get you settled in town. While your mom uses your car, you'd be able to walk to work if you stayed in the Sunday house." Her lips tipped up. "A tiny space of your own."

Gwen's pulse tripped. She loved the Zimmermann Sunday house, and privacy—well, it was something she'd seldom been afforded. Maybe she could study or even take an online class since the library was so close. They probably had a hotspot for Wi-Fi.

"I like this plan." She smiled at her aunt then looked at her mother. "What do you think, Mama?"

Hannah pinched the bridge of her nose, her elbow propped on the table. After a deep sigh, she glanced at her daughter, eyes welling with tears. "You'd be okay with this?"

Gwen nodded.

Her mother stared at her for a moment then slapped her hands on the table. "I think we girls might have saved the day." She reached for Gwen's hand. "Thank you, darling girl."

Wi-Fi, privacy, some spending money? "I'm very willing, Mama." She reached out her other hand to her aunt. "Deal, Aunt Katie?"

Katie laughed and squeezed Gwen's fingers. "Deal. Now the bossy aunt is your boss."

Chapter 3

Gwen plopped her loaded suitcase on the white iron bedstead and stepped to open a window. She'd forgotten the lack of air-conditioning in the tiny quarters, which would be brutal during a Texas June. She flipped the switch on a small oscillating fan, stirring the hot air, and pulled her ponytail tighter. "I can do this. I can do this." Perspiration dotted her lip, and she wiped it away with her shoulder.

She'd always loved the loft and chosen it over the small bedroom downstairs. It felt. . .safer upstairs. The loft held three beds. She'd chosen the twin bed closest to the window, despite the lumpy mattress. She eyed the two full-sized beds covered in matching quilts. Wedding ring pattern with faded, yellow backing. "Imagine clumping up in here with the whole family." Gwen frowned. "I'm not so sure I'd enjoy that. Even once a week."

She hung her blouses and jeans in the small armoire and pulled a bag of toiletries from the suitcase to carry downstairs to the tiny bathroom. She thought of her university dorm room and her suite mates. Privacy here—a true luxury—but lonely. She'd have to find something to do in the evenings. With no television, she'd be driven to the library with her laptop. Driven into air-conditioning, too. "Lord, let there be an online class I can take while I soak up cool air."

A loud clatter from outside caught her attention. She peered out the window. The racket came from the small house next door—another Sunday house belonging to a family she hadn't seen in ages. Something moved about inside. Gwen bit her lip. An intruder? She bent low in an effort to see in the kitchen window. A large shadow crossed the floor.

"Someone's definitely in there." Gwen rose on her tiptoes to look at the driveway. No car. Should she call Aunt Katie? The police? "Or mind my own business." She stepped away from the window, tucked her cell phone in her pocket, and climbed down the loft ladder.

Curiosity stirred and she crept onto the front porch. Since the little houses were less than thirty feet apart, she tiptoed across the noisy boards. If it were an intruder, she'd call the police for sure. But how would she know?

Gwen stepped off the porch and sidled up to the window of the Wurst house. She could hear a fan whirring and something clumping about. She tipped her head, her face nearly brushing the stonework between the windows.

"Ridiculous." A deep voice rumbled. "Just stupid."

A stomp and another clatter startled Gwen. She rose to peek inside.

Whump.

Something crashed against the window frame. Gwen jumped backward and fell with a loud *oomph*. She rolled to her side and gasped for air.

"Who's out there?" The voice roared.

Gwen scrambled to her feet and dusted her capris. She stared at the man framed by the window, then tipped her head and glared at him. Where had she seen this guy?

"What are you doing looking in the window?" The man shook his finger at her. "Some kind of Peeping Tom?" His hand stilled and he frowned. "You?" He leaned forward and propped his hands on the windowsill. "You were at the hospital."

"Hospital?" Gwen squeaked.

"Breathe deep. Breathe deep." The guy singsonged in an imitation of Gwen.

"Oh, Mr. Polite." Gwen brushed her hands together, her palms stinging from the fall.

"I see you continue your butt-in-ski ways." He waved his hand toward her.

"I do not." Heat crept up Gwen's cheeks and she floundered for words. "Being a good neighbor, I was—I was—concerned about the Wurst house when I heard all the commotion."

The man sighed and ran a hand through his hair, deflated. "Yeah, well, sorry about that. I'm battling major frustration right now and took it out on this." He raised a crutch. "Launched it farther than I intended."

Gwen swallowed. The man's brown eyes held a hint of sadness. A stick of copper-colored hair formed a definite cowlick. His damp university T-shirt clung to a well-developed set of muscles.

"Really hot today." Gwen swallowed. Interesting topic of conversation. Then again, why did she want a conversation with him? "Are you visiting the Wurst family?"

"Not really." He pointed down. "Tore something in my knee. Can't continue the Enchanted Rock excursion, and right now there's no one to drive me back to College Station, so the professor stuck me here." He rubbed a hand over his face. "And you are right, it is hot." Droopy eyes gazed back at her.

She hesitated. "Would you like something to drink? I have lemonade." *Gwen. Seriously?*

His eyes brightened. "That would rock." He laughed. "Maneuvering about and carrying stuff still isn't in my act."

Gwen smiled. "I'll be over in a second." She wheeled about and jumped onto her porch. Inside the bathroom, she ran a damp washcloth over her face and tightened the scrunchie holding her ponytail. She reached for her makeup bag then stopped. "What am I doing?" She looked at her reflection. "Gwendolyn, do not make a fool of yourself. Just be polite. Neighborly." She blinked. "And overlook the fact that he is a hunk."

Clay hopped on one leg to the bathroom. He washed his face and swiped at the ever-present cowlick. He'd change shirts and freshen up, but in this heat it was pointless. He sniffed an underarm then swiped on another layer of deodorant.

"How did settlers ever stand each other in close quarters?" He eyed his reflection. Would have to do. He wasn't shaving for some welfare woman he didn't even know. But it was company. Someone to talk with. He missed people.

The rap at the front door startled him. "Come in." He

tilted around and hopped through the small kitchen to the living room.

Using her foot, the woman shoved the screen door against its frame with a *pop*, then caught it with her hip to swing it open. She tipped her head. "Way to open the door with no hands." She carried two large mugs. "Frosty lemonade." She waited until he collapsed on the plage—he now understood the nickname devil couch—then handed him a glass.

"Thank you, ma'am."

She held up her glass. "I know these are beer mugs. I don't drink beer. But someone left them in the freezer and I decided they'd be really good with the lemonade. I don't like beer. Tastes nasty. Of course, in this area many people do drink beer, and if someone did, I suppose a glass like this would make it—"

Clay smiled. "I appreciate the lemonade and understand the use of the mug." He pointed to a ladder-back chair. "Won't you sit down?"

She inched toward the chair, her eyes never leaving his face.

He lifted the glass. "I'm Clay Tanner, and I appreciate your thoughtfulness."

"Gwen Zimmermann." She looked past him. "You're welcome."

"Hot, isn't it?"

"Yes." She sipped and nodded toward the small fan. "You need to put that closer to the window."

"Um-hm. Haven't figured out the logistics of moving it yet." He tapped the brace on his knee. "This slows me down."

"Oh." Gwen shot to her feet. "I'll take care of that." She dragged a small TV tray in front of the window, unplugged the fan, and set it where it could catch a good breeze. She pointed it at the sofa. "There. That will help." The breeze lifted hair from her forehead, exposing freckles.

"Thanks."

She glanced at his brace. "How long do you have to wear that?"

"I return to the doctor next week. We'll see." Clay swallowed the sweet, cold lemonade. "How's your dad? Was it a heart attack?"

"No. Thankfully." Gwen rolled her eyes. "He's so ornery. He has to rest for a few weeks and that's like tying a hawk to a post. I'm not envying my mom." She ran her finger through the condensation on the glass. "I'm in town to work for my aunt. She has an antique store on Main."

"Maybe I can visit when I'm more proficient on these sticks." Clay sighed. "I'm bored out of my mind." He lifted his cell phone. "I know this is smart, but it's not a great companion 24-7."

"Won't your family come get you?" Gwen sat down.

Clay bit his lip. "My parents are overseas right now. I'm not even sure where." He watched her eyes widen. "They are archaeologists and travel extensively. Having lived in boarding schools for years, you'd think I'd be happy for solitude."

"You lived in a boarding school?"

"I did. For four years." He smiled as she gaped at him. "It's not *Oliver Twist* or anything. They did feed us more than porridge and I received a great education." A twinge of loneliness swept over him. "And I had some holidays with my parents."

"Wow." Gwen drank deeply from her glass. After a moment she sighed. "I've never ever known someone who went to a boarding school. Sounds so—expensive and fancy. Like on TV or in the movies."

Clay laughed. This girl seemed quite transparent. Whatever entered her brain exited her mouth. He wondered if that was a good trait.

"And you're an Aggie." She pointed at his shirt. "Great school."

"Amazing school." He plucked at the damp fabric. "I've made lasting friendships there." He lifted his head. "And many of my geologist buddies are on Enchanted Rock as we speak."

"Bummer."

"Pretty much sums it up." Clay shifted from the coiled spring stabbing him. He reached for a throw pillow and lifted his leg. Before he could lower it, Gwen was at his side. She tugged the pillow from his hand and placed it beneath his knee. "Thank you." She smelled sweet. He hoped he did, too. He felt his ears redden at the thought. "You're pretty handy."

"I've done some nursing. Can't have a clumsy brother and not do some patching up." She returned to her chair.

"You lived in Fredericksburg your whole life?"

"Um-hmm. But I'm in school now. In San Antonio." She sipped. "Was going to summer school, but then family duty called." She groaned. "Seems like I'm marching in place."

Clay nodded. "I hear you. Feel the same way. Supposed to finish up this project for extra credit and grab my master's degree in August." He shook his head. "Now what? With this setback, I'm not sure."

"Your degree will be in geology? What will you do? Teach?"

A good question. "Have to see what opens up. My parents, of course, want me to join them. Use what I learned about formation of sites through geological processes and the effects on buried artifacts. But I don't know—" Heat crept up his face and his throat tightened. The idea of following in his dad's footsteps always made his throat tighten and pulse race. He sighed.

"Leg feel okay? You need ice?" The girl's piercing brown eyes probed his face.

"Yeah, it's fine. Thanks."

She reached for her half-empty glass. "Guess I should go."

Clay took a swallow of lemonade. "If you have to."

"Well, I don't have to. I mean, I don't go to work until tomorrow." She perched on the edge of the chair and leaned forward. "The store is just a couple of blocks from here. I'll walk over because my mom is using my car, since my brother has to have the truck at the orchard. Rob, my brother, will keep things running while I'm in town. He's Dad's right-hand man, but doesn't like working at the peach stand or the orchard. Me, I always wanted to farm. So I'm learning about horticulture and studying business. I hope, I mean, I'm—" The words stopped. She blushed a deep red. "I talk a lot when I'm nervous."

Clay chuckled. "I noticed."

Her eyes widened. "You don't have to be rude." She started to stand.

"Hey, butt-in-ski, sit down." He grinned. "You're better than TV."

Chapter 4

Gwen leaned against the store counter and watched passersby on the sidewalk, her mind drifting to Clay. Besides being handsome with that copper-colored hair and almost golden eyes, he was good company. After she'd gotten over her aggravation at another nickname, she'd enjoyed their evening of chatter. His love for all things Texas A&M became obvious when he discussed his school.

"I'd never be here without my scholarship." He bragged on the corps of cadets and their service to the country and the football team he'd played on. Since Gwen hadn't followed sports closely other than their local high school, she listened intently. You couldn't live in Texas and not know about the rivalry between his college and the University of Texas. She couldn't wait until he met Aunt Katie, a rabid UT fan. The thought made her chuckle. She wished she could have seen Clay in a football uniform. A flush crept up her cheeks.

An older woman approached the counter, interrupting her daydream. Gwen tallied her purchases and punched the total in the cash register. The golden antique whirred and chimed—a sound she'd loved since childhood. The musty smell in the antique store had never bothered Gwen, though she'd heard some customers complain and march out through the doors. She loved being surrounded by things from days gone by. And she loved hearing the *oohs* and *ahhs* when people recognized items perched on the shelves. So many memories were stirred by the books, lamps, dolls, and clothing her aunt stocked.

"Seventeen seventy-five, please, ma'am." Gwen smiled at the lady.

"Do you know my mama's flour canister was exactly like this? Can't wait to show my sister. This has a name. Can't recall right off. Do you know?"

Gwen lifted the ivory container trimmed in gold and looked at the sticker affixed to the bottom. "German luster." She wrapped it in heavy paper and slipped it inside a bag. "I hope you will enjoy sharing it."

"Thank you, dear." The lady tucked the parcel under her arm and surveyed the bookshelf next to the counter. "Think I'll browse here, too, if you don't mind."

Why would I mind? Gwen smiled. "Enjoy." She grabbed a long-handled feather duster and stepped across the aisle. She flicked the feathers across the top shelf, dust flying from the Radio Flyer wagon on display, the cut-glass candy dish, and a black rotary-dial telephone. A loud sneeze startled her. She swiveled about, the long-handled duster slapping into the woman's elbow. The lady lurched forward, and her package flew from under her arm.

"Oh my word." The woman howled. The antique canister angled for the floor and its demise if Gwen hadn't wrapped it securely. Inches from a crash, a large hand looped through the twine handles and caught the sack.

Clay held up the bag and smiled at the customer. "I believe this belongs to you?"

"Thank you, kind sir." The woman actually batted her eyes at him and simpered, "You have no idea how much I appreciate your kindness. This antique is so special to me."

Gwen stifled a laugh.

"I hope it holds only pleasant memories, ma'am." Clay ducked his head. Gwen realized if he were wearing a hat, he'd tip it. Her chest hurt. She held her breath, and finally let it out in a *whoosh*. Clay looked at her, his eyes twinkling. Then he touched the lady's elbow. "Have you had an opportunity to look at the other priceless antiques in the store? I believe downstairs holds more treasures."

The lady's eyes brightened. "Really? I haven't been down there." She placed her package by the cash register and turned to Gwen. "May I leave this here, dear? And shop some more?"

Gwen nodded, afraid to speak lest her laughter annoy the woman.

The lady's gaze roved over Clay's face and down to his knee. She sighed and turned toward the stairs. "I'm sorry you're injured. I'm sure you'd enjoy seeing the items down here, too."

"Maybe another time." Clay's smile left once the lady disappeared.

Gwen flapped the feather duster. "You made quite the impression. How did you know there were other 'treasures' downstairs? Have you been here before?" She walked behind the counter and tucked the package on a shelf for safety's sake.

"No. But when you go in one antique store after another, you can bet you will find treasures." He chuckled. "Or so my mom always said." Clay swiped at the lock of hair dangling across his forehead. "At least it's air-conditioned in here." He pointed a crutch toward a stool. "May I sit on that? Will it hold me?"

Gwen stepped to the end of the counter and tugged the stool closer to him. "Yes, it will hold your brawn. Sit." He perched on the stool and she leaned against the counter. "You crutched all of three blocks? In this heat? Want some water?"

Clay reached into a fanny pack tucked around his waist. "Got some."

"Nice accessory." Gwen pointed to the fanny pack. "Stylish. At least on the senior citizens and winter Texans."

Clay laughed. "Hey, it's inventive. I need something to carry stuff. Stopped at Dooley's 5 and 10 to purchase this baby." He lifted it from his waist and gave it a pat. "Cost more than five and ten, but it works."

"No maroon for A&M?"

"Nope." Clay watched two ladies enter the store. He bent forward and whispered, "Want me to charm them, too?"

"Work your magic, buddy." Gwen giggled. What was it about this hulking man that brought out the laughter? He was silly and she'd had too little silly in her life lately. The night before he had regaled her with tales of boarding school and college, and she laughed until her sides hurt. Clay was quite the entertainer.

He swiveled on the stool, leaned forward, and waved his hand. "Welcome, ladies. Is this your first time in Fredericksburg?"

"Why, yes, it is." A gray-haired lady, perfectly coifed, and in a stylish jogging suit, which probably never felt a tinge of perspiration, stepped closer to Clay. "It's a lovely town. Are you a local?"

"No, ma'am, but I got here as quickly as I could." He flashed a bright smile. "Please feel free to browse, especially the area downstairs with other treasures from days gone by. However, I'm sure you're too young to recognize most of the—"

The lady's cheeks turned pink and she placed her hand on her face. "Oh my goodness. You are full of smooth talk, young man." Again, a woman simpered in front of Clay. Gwen bit her lip. No laughing at customers allowed. She watched the interaction with amusement until the women trailed down the steps in search of more reminiscences.

"You've got that sales spiel nailed. Guess my aunt will need to hire you as a pitchman." Gwen ran her hand along the glass countertop. "Maybe you could stand outside with placards, like a sandwich man, and advertise."

Clay swept the hair from his face. "Not outside. That's why I'm here. In search of cool." He flapped his T-shirt from his chest. "I can only take so many hours sitting in front of a whirring fan. The white noise makes me sleepy; I topple over on that devil-couch and wake up drenched and wrenched." He glanced at his watch. "You get any break for lunch?"

Gwen nodded. "Aunt Katie will be here soon."

A frown crossed Clay's face. "Katherine Zimmermann?"

"Yep. My aunt."

"She's going to cook for me, Professor Wurst said."

Gwen held out her hands, palms up. "News to me. But for sure I won't be the cook, because that is so not my strong suit."

Clay smiled his bright smile. "Even for poor injured me?"

"Even for poor injured you." Gwen sighed. "My mama had me in the kitchen as a teenager and then finally gave up. Just not something I do well."

The door opened and a *whoosh* of hot air blew in along with Gwen's aunt. She stopped and eyed Clay and his crutch. "Now you wouldn't be the starving, injured college student I'm to feed, would you?"

Gwen laughed. "Does he look like he's starving?"

Clay held out his hand. "Clay Tanner, Miss Zimmermann. I'd be very grateful for a cup of soup or a crust of bread from you."

Katie threw back her head and let out a guffaw. "That's pure blarney. Are you Irish?"

"No, ma'am." He pointed to his T-shirt. "I'm an Aggie."

A frown crossed Katie's face. "Well, you might be getting only a crust of bread then. I bleed orange since I began dating a Longhorn."

"University of Texas is an excellent school, ma'am." Clay's eyes brightened. "I'm sure there are many wonderful reasons one chooses to go there." He bowed his head. "However, football is not one of them."

"Young man, you think you'll want to eat something I cook after that declaration of war?" She shook her finger at Clay. "Best be scared, very scared." A grin crossed her face. "Gwen, get him out of here and go to lunch."

"Will do. Be back shortly." Gwen grabbed her purse and pointed at the steps. "There are three ladies downstairs"—she glanced at Clay—"searching for treasure."

Her aunt's brow furrowed. "Treasure?"

Clay and Gwen laughed. He crutched to the door and opened it. Gwen flashed a look over her shoulder and said, "Explain later, Auntie-dear." She held the door for Clay to exit and followed behind him onto the crowded sidewalk. "Maybe I'd better walk in front and blaze a trail."

"Nah, I'd rather you walk beside me, so we can talk."

A soft glow kindled in Gwen's heart and spread through her middle. She'd not had a gentleman interested in talking with her in a long while. She'd been so focused on school that frivolity and relaxing in the presence of a man had escaped her. She slowed her steps to Clay's pace. "So talk, buddy. What's new this day?"

What's new? Clay wanted to tell her how he'd tossed and turned during the night. Not because of his knee or the heat, but because of a brown-eyed girl next door. He'd been captivated by Gwen's lack of pretense. The college women he'd dated in the last few years had been all about themselves, trying to leave the right impression. Hunters. That's what he had termed them. And he wasn't ready to be bagged by anyone. No. Gwen Zimmermann had plans for the future like he did, so there were no expectations. Clay had relaxed and enjoyed a couple of hours of pure fun. He awoke missing her presence and made a decision to seek her out.

After a cold shower—Professor Wurst needed a new hot-water heater—Clay dressed and headed toward town. He was grateful for benches along the crowded walkway, the open doors of some shops that blasted cold air outside, and made it to the right antique store after he'd dived into three others. Finding Gwen with a feather duster in her hand brought a smile to his face. Domestic? Maybe not. Intriguing? Definitely.

"That place serves wonderful food." Gwen pointed to the Auslander Restaurant. "And we only have to cross one street." Her brows lifted.

"Fine with me."

Inside the restaurant a cacophony of sound met his ears. Music, chatter, a television broadcast, and the clatter of dishes indicated tourists found this restaurant worth visiting. A saucy waitress showed them to a plank table near the wall, where Clay propped his crutches and slid into a chair.

The tantalizing aroma of smoked meat filled the air. "Smells good." A large fireplace centered on one wall held up a deer's head with the largest spread of antlers Clay had ever seen. He spotted another one on the sidewall. Over the bar was a stuffed Longhorn. Definitely not a PETA-friendly place.

"Do you like sauerkraut?"

Clay wrinkled his nose. "I don't think so."

Gwen laughed. "Worth trying, especially here in the heart of German cuisine." She bent over the menu and skimmed the page. "Awesome schnitzel, too."

"Kraut, links, and beer." Clay laughed. "Sounds like a winning combo to me."

"Except for the beer part, you're right." She sighed. "So many choices, so little time. But I think I'll opt for today's special."

The waitress took their order and returned with heaping plates of sausage, fried potatoes, and red cabbage. Clay shoved the red part to one side. He cut into a link and sighed as he chewed.

"Best food I've had since I've been here." He looked up to see Gwen's bowed head and became silent, embarrassed that he'd interrupted.

She didn't seem to notice as she took a bite of cabbage and wiped her mouth on a napkin. "Wait until Aunt Katie starts to feed you." She smiled and her eyes brightened. "Request a peach bread pudding. She makes the best, according to her friend, Phil. He seems to be an expert on bread pudding since he's a world-traveler."

Clay looked around the room. "Do you see our waitress? Think I want her to pull me a pint."

"Beer? " Gwen stiffened in her chair.

He watched her face grow red. "Would you rather I not drink?"

She nodded.

Clay lifted his water glass in a toast. "Then I shall defer to the lady." He continued his meal, but curiosity niggled at him. "Your family teetotalers?"

Gwen's mouth tightened. "Had one in the family who abused alcohol. Just doesn't go with our lifestyle now, let's put it that way."

"And what lifestyle"—Clay drew quotes in the air with his fingers—"would that be?"

She toyed with her knife. "I try to live a Christian life. And I just don't believe drinking fits in." Gwen shook her head. "I'm not saying a bit of spirits every now and then is wrong. It's not my place to judge anyone or tell you what your convictions should be. It's just not something I'd do."

Clay nodded. "I see." He cut into another piece of sausage and chewed slowly. *Christian, praying before meals.* Might draw a line in the sand for their friendship. But who would he talk with during this forced time of rest if he alienated Gwen? He felt his middle tighten. He'd miss her presence too much.

The waitress returned with their bill. Gwen reached for the leather case at the same time he did and their fingers touched. Clay jerked back as though he'd hit an electrical current. He rubbed his hand down his thigh, the tingle still evident.

Gwen tapped the folder. "I'll get this one. You're my guest today."

His dry mouth wouldn't form words. He watched her open her purse, wrinkle her cute nose, and peer into a wallet. She pulled out several bills and stuffed them in the folder.

"You ready?" Gwen slid his crutches within easy reach

and stood. "I'm really glad you were able to lunch with me."

"Sure," he croaked. He wanted to examine his hand and see if it was branded. "Next time's my treat." Was he ready? Clay could hardly wait.

Chapter 5

An annoying chime from Gwen's cell phone jolted her awake the next morning. She groaned and groped about to find it under the bed.

HEY. CAN U GET CAR?

A smile tugged at her lips. Why shouldn't she be awakened by the one about whom she'd been dreaming? She rubbed her eyes with the back of her hand and tapped letters. MAY B. WHY? Last night she had pulled wicker rockers from the storage shed to Clay's front porch and heaped Blue Bell Rocky Road ice cream in two bowls. They'd sat in the creaking rockers, eating, and she'd spilled her dreams.

"I've always loved wildflowers, and this area is famous for the Fredericksburg Wildseed Farm." She waved her hands, almost upsetting the bowl in her lap. "It's gorgeous in spring, every color under the rainbow spread out before you. I'd like to develop the unused property behind our family's orchard. It's already a field of wildflowers, planted by my great-grandmother, but if it were properly cultivated—"

Clay licked his spoon and pointed it at her. "You could make a profit."

"Exactly." She spun to face him. "Daddy doesn't have time, especially now, and I'd love to put that land to use. Why, we could make good money from just lavender. Think how many

lavender products there are. From lavender baby shampoo to shower gel at Bath & Body Works to natural sleep aids. And it smells so wonderful—imagine a whole field, almost purple in the sunset. I don't think it would be that difficult. I've been studying horticulture websites about the actual planting and I could use my associate business degree to get the business started. Since the store is already there, the peach stand would be a good place to set up shop. And we could supply worldwide with the use of the Internet. I envision—" She flopped against the wicker rocker out of breath. A flush crept up her cheeks. "Here I go, rattling on." She took a huge bite of ice cream and an immediate brain freeze burned in her head.

"You aren't rattling." Clay patted the arm of his chair. "You're dreaming big. And that's a good thing." He rocked back and forth. "Maybe I'll dream big someday," he murmured around the chocolate in his mouth.

Gwen ran her hand over her hair and yawned, struggling to wake up. She sighed and glanced at the silent phone. She crawled out from under the sheet and made a trip downstairs to the bathroom, cell at the ready, and picked up her toothbrush. She squirted toothpaste on the brush and stared at her reflection in the mirror.

Never did spill his dreams.

The phone chimed. Gwen rinsed her mouth, dried her hands, and picked it up.

Trip to Ench Rock. Get my equip. Can u?

Enchanted Rock? She glanced at the clock in the living room. No reason they couldn't make it out there and back before she had to go to work. She'd ask Rob to bring her the car. One tap of speed dial and her brother answered on the third ring.

"Seriously, Gwen? I've got work to do," Rob grumbled.

"Please, little brother. You'll get to meet Aggie-guy. You two can talk football."

Silence met her plea. "Rob. Please. It won't take but twenty minutes to get here, and we'll drop you off on the way to the rock." She added a little whine, "I've been stranded for days without wheels."

Rob groaned. "You'll have to use my truck. Dad gets released from the hospital today, and Mom will need the car."

"He's coming home?" Gwen's pulse picked up speed. "Mom didn't tell me that last night."

"She didn't know. Doctor told her this morning." He blew out a breath. "Okay. Let me unload and I'll be there by nine."

"Thanks, little brother." Gwen tapped END and then a 2 to reach her mom. The call went straight to voice mail. "No reception in the hospital, I guess." She rushed to the loft and tugged on clothes then climbed down the ladder and walked to the kitchen window. "Aggie-man," she yelled.

Clay appeared at his window. "Good morning." He lifted a coffee cup in salute. "Hope my text didn't wake you."

"Not really." She'd been in the gray area of sleep, dreaming of him, not wanting to awaken, but she'd never admit that. "My brother's bringing his truck, so we can get your stuff. He'll be here in about thirty minutes."

"Thanks, pal." Clay set the coffee cup on the windowsill and slid a crutch under his arm. "I'll be ready in a few."

Gwen listened to the *thump*, *thump* of his receding steps

and grinned. She reached into the fridge and grabbed a cola then cut up a peach and nibbled it for breakfast, bent over the sink to catch the juice dribbling down her chin. She wiped her face with a dish towel. "Umm. Nothing like a fresh Fredericksburg peach." Surveying the kitchen counter, she noted only a few were left. She'd have to pick up more when they dropped Rob off.

After washing her hands, Gwen found her flip-flops, purse, and scrunchie. She closed the front door behind her and sat on the front steps. An early morning breeze kissed her cheeks, and a mockingbird chattered at her for invading its space. "Don't worry, buddy, I'm out of here in a minute." She scooped hair from her neck, wound the scrunchie from her wrist, and pulled it into a ponytail.

Clay hitched across the yard and joined Gwen, collapsing on the step and bumping her shoulder. "Who you talking to?"

A subtle hint of cologne tickled her nose. The morning light brought out flecks of gold in his irises and a stubble of red whiskers along his jawline. "Just a bird." Gwen watched as he stretched his long leg out next to hers. She felt heat rush to her cheeks.

"Really appreciate your help. I hate to leave my stuff with the others." Clay sighed. "And there are a couple of books I'd like to retrieve." He ran a finger under the edge of his brace. "Something to read and relieve the boredom."

"How's the leg doing?"

"Okay. Just an aggravation." He huffed. "I'm tired of sitting around, but it's such a hassle to go anywhere."

"I'll keep a mode of transportation, and you can go to

church with us in the morning. Change of pace." Gwen bit her lip. A sudden desire to see Clay at worship services flooded her.

Clay leaned back on his elbows and eyed her. "Church?"

Well, in for a penny, as her dad used to say. "Yes, we go to Fredericksburg Community Church every Sunday morning. I'll keep the truck and we can go. Doesn't start until eleven, so you can get your beauty rest."

Clay fixed his eyes on something across the street. "I haven't been to a church service since I was a kid."

"Really?" Gwen's stomach knotted. Did this man know about Jesus? She winged a prayer heavenward. "Won't you come? Mom and Dad would like to meet you. He comes home from the hospital today."

"And he'll be in church tomorrow after being in the hospital?" Clay's brows lifted.

"Most likely. And we can pick up fried chicken to take home and eat. Surprise my mom. She usually cooks a big dinner, but I imagine she'll have her hands full with Daddy." Gwen bumped Clay's shoulder. "Sound like a plan?"

Clay chuckled. "Maybe so. Again, anything to relieve the boredom."

Gwen pressed her lips together. Getting to know the Lord would surely relieve his boredom. She'd have to talk to Him about how she could help present the plan of salvation.

A horn honked and Rob pulled into the driveway. Gwen slid a crutch toward Clay and he clumped to the passenger door behind her.

"Let me climb in the backseat, and you'll have more room

to stretch out your leg," she said and clambered in. "Rob, this is my neighbor, Clay Tanner."

"Thanks for bringing us a mode of transportation." A sheen of perspiration crossed Clay's forehead after he settled into the seat.

"Not a problem." Rob flipped the air-conditioner switch to high. "Bet you could use some cool air. I don't know how y'all are standing those accommodations." He reversed the truck and pulled onto the street. "Aggie, huh? My dream."

Gwen sat back and listened as the two talked. Rob spilled out college plans she'd never heard. He'd been out of high school a year and she worried he'd not further his education. Such a smart guy, it would be a waste if he didn't. The cool air, drone of their conversation, and the truck's motor soothed her.

From her vantage point, she could see Clay's strong profile, long eyelashes, and crooked grin. Her heart sped up. This sudden attraction to a man surprised her. She'd been so busy with college and her family, there'd been no time to date. And certainly none of her high school classmates who'd labeled her Peach-girl interested her. But Clay certainly did. Yes, he did.

Rob chattered, much to Clay's relief. It distracted him from the throb in his knee. Climbing up into the truck might not have been the best idea of the morning. But here he was. On the way to Enchanted Rock where he'd have to repeat the process. He glanced back at Gwen and gave her a smile.

Her brown ponytail, a bit off center, swung back and forth when she shook her head, feigning chatter and pointing at her brother. Clay stifled a laugh. The Zimmermann kids did have a gift for gab.

Clay shifted and straightened his leg, relieving some of the pressure. He patted his new accessory, the fanny pack, and felt the bottle of pain meds. Might need one of those for the trip back. With thoughts of his brown-eyed neighbor and physical discomfort, he'd not slept worth a flip since his injury.

"—church?" Rob looked at him.

"I'm sorry, what did you say?" Clay suspected the question was the same one his sister had asked a few minutes earlier. How did he feel about attending a church service?

Rob turned from the highway into the parking lot of the Zimmermann Orchard store.

"Our humble home away from home." Rob thrust the gearshift into PARK and turned to face his sister. "Plenty of gas. See y'all in a bit." He opened the truck's door and reached for the cab door to let his sister out. "Hope to see you in the morning, Clay."

Gwen slipped from the truck and into the driver's seat. She pushed a button and arranged the seat to accommodate her small frame. "Thanks, bro."

"Yeah, thanks, Rob. See you later." Clay didn't agree to "in the morning." His stomach churned at the thought of a dreary service, a droning pastor, and a heavy-footed organist. He'd attended services with his grandmother in Connecticut and found little to enjoy. He was sure church in Fredericksburg would be no different.

"All set, buddy?" Gwen grinned at him.

Clay nodded and smiled, her grin infectious. The cool air in the truck's cab was filled with Gwen's sweet scent. Not a heavy perfume, something light. She wore cutoffs, flip-flops, and no makeup and certainly hadn't spent hours before the mirror fixing her hair. Maybe an hour worth of misery in the morning would be time well spent. And it would be cooler. "All set." He'd give her his answer on the way home. This no-frills woman intrigued him.

Chapter 6

Gwen pulled onto the highway for the thirty-minute drive, and a misty rain began to brush the air. She flipped on the wipers and groaned at the muddy mess on the windshield. "Been so long since we've had rain, I'm surprised these even work."

Clay heaved a sigh and stared out the window. "All this means is a slippery slope for me. I don't see how I can climb the rock with crutches and rain." He stomped his good foot against the floorboard. "Makes me furious. Three steps forward and two back."

"Crippled steps at that." Gwen's lips tipped up.

"It's not funny."

"Sorry." She shot him a glance.

His dark eyes clouded with worry. "Dad pulled a lot of strings for me to go on this excursion and now I will tick him off. Again." Clay worried the hem of his shorts. "The story of our relationship, nothing new."

Gwen had no words to add since she was close to her dad. She couldn't imagine being separated from her family for such extended periods of time. Boarding school? She pressed her lips together and steered the truck around a slow-moving tractor on the shoulder of the road.

"Sorry, Gwen." He gave her a quick look. "Sound like a petulant brat."

She shrugged. "You don't owe me an apology."

Relief softened his features.

"Do you think we can still get your stuff or should we wait for another day?"

"No, I texted Larry earlier. He said he'd meet us in the parking lot. I'll send him another one and tell him to lug all my junk with him." Clay shifted in the seat and pulled his phone from his pocket. He tapped the screen then placed it in his lap. "Just disappointing. I thought maybe we could walk a path and I could show you where we'd camped."

"Maybe next time." Gwen grinned at him. "This drive is rather relaxing. We can make it again, maybe have a picnic." She bit her lip, her heart pounding loudly in her ears. Was *she* asking *him* on a date? No, just friends hanging out. *Right, Gwen. Clay Tanner is just a buddy.* Her breath caught in her throat and an unexpected ripple of excitement tickled her stomach.

She made the turn off Highway 16 onto a road leading to Enchanted Rock State Park. The mist had dissipated, leaving bright sunshine bouncing off the arid ground. Cactus, cedar bushes, and mesquite trees dotted the sides of the road. A few cows searched for bits of grass. She hit the brakes to cross a cattle guard just as a jackrabbit darted across the road.

Clay chuckled. "Guess he knew a woman was behind the wheel."

"Watch it, Aggie." Gwen's pulse picked up speed. His attitude had brightened with the morning sun.

Ahead, the amazing pink granite dome rose in splendor.

"Ahem." Clay cleared his throat. "As your official

geologist, here are some facts. The rock is a huge, pink granite exfoliation dome that rises 425 feet above ground, 1825 feet above sea level, and covers 640 acres. It is one of the largest batholiths in the United States."

"A batho—what?"

"Batholith. Means an underground rock formation uncovered by erosion." Clay straightened in his seat. "The guys at the camp are in undergrad—well, most of them—and are here to study the different rock formations. Larry and I are in charge of one group. Part of my last class before graduation." He pointed to the entrance and scooted up to grab his wallet from his back pocket. "I have a pass to allow us in. Just park and hand it to the ranger."

Gwen followed his instructions and carried the pass to a waiting ranger at the desk. "We won't be long."

The ranger extended a map and brochure, which Gwen tucked under her arm. She didn't want to rain on Clay's parade, but she'd explored this rock more than once with her family. However she'd never seen it through his eyes.

Inside the truck, Clay held his cell phone up. "Larry is on his way. Stop over there"—he pointed toward the huge rock—"and we'll meet him partway."

Clay clambered from the truck, his crutches banging the door and fender, hopped on one leg then steadied himself against the truck bed. Gwen circled around to meet him and gave a soft laugh. He looked like a school kid ready for a field trip. He slid on sunglasses. "Let's explore a bit."

The wide walkway before them had subtle steps cut into the ground, each step edged with a mesquite plank.

They crossed a dry creek bed on a wooden bridge. Pink granite bricks ran along the border of the small bridge. In the distance, the pink dome glittered. The jagged rocks in front of them resembled LEGOs randomly stacked, jutting in every direction.

"Cool, huh?" Clay paused for a breath. He pointed a crutch. "Indians thought there were spirits in the rocks because of the noises it makes."

Gwen stopped in her tracks and wrinkled a brow. "A noisy rock?"

He grinned. "Yep. But it's not spirits. They heat by day and cool at night so they contract, thus groaning noises."

Gwen laughed. "Guess these rocks already do cry out to tell of our God."

Clay tilted his head. "What do you mean?"

"Jesus said if His disciples kept quiet about Him, then the rocks would cry out."

"Bible verses." Clay lowered his gaze and sighed. "I think the only one I ever learned was 'Jesus wept.'" He hobbled farther on the bridge. "One summer when I was about six or seven, my grandmother hauled me to a week of church with other kids."

"Vacation Bible School, probably."

He nodded. "Think so. 'Bout the only time I had fun at her church, I promise you that."

Gwen smiled. "Not all churches are boring, Clay. Ours certainly isn't." She followed him on the bridge. "Which I hope you'll find out in the morning."

A tall, trim man clunked down the slope, a backpack

slung over his shoulder. His dark hair, threaded with silver, curled at the back of his neck, and he was in need of a shave. "Looks like you're on the mend." He clapped Clay on the back and extended a hand toward Gwen, his dark eyes twinkling. "Larry Glen. Are you the keeper of this lad?"

"Gwen." She smiled. "Driver at least."

Clay said, "Dude, don't give her any ideas. If she's my keeper, she might dump me out here. As it is, she's trying to haul me to church."

Larry's brows rose. "Not a bad idea. I'm having my own service over there in the morning"—he pointed to the rock's dome—"to be closer to the Lord."

Clay ran his hand over his face. "So you need me to unload that backpack?"

"Nah, I've got another. Just take this one with you. When do you get out of the brace?"

"I see the doctor on Wednesday. Know for sure then if surgery is in the future or not." Clay heaved a sigh. "Man, wish I could be with you."

"No, you don't. Heat, critters, and undergrads. You won't miss a thing. And Professor Wurst went back to campus, so there's nothing to do. The guys are making their own observations for his class and I'm pretty much babysitting." He patted Clay's arm and gave a playful shove. "Go enjoy city life."

"Don't have critters, but Professor's place isn't air-conditioned, so there's heat. Just hate to let people down—"

"Clay, you aren't letting anyone down. You had an accident." Larry leaned forward. "And you're not disappointing your dad. He'll get it—he's in the field enough to know about accidents."

"Haven't even e-mailed them yet."

"Do it." Larry turned to Gwen and handed her the backpack. "Keep this guy out of trouble, will you?" He turned to walk back up the hill. "I'll be in touch." He shook a finger at Clay. "Don't worry." He took a few steps and stopped. "I sent you some good reading material."

"Thanks, man." Clay swung about to face her. "Ready?" He started up the path without her answer.

Gwen silently trailed behind, wondering again about Clay's unusual relationship with his folks.

Clay couldn't summon words to chat with Gwen on the way out of the park. His thoughts were filled with his mom and dad. He had so much he wanted to say to them, but he didn't know how. Here he was, twenty-two, and still concerned he'd hurt them. Why was it so hard to stand on his own two feet? A grown man shouldn't feel the need to please—

"Hungry?" Gwen guided the truck around a curve. "I'm in need of something to drink, at least."

"Yeah, I could eat."

When they reached Fredericksburg, Gwen parked in front of Winslow's. A sign across the window touted BEST HAMBURGERS IN TOWN. Clay's stomach rumbled.

Not many people were inside, so they had their pick of tables. Gwen walked toward the wall and said, "You can prop your crutches here."

Clay slid them from under his arm and leaned them on a chair, then lowered himself into the seat. The waitress took their orders, and within minutes a juicy burger sat in front of him. His stomach growled again and he clapped a hand over it.

Gwen giggled. "Guess this was a good stop."

Clay bit into his burger and swiped juice from his chin with a napkin. "Didn't know how hungry I was." He stopped and peered at her. Frustration bubbled up. He'd interrupted her prayer again.

She raised her head, winked, and chewed a bite of a french fry. She sipped her cola. "Good to know your professor won't be upset about your absence." She peeked up at him. "Sorry you are."

"Yeah. Bummer."

"So your parents don't know you've been hurt?"

Clay sipped his drink and said, "Haven't felt the need to tell them." He ran a hand down the condensation on the glass. "My family's not close like yours. I do good to see my parents a few times a year." His tone was a bit acerbic, but he didn't care. At the moment, anger rose within him and he resented her relationship with her parents. He recognized the unwarranted feeling because he'd had it so many times before and fought to tamp it down.

They ate in silence for a few minutes, then Gwen said, "What do you think about church in the morning?"

"Gwen, I've never—I mean, I'm not against church. It just isn't for me."

Disappointment flashed across her face, but she didn't say anything.

Clay's pulse raced. Here was a beautiful woman, maybe interested in him, and he was turning down an invitation to attend an event, which was an important part of her life. Stupid. He didn't have anything better to do with his time. And a church was bound to be air-conditioned. He cleared his throat. "But I wouldn't mind joining you." Her eyes brightened. "To try it out, I mean. I'd like to visit places in town." What a lame acceptance.

"Awesome. I'll keep Rob's truck, and after church we can grab dinner and take it to my house. I'd like you to meet the family. I'm sure Aunt Katie will be there, too. You can discuss your week's menu with her."

Clay toyed with a pickle spear. Her brown eyes twinkled and her cheeks were flushed a lovely shade of peach. He nodded. "Then it's a date."

Chapter 7

Gwen leaned toward the mirror and flicked mascara along her eyelashes. She blinked, growled, and wiped the smudge away with her finger. One more application then she stared at her reflection. "Best I'm going to do." She stuffed her makeup into a bag and zipped it. "Why should I care, anyway?" A flush crept up her neck. She knew. She'd replayed the words over and over all night long.

"It's a date."

She spun from the mirror and climbed the loft ladder. Selecting a peach-colored blouse from the armoire, she pressed it against her chest. Whirling in front of the mirror, she scanned her face. "Brings out the right color"—she pursed her lips and furrowed her brow—"for a peach girl." She tossed the shirt on the bed and reached for a green dress. "I'm *so* not the peach girl anymore." The high school label made her shudder—she'd been teased enough to last a lifetime.

Gwen stepped into the dress and slid the zipper up her back, almost to the top. "Great. Where's Mom when I need her?" She twisted and turned but no contortion worked, at least an inch remained unfastened. She'd have to find her mom or aunt before service.

All morning she had battled the decision to not wear jeans and dress up. But her desire to look her best in front of

Clay won out. *"It's a date."* Her heart fluttered as she slid on her black sandals.

Running through her thoughts all night had been constant prayers for his salvation. "Lord, I know he seeks his dad's approval"—Gwen clomped down the ladder and gathered her things—"but he needs to know You." She closed her eyes and clutched her Bible to her chest. "Please, Lord. Speak to him this morning."

Her heart thumped in anticipation as she dashed to the truck. She slid her purse and Bible in the front seat and walked next door. "Hey, sleepyhead. You ready to go?"

Clay, wearing dark jeans and a yellow T-shirt, stumbled over the threshold and onto the porch. His dark eyes fastened on Gwen and a flash of uncertainty crossed his face. "I don't have a suit."

Gwen laughed. "Pastor Mike won't even be in a suit. Don't worry, our church isn't formal, you'll be fine."

He shut the front door and hobbled down the steps to the truck. He slid the crutches into the truck bed then climbed inside the cab. "Figured those would be okay back there on a short ride. I'm tired of messing with them."

Gwen turned the key in the ignition.

"Wait." Clay's fingers brushed her neck.

Her ears burned and her heart pounded in her chest.

"Your zipper needs—" He tugged it up. "There."

"Thanks," she whispered and backed onto the street, her pulse racing. What would Clay think of the next few hours? And why did it matter so much to her? Oh, she knew why. This man had wiggled his way into her heart.

The church's parking lot filled up quickly. Gwen spun into a slot, and they walked toward the front doors.

A whistle split the air. "Is that my Gwennie?"

Gwen spun to see her mom and dad behind her. "Dad." She hugged her father tightly, then held him at arm's length to study his face. "You feeling okay? You look good."

"Thanks, daughter. I'm feeling fine." He nudged his wife. "But your mom has me on a tight leash, that's for sure."

"Just for a while, dear." Gwen's mom winked. "Following doctor's orders, you need rest."

Gwen reached out her hand to Clay. "Want you to meet my new neighbor."

Clay lurched toward her parents, clutched a crutch under his arm, and extended his hand. "Clay Tanner."

Gwen's dad smiled, his eyes crinkled. "Heard a bit about you from my sister. She said you have quite an appetite."

"I'm grateful for the meals she's brought me."

"Welcome to church, son. Glad you're here." He clapped Clay's shoulder and steered him around toward the sanctuary. "Let's grab a seat."

Gwen followed her family, a light perspiration dotting her lip, her mouth dry.

A number of friends welcomed them to the service. Gwen's dad motioned to a back row. "You two might be more comfortable here, where he can stretch his leg out." Gwen nodded and slid into the second seat, leaving the aisle seat for Clay.

A young man bounded up, hand extended. "Hey, good to see you. I'm Pastor Mike. Who's the new guy?" After a quick introduction, he headed toward the stage and grabbed a guitar.

Clay's eyes widened and Gwen stifled a grin. Her pastor, Mike Hooper Jr., wasn't a typical minister. Young, fresh, and bold, he believed in meeting people at their point of need. He was all about relationships—with Jesus especially. And he didn't think his church met the suit and tie dynamic.

The worship team began to play and the congregation stood. Gwen leaned toward Clay. "If you get tired, sit. No one cares."

He nodded, a strained look on his face, a muscle in his jaw working.

Okay, Lord. Let's see what You have in store.

Gwen relinquished her spirit to the music, clapping her hands and entering into praise, her heart so full, she felt it would burst.

Clay, leaning on his crutches, peeked at Gwen from the corner of his eye. Hands raised, she sang with gusto, even if it was a tad off-key. In front of them, her parents worshipped the same way. He rolled the picture through his brain. *With abandon.* He'd heard that phrase in a church context. Now he saw it lived out before his eyes.

The words of song after song flickered on the large screen beside the stage. The contemporary music, the band—a guitar-playing preacher—not anything Clay had ever experienced. Certainly no organ. His knee began to throb. Shooting a furtive glance about the room, he noted a number of people had taken a seat, so he dropped into his chair. From that vantage point, he could watch Gwen. Her face—glowed. No other word seemed to fit. She had given herself over to the music and lifted her hands, a sense of awe sparkling in her eyes. Clay was spellbound. This was no act or showing off. He could tell her faith was the real deal.

After the music, introductions, and money collecting, the preacher began his spiel. Clay settled against the back of the chair to tune out, but Mike's words caught his attention.

"Elisha is with his followers near a river to cut down trees for a new meeting place. A guy loses the head of his ax in the water and is distraught. 'Sir, it was a borrowed ax.'" Mike paced the stage. "Poor guy. Freaking out. So Elisha tossed a stick in the water and the axhead floated to the top." He paused. "Imagine that. Do you think it was Elisha's magic or God's power at work?"

Clay shifted in his seat. Such unbelievable tales in the Bible.

"The axhead can represent our dreams in life. Our dream is like the borrowed axhead. God gave us our dream. . ."

Clay sighed. His dream—to work the land, have a place of his own—could never be a reality. He was expected to dig in the dirt all right, but for relics and artifacts with his dad. Not to plant and harvest. His ears perked up.

". . .where did you lose your dream? Whenever you lose the cutting edge, and don't hear God's voice, go back to the last time you obeyed Him and start over. A dream can be restored." Pastor Mike lowered his voice. "The wooden stick Elisha tossed in the water resurrected the axhead. The wooden cross touches our lives and resurrects. Reach today for that wooden cross and let it change your life."

Clay stared at his knee brace, lost in thought. The last time he heard God's voice? Had he ever heard that voice?

A picture of his grandmother floated through his mind. *"I love you and Jesus loves you, I'm praying."* She ended every visit with that statement. He'd rolled his eyes at Gran with her old lady's religion and preaching, because it always made him uncomfortable.

Clay nudged the negative feelings aside and glanced at Gwen. His heart stirred. She certainly didn't exhibit an old lady's religion, and he could tell she cared—about him. He shifted in his seat and realized he'd come to care about her. In just a few short days, this woman had captured his free-roaming heart. He gazed about the room. Church and Christianity would definitely be a hurdle to any relationship with Gwen.

Dinner with the whole Zimmermann family had been a riot. Rob and Gwen's sparring, Aunt Katie ribbing him over their rival football teams, Mr. Z's goofy jokes. Clay had laughed until his sides hurt, and eaten a heap of fried chicken, okra, and mashed potatoes. Comfort food, Mr. Z called it.

Back at the Sunday house, Clay groaned and settled onto the devil couch, the small fan pointed at his face. He wasn't sure comfort was what he felt at the moment. He shifted against the springs and straightened his leg to relax muscles. That helped.

But he couldn't rearrange the inner convictions roiling in his middle. He'd never experienced a service like today—witnessing Gwen's obvious joy at being in God's presence made him uneasy.

He dug into Larry's backpack and pulled out an assortment of notebooks and three paperbacks. He dumped the lot on the floor, tugged a textbook into his lap, and thumbed the worn pages.

Rocks. Escarpments, anthracites, fossils. All interested him, but none was his passion. He scooted lower on the sofa and closed his eyes. A tractor, a fertile field, a small farmhouse...

An ache, a longing, started under his breastbone. Gwen's face flitted into his dream—a purple haze surrounded her. Lavender. Gwen Zimmermann's lavender fields.

Clay's eyes popped open and a sudden realization raced through him. He and Gwen shared the same passion. Planting and harvesting. He swung his good leg to the floor, grasped the couch arm, and stood. He pinched the bridge of his nose. Another vision filled his senses. A wooden cross.

Tears flooded Clay's eyes and a sense of loneliness tore through his middle. He couldn't have his dream. His dad helped so much with the expenses of his education, Clay had to fulfill his father's expectations.

And Gwen? He heaved a sigh because he did not fit into the church mold—not any church, even in Fredericksburg. Same routine everywhere he turned. Round peg, square hole.

Clay closed his eyes and silently voiced his first prayer. "God, if You're there, I think we need to meet. I really do care about this woman." He heaved a sigh and slumped on the devil couch. No lightning bolts or whispered words from above, but his heart felt lighter. What was the possibility he could gain his dream?

And become one step closer to Gwen.

Chapter 8

Gwen's heart sang Monday morning, despite her lack of sleep. Her night had been filled with Clay dreams. She'd enjoyed the time with him and her family—he had fit in like fingers in a glove. Her daddy's teasing hadn't seemed to faze him, and he'd won over her mother after his third helping of peach cobbler. Rob already raved about the Aggie scholar.

To top it off, he'd gone to church. She giggled. Clay Tanner had gone to church.

And what a sermon Pastor Mike had preached. One of those pastor-read-my-mail kind. Surely Clay's heart had been touched. She didn't open her eyes during the closing invitation, but her fervent prayer had been for Clay's salvation. God must've heard her pounding on the door.

Gwen sank on the stool behind the counter, her heart sinking, too. She could pound all she wanted, but unless Clay knocked and asked Jesus into his heart—

Wednesday, Clay had a doctor's appointment. What if he left after that? She mindlessly doodled on a scratch pad then noted the intertwined hearts. She groaned. That's how she felt. Like they'd become intertwined. Yet she didn't know if he was a Christian. And she knew she didn't want to be married to an unbeliever.

Gwen propped both elbows on the counter and placed her head in her hands. "Lord, lead Clay to Your feet if he didn't go yesterday. Please. Even if he leaves Fredericksburg and I never see him again, he needs to know You." Gwen brushed tears from her eyes with her thumbs. "And Father, give him peace with his mom and dad."

The door opened and a man and woman trooped inside. Gwen pasted a smile on her face. "Good morning, welcome to Katie's Kupboard. If there's anything you need, let me know."

"Thank you." The lady waved her delicate hand, a large diamond sparkling on her finger. "My husband and I always appreciate the welcome in this friendly town."

Gwen's lips tipped up. "Glad you feel that way."

The lady strolled about the store and stopped with a gasp in front of a piece of furniture. "David, look at this pie safe. Don't think I've seen anything like it before." The woman pulled the doors open and peered inside. "Clean as a whistle, too." She fingered a price tag and glanced at Gwen. "When could you ship this?"

"Today, most likely. Are you interested?"

"Oh my, yes." She glanced toward her husband, her hazel eyes twinkling. "Aren't we, dear?"

David gave a crooked grin and nodded.

Gwen jerked an order form from under the counter and peered at the lady. "Where will it go?"

"San Antonio. My name is Jo Ann," she recited her full name and address. "My husband remodeled our kitchen for our fortieth anniversary and this will finish it perfectly." She beamed at her husband and interlocked fingers with his. He leaned forward and gave her a peck on the cheek.

Gwen's throat tightened as she watched them. Forty years. She longed for a husband with whom she could share a lifetime love. "You seem so happy." Gwen clapped a hand over her mouth after she blurted out the words.

David leaned on the counter. "We're very happy. God's blessed us." His brow wrinkled. "Don't get me wrong, life's handed us trials"—he squeezed his wife's fingers—"but with Jo Ann and God on my side, there's nothing I couldn't handle."

Jo Ann winked at him. "Back atcha, Papa."

Gwen giggled and completed the paperwork. David wrote a check and the couple left. Gwen watched out the window as he slung an arm over Jo Ann's shoulders and gave a squeeze.

"See, Lord. That's what I want."

"What do you want?" Aunt Katie asked. She climbed up the last step and walked behind the counter next to her niece. "Some chocolate?" She handed Gwen four M&M's.

Gwen popped them in her mouth, chewed, and swallowed. "Yum. I always want chocolate." She scooted the form toward Katie. "Sold that pie safe, so it needs to be delivered."

"Hooray." Katie beamed. "You're doing one fine job, Ms. Zimmermann." She flicked her nails on the glass countertop. "What were you and the Lord discussing?"

Gwen felt a flush creep up her cheeks. "Nothing much."

"Ha. Only a muscle-bound Clay Tanner, I betcha."

"Maybe." Gwen ducked her head and toyed with her ponytail.

Katie patted Gwen's hand and circled around a bookshelf

toward the back of the store. "Be careful, sweetie. Don't want you to follow in my footsteps."

Gwen watched her aunt and swallowed hard. "I'm praying for God's direction for everything in my life. Including Clay."

"Including me in what?"

Gwen froze. She hadn't heard the front door open. She swiveled around and stared at his sweaty T-shirt, which clung to hard biceps and a broad chest. He swept his cap off and the ever-present cowlick stood at attention.

A boyish grin crept across his face. "Can you ditch this place?"

"Already?" Gwen pointed to the black kitty-cat clock. "I've only been here an hour."

Clay shrugged. "Thought I'd give it a try." He chuckled. "You still have the truck."

"Um-hmm." Gwen crossed her arms over her chest. "Where do you want to go?"

"Zimmermann Orchards."

Gwen straightened. "Why?" She stepped around the end of the counter. "What do you need to do out there?"

He shrugged again. "We don't have to go right now. I'd just like to return while you have transportation."

Curiosity nibbled at her brain. "What's the mystery, Aggie-man?"

"No mystery. I'd just like to look at the field behind the orchard." Clay shuffled forward. "The one for lavender."

Gwen started. "Lavender?" she squeaked. "You want to look at my field of dreams?"

Clay pointed a finger at her, pistol-style. "Bang. You're on target." He parked on the stool and surveyed the room. "I can feather dust if you want me to while you work."

Aunt Katie approached the two. "No need. Gwen's earned a day off since she sold one big piece of furniture today. Shoo. Go." She flapped her hands.

Gwen raised a brow. "Are you sure?"

"Positive." Katie grabbed Gwen's purse and tugged her toward the exit. "Get a move on it, both of you. I've got work to do." She laughed and opened the door.

Clay smooched Katie on the cheek. "Thanks, Chief Chef. Appreciate it. And thanks for the potpie last night. Grateful for all this food you've sent my way."

Katie waved a hand and Gwen scooted out the door, not sure what adventure lay ahead. Whatever it was, she would be with Clay another day.

They climbed in the pickup and drove toward home, and Clay wouldn't answer one question.

Clay smiled as he surveyed the acreage behind the Zimmermann orchard. Left unattended, scrub oak, mesquite, and cactus dotted the landscape. Patches of brown grass swayed in the breeze.

"Want to tell me why we're here?"

Clay shoved his sunglasses on his cap, knelt, and fingered the soil. "Wildflowers take hold pretty fast, huh?"

Gwen's eyes sparkled and she dropped beside him. "Oh Clay, you should see it after a rainy season. Bluebonnets and Indian paintbrush. Greenthreads, yellow flowers like this one, cover the ground." Gwen fingered a lone flower. "We've taken more than one family portrait plopped in the middle of this field." Her tone softened. "Can't you just see it? A money-making project with just a small amount of effort. I mean, it would take irrigation, because in Texas we sure can't depend on rain. Have no clue how I'd be able to afford that. And then there's—"

"You'd need a bank loan."

"Now that would take a miracle. But then, He's in that business." She stood, lifted her eyes heavenward, and hollered, "Lord, if I'm to create a lavender field, You'll have to figure out a way." Gwen stomped on a clump of dirt, raising a powdery dust. "I know He heard that one."

Clay sneezed then coughed.

"Oops. Sorry." Gwen giggled. "Didn't mean to choke you."

"Gwennie?" Mr. Zimmermann's voice echoed across the field. "What you doing? Need anything?"

"No, Daddy. We're fine. Be there in a few." Gwen waved and her dad retreated into the store.

Clay pushed up and settled his crutches under his arms, sweat trickling down his back. He swiveled about, and on the turn, his crutch stuck. He jerked it free and stumbled forward, crashing down onto the edge of a large flat rock with his good knee. Pain jolted through him and he squeezed his eyes shut.

"Are you all right?" Gwen knelt beside him, concern etched across her face.

Clay stared into her brown eyes, the simple prayer she'd voiced piercing his heart. "I bet you prayed for a pony when you were a kid."

"What?"

He rubbed his knees and rose. "Never mind. Let's get something to drink."

The two ambled through the peach trees to the store. Mr. Zimmermann held a small box, pulled out two jars of peach goods, and set them on a shelf. "What y'all up to, out there in the back forty in this heat? Water bottles and sodas in the fridge. Best drink up and rehydrate after all your sweating, I can smell you from here." He grinned.

"Daddy, that's rude." Gwen lifted her ponytail and stood in front of a small oscillating fan. "Ahhhh."

Her father laughed, then a frown crossed his face. "Young fella, your good knee is bleeding." Mr. Zimmermann pulled a napkin from a dispenser and held it out toward his daughter. "Wet this so he can clean that cut, then we can see about a bandage. What happened, Clay?"

"Met up with a huge rock, Mr. Z." Clay took the napkin from Gwen and dabbed the blood away.

"Probably the gazebo." Mr. Zimmermann handed each of them a bottle of water. "Too hot to be wandering around outside." He pointed to the box. "If you need something to do, you can always help me stock the store."

"On my day off?" Gwen popped her dad on the arm. "I'm going to show Clay the sights, play tourist. We're headed to the pioneer museum. He's experiencing a Sunday house, might as well see how our peeps lived long ago."

Clay tossed the napkin into the trash. "What gazebo?"

Mr. Zimmermann leaned against the counter and folded his arms across his chest. "When my great-grandpa, Hank

Zimmerman, married, he built a gazebo in a field of wildflowers for his bride. That rock is the foundation symbolizing their faith in Jesus Christ." Mr. Zimmermann's eyes locked with Clay's. "And though the winds came and took down the gazebo, the solid rock is still there. Just like Jesus."

Clay ducked his head, he couldn't hold the gaze, and murmured, "I see." He didn't see—this blind faith of Gwen's family baffled him, and he didn't see how he could fit in. The gnawing on his insides intensified, making him jittery. "Guess we'd better go, Miss Tourist Guide." He gulped out a thanks to Mr. Zimmermann and hobbled toward the door as though he were being chased.

Chapter 9

A tall, heavyset nurse led Clay to Dr. William's exam room after his X-ray. Clay perched on the paper-covered metal table and nervously picked at the brace wrapped about his knee. Waves of acid welled up from his stomach and sweat prickled his brow. Would surgery be necessary? He longed for Gwen to be at his side and hold his hand. She'd offered to bring him, but he'd chosen to grab a taxi. She also said she'd pray.

Prayer. The foundation of the Zimmermann family. Mr. Z's explanation of the rock on which he'd stumbled three days ago haunted him. Why did faith seem easy to them? They struggled for money, Mr. Z had health problems, Rob wanted college but seemed locked to the orchard, and Gwen—

Gwen. Beautiful brown eyes, freckles peppered across a turned-up nose, and a smile that lit up his heart. She was a giver who seemed to expect nothing in return. Such a lack of pretense. He thought of the few girls he'd dated in college. What a difference. Not only was Gwen Zimmermann beautiful, she was a true believer.

His throat constricted. A woman who'd never choose him because of his obvious lack of belief.

Clay pictured his father and mother in the Fredericksburg Community Church and he pressed his lips together. Roger and Evelyn Tanner prided themselves on their modern-day opinions. He'd heard his mother expound more than once when, as a youngster, he'd questioned why they didn't go to church. "Man is incapable of providing sufficient, rational grounds to justify God exists, so why would we bother?"

His grandmother shook her head at her daughter and wiped away a few tears. She assured Clay God loved him. "Faith, my dear child, is the substance of things hoped for, the evidence of things not seen." Clay's pulse picked up speed.

Larry had included a Bible called *The Message* in his pile of books, and Clay tugged it from the fanny pack while he waited for the doctor. He thumbed the pages. It wasn't like any he'd seen before.

Larry had highlighted many passages but circled and starred Romans 10.

Clay read it again.

> *The word that saves is right here, as near as the tongue in your mouth, as close as the heart in your chest.*
> *It's the word of faith that welcomes God to go to work and set things right for us. This is the core of our preaching. Say the welcoming word to God—"Jesus is my Master"—embracing, body and soul, God's work of doing in us what he did in raising Jesus from the dead. That's it. You're not "doing" anything; you're simply calling out to God, trusting him to do it for you. That's salvation. With your whole being you embrace God setting things right, and then you say it, right out loud: "God has set everything right between him and me!"*

Was it really that simple?

The exam-room door swung open. "Mr. Tanner?" Dr. Williams strode into the room, an air of confidence swirling in with him. He shook Clay's hand, perched on a small stool, and scanned the reports. After poking and prodding the injured knee, Dr. Williams fastened the brace and gave a reassuring smile. "Things look good. From what I see, surgery won't be needed at this time. However, you will need some physical therapy. We can have the girls up front schedule it here in town or back in College Station. I think you'll be fine in the long run. Do start out easy."

A *whoosh* of air left Clay's lungs and they both laughed. The doctor clapped him on the arm. "I'd be holding my breath, too. See you in two weeks or"—he handed Clay a slip of paper—"here's the name of a doctor in Aggie-land, if you trust those kind of guys." He raised a brow, laughed, and exited as quickly as he'd arrived.

Clay sagged with relief. The nurse handed him the crutches and he hobbled to the front desk. "I'll call and let you know my plans if I need another appointment. Thanks so much."

He lurched into the waiting room and jerked around at the sound of his name.

Gwen reached out her hand and he clasped it. "Will you need surgery?"

"Why aren't you at work?"

Her eyes narrowed. "Will you need surgery?"

He shook his head.

"Praise the Lord." Gwen laced her arm about his waist and

pulled him close. With one arm and a crutch, he attempted to return the hug.

He stepped back and stared into those big brown eyes, a flood of tears welling up, nearly choking him as he held them back. "What are you doing here?" he whispered.

She pursed her lips and shrugged. "Did you really think I'd let you go through this all by yourself? You don't have family in town, so I figured I'd come."

Relief coursed through his middle, along with another feeling he'd come to recognize. A desire for her presence. He longed for Gwen Zimmermann to share his days. Clay felt a flush sweep up his cheeks and his mouth went dry. Suddenly he realized he had fallen in love.

Gwen turned the key in the ignition and headed toward Enchanted Rock, her chest heavy. Clay wanted to return to the team since the doctor had given such a good report. He hadn't emptied the Sunday house, but she felt sure Larry would help him do so pretty soon. His eagerness reminded her of the family's Lab. Clay wasn't panting and bobbing about, but he might as well have been. And she felt lower than a snake's belly.

"Can't do much climbing, that's for sure"—Clay beamed at her when they turned in to the state park—"but I can help the guys catalog and answer questions. It's going to be great to feel useful again."

"Um-hmm." Gwen nodded at the ranger and pointed to the parking lot. "Just be a few minutes." The ranger waved her through.

Gwen swung into a parking slot and swiveled to face Clay. "Well, Aggie-man, here you be. Back with the menfolks." She struggled for a smile, blinking back tears.

"Larry's coming down to grab my gear." Clay swung the door open and dropped a backpack on the ground. He slid out and pulled the crutches from the truck's bed, then leaned inside the cab. "Come with us so you can see the campsite."

"I need to get back to work, Clay. Maybe another time." When the dull gnawing inside of her subsided.

"Come on, Peach-girl." He stuck a crutch inside and poked her ribs.

A flush crept up her cheeks. "Peach-girl?" she squeaked. "Peach-girl? I am so out of here." She shifted into REVERSE.

"Gwen." Clay squinted at her as though to say something then tugged his sunglasses on and backed up. "I'll call you." He slammed the truck door and tugged two backpacks over his shoulder.

Gwen caught sight of his wave as she pulled out, tears blurring her vision. She drove up the road, out of sight of the park's entrance, pulled to the side of the road, and cried.

Exhausted, she slumped in the seat and surveyed the bleak surroundings. As dried-up and barren as her spirit. A guy she'd known a week had worked his way into her heart and life, and now he was gone. Oh sure, she might see him when he moved out. Or he might breeze through town to visit the doctor one more time. But he wouldn't be her next-door neighbor, the guy who sat on the front porch munching ice cream and sharing dreams. That pocket of time had dissolved.

Gwen sat forward, glanced in the mirror, and groaned.

She rubbed her eyes and jerked her scrunchie tighter, then ran her fingers across her lips, the desire to kiss Clay so strong she almost turned the truck around. She closed her eyes and breathed deeply. Feeling calmer, she turned onto Highway 16 and headed toward Fredericksburg.

"Enough moping. Back to work. Guess you had a summer romance, Zimmermann." If only summer lasted forever.

Chapter 10

With a click of the mouse, Gwen sent her final online essay to the professor, completing the last of her three summer courses. If she could take twelve hours on campus in the fall, she'd graduate in December. "And haul that diploma to the peach stand."

She sighed and slapped the laptop closed without checking her Facebook or e-mail. Clay had disappeared, just as she knew he would, without a face-to-face good-bye, but she heard from him online constantly. Her heart had shriveled once he left, and she poured herself into work and school for the rest of the summer. Now it had been ten, long, grueling days of silence. "But who's counting?"

Her words echoed in the quiet room of the Gillespie County Library. She stared at the tall shelves jam-packed with books and the lovely antique tables and chairs. How many high school book reports and research papers had she completed in this room? And here she was at twenty, still in the same place with the same people and the same books. "I did finish college-level work, though." She shook her head. This internal battle longing for more resulted from frustration stirred up by one Aggie-man. She had to move on. Question was, move on where?

Gwen slid the laptop into its case, gathered her purse and

papers, and plopped it all in the front seat of her car on her way to Greater Grace Christian Coffeehouse to celebrate with a latte and a muffin. Aunt Katie and her friend, Phil, sat on the huge back deck, cups in hand.

"You done, girl?" Phil grinned, his long, gray ponytail blowing in the breeze.

"Yep, I'm a done girl." Gwen slid onto the redwood bench beside her aunt, toying with the giant chocolate muffin. "Now if I can get to San Antonio and finish—"

Katie grasped her niece's hand. "We were just discussing that, honeybunch. I have an opinion, want to hear it?"

Gwen laughed. "Auntie-dear, when have you ever kept an opinion to yourself? You ask that question and dish it out. So, yes, I want your opinion."

Phil leaned forward. "Actually, it's my idea, so I want credit." He raised a gray eyebrow.

"Duly noted." Katie tugged a sheet of paper from her purse and flattened it with the palm of her hand. "*Phil the philanthropist* wants to pay for you to finish your degree. In turn, you will keep the books on his irrigation business for a year." She pointed to a column of figures. "Once your 'indentured servant-hood'"—Katie fashioned air quotation marks—"is paid off, and if he's satisfied with your work, he's offering to pay off any outstanding college debts." Katie's eyes twinkled. "Think that's a pretty good deal?"

Gwen stared at her aunt then shifted her gaze to Phil. "Why?" she gasped.

"Because I can." He sipped his coffee and smiled. "It's a win-win. I need the help and so do you."

"I'm speechless." Gwen scanned the paper, her pulse racing. "Mr. Mitchell, I don't know what to say."

He tipped his head. "I've watched you diligently work for Katie this whole summer, knowing you gave most of your paycheck to your family. That kind of selflessness is unusual, Gwen, in these times. Especially with your age group. You never let your family down and I think it's time you were blessed." Phil settled his elbows on the table. "Let me bless you."

Tears welled in Gwen's eyes. "Thank you," she whispered. "I appreciate your offer." She faced her aunt. "What about Mom and Dad? They still need income—"

Katie extended a hand with a flourish in her friend's direction. "Fill her in on that idea, Mr. Mitchell."

Phil swung his long legs astride the bench and beamed. "Your dad and I've discussed my investing in the orchard. I like his storefront idea, and with extra capital, he could certainly expand. Gwen, the burden for extra financing won't be on your shoulders any longer."

A tight band around Gwen's middle loosened at the same time a niggling worry began. To accept this offer meant staying in Fredericksburg. Earlier in the summer, the lavender fields permeated her thoughts—as long as she discussed them with Clay. Now her dream felt empty, hollow. But debt-free? She couldn't pass that up.

"Mr. Phil Mitchell, I think this is a fine idea and I am ever so grateful." Gwen reached out a hand. "Shake?"

He enveloped her hand with both of his in a warm clasp. "Bless you."

A warmth ran through Gwen and she felt lighter. A blossom of hope took root, defrosting her heart. Summer's end and a fresh start. She raised her latte. "A toast. To new beginnings."

Clay's mother held his diploma at arm's length. "I'm quite proud of you."

"Thank you, Mother." He forced a smile.

"About time you joined up on our next expedition." Clay's father nodded to a colleague and turned back to his son. "We'll leave in September."

Clay pressed his lips together and closed his eyes. A featherlight touch caught his attention. "I've sensed a change in you, Clay." His diminutive grandmother tilted her head and looked into his eyes. "And I like what I see. Would a certain young lady have anything to do with this glow?"

"Partly, Grandmother. She's the one who got the ball rolling again." Clay clasped her hands. "You are the one who started it." He drew her close and whispered into her ear. "Your prayers have finally paid off. I know Jesus loves me and I love Him, too."

His grandmother threw her arms about his waist. "Oh Clay. If only you knew how long I've waited to hear those words." Tears soaked Clay's shirt. "I'm blessed and thrilled beyond description."

Mrs. Tanner closed in on them. "What are we celebrating, Clay?"

Clay leveled a look at his mother and father, wet his lips,

and said, "My decision to accept Jesus as my Lord and Savior."

"Posh. What nonsense." Mrs. Tanner dismissed the idea with a flutter of her hand.

"No, Mom, it's not. I learned God has a purpose and a plan for me"—he faced his father—"and it doesn't include archaeology. I am going to farm. Maybe even raise lavender."

Grandmother Tanner giggled. "I knew it, I knew it. She must be one special young lady. I can't wait to meet her."

"What young lady?" Clay's mother frowned. "A girl has made you change your entire vocation?"

Clay threw back his head and laughed. "No, Mother. Jesus has. Come on, Gran, let's grab a cup of coffee. I've so much to tell you. How you planted the seed, Gwen and her church watered, and my buddy, Larry, helped me harvest." Clay pulled her along and spoke over his shoulder to his parents, "If you want to know more, you'll need to follow and just. . .listen."

Gwen slid into her jeans and pulled a blouse over her head. She swiped her hair into a ponytail and stepped into flip-flops. She should be excited about leaving for school next week, but a cold fist gripped her heart. Yesterday a young man had entered the shop wearing an Aggie T-shirt, and she'd left the counter to Aunt Katie before she burst into tears. Despite numerous e-mails and Facebook pictures to keep her updated, Gwen ached to see Clay—ached to hold his hand, to hear his voice. She clutched her stomach. Ached to have him embrace her. Ached for a kiss.

"Peach-girl, get a move on it." Her brother clattered

about downstairs, closing windows and locking up the Sunday house. She choked back tears, fastened the clasp on her suitcase, and walked to the loft ladder.

Rob peered up at her. "Toss that down."

"Oh sure, I'll gladly give you a concussion." Grasping the suitcase handle and the ladder, Gwen descended from her tower for the last time this summer.

"Come on. Church starts in a few minutes."

"Did you get the peaches from the fridge?" Gwen turned the fan off.

Rob pulled her suitcase from her hand and shook his head. "Nope. I'll wait in the truck."

She walked to the kitchen and pulled the sack of peaches and an apple from the refrigerator. She opened the freezer and spotted an almost empty carton of rocky road ice cream sitting on the middle shelf.

Gwen burst into tears. She sank into a chair at the kitchen table, scratching frost from the carton. Tears trickled down her cheeks. "Clay, I miss you so much. Do you miss me at all?"

She shuddered and stood. Time to get moving. She emptied the ice cream into the sink and tossed the carton into the trash bag Rob would collect later. She ran water and rinsed her face, then dried it with a paper towel. She surveyed the little bungalow one last time, thanking the Lord for the special summer then closed the front door.

The band had already begun when Gwen and her brother arrived at church. She slipped in beside her mother and tried to sing. Words lodged in her throat.

"Lord, give me a heart of worship. Wherever Clay Tanner

is, bless him, watch over him, and fill him with Your Spirit." Her whispered words mingled with the band's music. With a lighter heart, she began the next song and was soon lost in worship.

Pastor Mike had read her mail, too, because he spoke on awakening the spirit, and hers felt long dead. "Develop a spirit of expectation and belief. Hebrews 11:6 says He diligently rewards those who seek Him. . ."

Gwen stared at her folded hands in her lap. She'd thought so much about Clay, had she lost sight of diligently seeking the Lord? "Forgive me. Help me in my unbelief."

The worship band returned to the stage and music stirred her heart. She raised her hands and sang, "Holy, holy, holy, Lord God—"

She froze and closed her eyes. A familiar rich baritone caught her attention. She whirled around.

Clay winked at her and never missed a beat. Gwen stepped between the chairs and stood beside him, squeezing herself to quell the banging of her heart. He glanced down at her and pointed to the screen.

Gwen turned and joined in the song.

Their voices blended—"Holy, holy, holy. . ."

Epilogue

G wennie, Clay needs you." Mr. Zimmermann shouted through the kitchen door.

"Coming." Gwen hop-skipped through the living room, weaving around boxes of jellies and jams from local farmers.

Phil grinned at her. "This last shipment should be done soon. Then I'll be out of your hair while Katie and I take our cruise." To Gwen's astonishment, Phil and Aunt Katie had married, purchased a yacht, and made plans to sail the ocean's blue, as her aunt put it.

Gwen smooched his weathered cheek. "Promise me a postcard from every port. I love you." She fluttered her fingers and headed toward the store.

"There you are." Her father propped his hands on his hips. "Clay's waiting."

She looked around the store. "Where?"

Her dad pointed to the orchard. "Outside, back of the orchard."

Gwen's eyes lit up. "Did he and Phil get the last of the irrigation pipes in?"

Mr. Zimmermann shrugged, his eyes twinkling.

"Daddy"—Gwen giggled—"you men are keeping way too many secrets."

Her mother popped up from behind a counter. "Just happy your daddy feels well enough to have a secret or two. Now scoot. Geologists are often impatient."

Gwen dashed out the door, letting the screen slam behind her. "Clay?" She bent forward and scanned beneath peach trees for his lanky legs. "Come out, come out, wherever you are." Her heart swelled at the words. After his graduation, Clay had returned to Fredericksburg and worked alongside her father and Phil to build Zimmermann Orchards business. He'd visited her every weekend in San Antonio while she finished her degree.

"This way, Peach-girl."

She bit back a retort and followed the sound of his voice, weaving between peach trees in full bloom, the sweet scent of their blossoms tickling her nose. "Are you irrigating? Did you get the pipes finished? I saw Phil and he said they were about to sail. If you have any questions, you might want to address them now, before they leave. No telling when we'll make contact. Of course we can Skype, but you know how he likes to sketch out details—"

Gwen's breath caught in her throat. Clay stood beneath a rough-hewn gazebo, the boyish grin she loved so much spread across his face.

"What—what—" she sputtered and stepped onto the rock, her hand covering her mouth.

Clay reached out his hand and tucked a strand of hair behind her ear. "Miss Gwendolyn Constance Zimmermann, I wondered if next spring, when the wildflowers and lavender are in full bloom, if you'd do me the honor of marrying me?"

He glanced at the partially built roof. "Under this roof"—
he looked down—"and on this foundation. An age-old
foundation created by love and built on Jesus Christ." He
held out a red velvet box, the lid tipped open. A burst of rays
spread forth from the sun-kissed diamond.

Tears streamed down Gwen's cheeks and she nodded, too
breathless to speak for a moment. She cleared her throat. "Mr.
Clay Scott Tanner," she choked out, "I would be honored."

Clay slid the ring on her finger and clutched her to his
chest. She leaned back and gazed into dark brown eyes full
of promises for a lifetime. He cupped her face with his hand.
She stroked his strong jawline, the diamond glistening, and
smiled.

Gwen slid her hand around the back of his neck, pulled
his face closer, and whispered, "Thank You, Lord."

Her lips met his.

Eileen Key, freelance writer and editor, resides in San Antonio, Texas, near her grown children and three wonderful grandchildren. She's published ten anthology stories and numerous devotionals and articles. Her first mystery novel, *Dog Gone*, from Barbour Publishing, released in 2008. Her second book, *Door County Christmas*, released in 2010. Find her on the Web at www.eileenkey.com.